MAZE

MAZE

J. M. McDermott

An Apex Publications Book
Lexington, Kentucky

Maze
ISBN: 978-1-937009-21-2
Copyright © 2014 by J.M. McDermott
Cover Art © 2014 by Angela Giles
Title Design © 2014 by Deanna Knippling
Typography by Maggie Slater

Published by Apex Publications, LLC
PO Box 24323
Lexington, K.Y. 40524

www.apexbookcompany.com

My name is Jenny.

I was in a city inside of a city inside of a city. In the shadows there, I slept. I knew only my name—nothing else—and nothing, and nothing else for a very long time. I slid from behind a shadow and a shadow. I saw you sleeping here.

Put me in your lung.

Breathe deep.

Maia
Station's
Maze

1: Who Am I?

My name is Maia Station.

I was born in the sky, on a station. I never expected to be anywhere else. I was a scientist, but I can't remember how to do anything scientific after ten years surviving in this maze. The tools I took for granted before this life are gone. The great coils and conductors and artificial constructs that I used to treat like toys are as distant as the stars in the sky. My memories of the station and my memories of here are all disjointed, as if everything before the maze is wrapped in silver gauze—my mother, my childhood friends, all the things I did and learned—until the tear, when I woke up in the maze, and sand ground away my mind.

I think it would help if anyone believed me among the other survivors I found here. No one else came from the sky, or even from a time when such a life was conceivable. I'm alone here, with my daughter, Julie. She doesn't believe my stories, either. She only knows the maze.

I don't know how it all happened—how I arrived here from there. None of the others do either. I remember entering my private chamber on the station. I closed my eyes to sleep. I don't know what happened next. I was awake in what seemed like moments, though centuries had passed, swallowed up by speed and light, and the station was long gone and I was here, in the maze, alone.

It has been years since I woke up. I found a tribe of people who found themselves here, like I did. My daughter, Julie, was born here. I was pregnant with her when I found the tribe. Before I came to this tribe, I met Saitan. I met his satyr. I met Julie's father. I met myself.

I never speak of what happened when I first arrived here, because I want my daughter to be safe, accepted, and loved by all the people here. The blood in her veins will keep her safe just as it kept me safe when I was pregnant with her, as long as I never tell anyone what happened.

I have a nightmare of the satyr of Saitan, hunched over the corpse that birthed him, devouring himself. In the nightmare, I see my daughter, Julie, devouring there, with him, like a monster. But I wake up and I look at her and she's not like the satyr was. She's a beautiful girl, and she looks just like me when I was a child. She's clever. She has friends among the tribe. No one thinks she's different. She's my daughter, and I love her, and I'm not afraid of the light. The maze is dangerous enough without being afraid of my own child. I wonder—half-hoping—if the blood of the maze will protect her even when the dangerous things would devour the rest of us. I wonder—half-hoping—if Julie's blood will protect the people here like it protected me.

Julie, my beautiful daughter, sat down to eat the flatbread I had made for her from the wheat and rice we grew by the pond and the acorns of the trees that grew here, where a lake used to be, among the maze walls. Julie had been playing all day long.

I had been teaching her to count and she told me that there were exactly eight trees. She was off by a hundred or so, not counting the saplings we had cut down for wood and spears, or the bushes that grew in the marshy waters of the pond. Julie explained that she had decided only eight trees were large enough to count. I suspected she forgot what came after eight.

There was no school in the maze. There was only survival.

Julie reached for food, but I took her hand in mine and turned her around. She had blood on her arm, near her shoulder.

"Julie, are you okay? Did you cut yourself?"

"No, Mama."

Was it hers? I ran my hand around the blood and puckered her white skin for any sign of cuts. She was unhurt.

"Where did this blood come from?"

She shrugged. She reached for her food. I stopped her hand.

The children had all seen death before. They could not be protected from it here. Each spring the dancing women dressed up the children in feathered costumes like vultures and banged drums for them and the children danced around a fire. When they reached the center, they threw their costumes into the flames with a cheer. Some of the people here treated this like a prayer against death, but I told Julie it would never work. We knew better because we—Julie and I—were scientists, and this festival was only good for the fun of dancing.

2

I brushed Julie's hair away from her face with my hand. It wasn't her blood.

"How did you get blood on your arm, Julie?"

"I don't know, Mama."

"You must have rubbed up against something. Go take a bath."

"What? Why?"

"Blood is dirtier than mud."

"Mama..."

"Don't argue with me, Julie. There are things in blood—in everyone's blood—that you cannot see. Very small things that are like ants nibbling at you. There are tiny things in your blood that try to kill the ants, like spiders so tiny you cannot see them."

"I don't believe that, Mama. That's stupid. Why can't I believe what others do? It's just blood. Lucius says we should drink blood. Saitan smears it on the lips of his dead family's souls."

"We are scientists, Julie. We are not like Saitan at his grandmother's idols, or Lucius kneeling for two sticks, or Joseph and Gokliya leaving flowers on graves to speak to the dead, or Huzzar, the Mahometan always washing his hands in dirty water, or the dancing ones. Julie, we focus on what is known, what can be proven repeatedly. Listen, I'll prove that blood is dirty to you, too. Just go take a bath first, while I get the experiment ready. Find a good stone and scrape away all that sweat and mud."

"I don't want to."

"Right now, Julie. Go."

Like I said, my name is Maia Station.

I was born in space, on a beautiful station, and that was what everyone called me because I told them about it when I learned the language here. I still don't know how I came here from there.

Here, time is blood; blood is time.

We know our trails, and we know our village, but I know that traveling too far changes the age of the air. I saw it for myself, crossing trails underground. Time flows through these hallways, but it happens on a scale so big it's hard to for us measure—maybe impossible.

The maze's stone hallways open to an empty sky. Seasons roll in and away, and as long as I hold still, all things are the same—and stable.

Stay where you are, if you find a good place where there's food and fresh water. That's what Enyo Gyoja says. He's the leader of our nameless community, if anyone is. I think he's right. If I don't know how I came to be here, I don't know how to go home. If I don't know how to go home, I had best make my home where I can, raise my daughter, and hope for her the best future I can give to her.

I can live with anything, even death, if I know my daughter will have a better life than this.

2: Here

Before I came to the maze, I was asleep—in deep soma; I had no dreams. I was amniotic. I was saline. I was still. Somewhere in the hidden places of my consciousness, the high whine of engines spinning slipped into silence.

I couldn't breathe. I grabbed at my neck, but I couldn't reach it. My helmet was in the way. I clawed at it, gasping for air, and jackknifed on the ground. I was under a wall of stone bricks. Snow was on the ground. My faceplate cracked on something like a rock beneath the snow. A brick had fallen from the wall and had hidden itself beneath the white snow. The brick saved my life.

My face smashed against the brick inside the snow. My mask cracked clear. I could breathe. Behind me, the umbilicals were all torn. Wounded silicates oozed oils and liquid oxygen. I tugged at the lashes and bindings of the outer shell. I didn't have the tools to unwind myself from the steel. I did the best I could. I disconnected the draping umbilicus. I got my torso free, and one of my arms. I left the lost parts where they fell.

The helmet came off with help from both my hands and the life-saving brick.

I was alone.

I was in the maze, but I didn't know where I was, and I didn't know it was a maze. Too thirsty to think, I swallowed the snow. It burned. It was so cold. I saw a bird flying overhead, small and soft, or it could have been an insect, hard with chitin that my blurry eyes had softened into a bird. My body was not ready to be alive.

I climbed carefully to the top of the wall. The stones were wet, but they could be climbed. I straddled the wall, cautiously. I looked all around at the new world I had found. The gnarled stone passageways crawled over the horizon to one side. To the other, a hill peaked, with a cliff and caves along the cliffs. I thought I saw something moving there. I squinted. My eyes ached from sunlight, when starlight and bioluminescence were all my eyes had ever known. I couldn't pull a shape out of the cliffside hints of motion.

MAZE

I found this maze: pathways, and all pathways, and all stone. From where I was, walls rose far past my head and rising and falling like jagged teeth where the bricks at the top had eroded away.

As I walked, I coughed up the blue sick of the liquid oxygen and mineral blends. I stripped away the small bits and pieces of my suit that hampered my movement. I was still not alive enough to feel the full weight of pain from my sudden transition.

I kept my boots on.

I struggled with my own weight. I was newborn. I stopped to curl up into a ball against a wall and rest my burning legs. My palms pressed into my empty stomach. I hadn't eaten anything in forty-two years. My body cried out for food, and I had none. I had snow that burned with cold.

(Geophagy: I would do anything to quiet my insides. My eyes scoured the ground for handfuls of dirt that wouldn't hurt. I drooled. I pictured stones cutting up my fragile intestines, where the bacteria hadn't yet rebuilt their devastated kingdoms beneath my skin.)

I was going the wrong way. I looked over my shoulder. The hill was behind me. I didn't have the strength to turn around. I walked forward. I came to so many crossroads. I didn't have the will to choose. I stumbled and fell.

I fell against a wall. I slept.

Pulled from sleep, returned to sleep. I had the numb certainty of death inside me.

Had we crashed somewhere? Had some unknown tractor beam hurled us upon an atmosphere where my pod had crumbled and spit me out among these bent pathways? There were no smoking ruins on the horizon. Nothing beeped inside of me. Nothing trembled in the air where the blast would have unwound the snow clouds, darkened them, and pressed a burning stink of devastation.

I awoke to darkness and silence. I blinked into the moonless night. I held still. The snow draped me in chill. I felt the melted snow seep into my clothes. My death would be miserable and cold. I did not have body fat to warm me. I did not have anything.

The sun rose a little bit. I was barely alive. I crawled. I crawled slowly.

I chose a path among the forking hallways. I turned a corner and crawled. I was at the base of the hill's cliff. I touched the rock. It was all limestone, white as the cliffs. I scratched at it with my fingers. I had no sense of geology here. The maze walls were bricks—I thought—but underground were, perhaps, bricks that had been weighted down to limestone.

The ground was covered in mud beneath the snow. Below the cliff, the mud was off-white with chalky cliff erosion and only just discernible from the snow.

There was a cave. Along the side of the cliff, the sheer white rock crumbled inward like a tooth's cavity.

I was hungry. I was cold. I could only crawl, sick as I was from coming up in a blink of an electron through what should have taken days.

I struggled into the black. I stopped when I couldn't move anymore. It was warmer underground, but only just. How long did I have until hypothermia set in and killed me? I had already lived far longer than I deserved.

Underground, I was out of the frozen breeze and the damp.

I stripped the last of my shell off. I peeled the elastane skinsuit away completely. I laid it out on the ground. I pulled myself to standing, to air out. I needed to lose the water against my skin, even if it hurt more. Water would freeze me to death.

I heard sounds echoing up from the depths, like the sound of the engine in my lost night sky. Something moved in a pulsing, regular, grinding way.

I waited, alone, for a thousand upon a thousand upon a thousand seconds, all of them terrible.

I knew I was going to go deeper underground, whether there were sounds or not. It was warmer there. I longed for lava and steam. I refused to be afraid of noise until I could deduce what was making the sound. I told myself that an animal would be just as afraid of me as I was of it.

When I was drier and too cold to stand it a moment longer, I pulled what I could of my clothes over me again. I was weak. I couldn't lift the remnants of the shell off the ground, much less pull it over my body again. I left it there.

It was warmer underground.

Crawling, afraid of sudden drops, I ran my hands over the ground ahead of me before pulling my weary body deeper into the black void.

My hand touched something cold and sponge-like, with a sticky sheen over it that smelled familiar. I explored it gingerly with my hands, found bones beneath the surface. I stopped touching it.

Toes. A foot. An Achilles' tendon.

Adrenaline doesn't just kick in. It takes a few seconds. I looked into the darkness. I imagined all sorts of shapeless, monstrous things. Adrenaline burst inside me like a fear balloon.

I heard the sound again, closer.

Too weak to run, I wanted to run. I thought I was going to die there. I curled into a ball. The noise came into the room, beside me. Turning my head, I didn't know what I'd see, if I could see it at all.

Light flickered in the dark, a puff of neon cotton floating in the air like a wind-blown seed.

It was speaking, I think. I could hear something like a voice at the edge of sound, pulsing like an engine in the background of the air.

"Did you say something?" It hurt to speak. My throat burned. I was rasping. I couldn't understand myself. I thought I tasted blood in my throat from speaking.

I listened closely.

Put-me-in-your-lung-put-me-in-your-lung-put-me-in-your-lung-put me-in...

"What are you?" My lips cracked, and I was bleeding. I licked at the blood with my tongue. It tasted good.

Help-me-put-me-in-your-lung-help-me-help-me-put-me-in-your-lung-help...

I wanted to. I wanted to help the light. I had been a helpful person on the station, where we were friendly to each other and tried to help. Whatever it was, I couldn't help it. How could I help the light if I was dying? "No," I said. I curled away. I was in a strange land. I was starving to death. "You need to help me. I need food and water. I'm dying."

Please-help-me-please-put-me-in-your-lung...

The light came closer to me. I backed away farther.

"Help me, and I'll help you."

The light quieted, like it was thinking.

Follow.

The light, in silence, descended beyond the body. It kept going and going. I could barely make it out. I waited in terror—trembled with it and choked down my moans of death terror.

What else could I do?

I followed the light. I would have followed it anywhere.

I wasn't sure where the light was taking me.

I scrabbled on hand and foot through the stone. We came to junctions where eternal darkness and a gust of wind, maybe a sound, drifted up from some great depth, only to die in moments at the turning path.

Follow.

Down and down and down. The flittering light approached a darkness I thought to be a great cavern, but the presence of the little light unraveled the illusion. It wasn't so large, when the light traversed it.

Follow.

We turned a corner to a stairwell of stone bricks, worn with age and countless misshapen feet. The stairs were the wrong size for me. They were tiny and awkward to crawl down. I couldn't have stood up, though, even if I had been strong enough for it. My knees hurt more than they had ever hurt in my life. I had scrapes and bruises. The lip of the stairs hurt me. I tried to bend into a beastly crouch.

Follow.

Down and down, until I could not move my joints. I collapsed.

Just before darkness, something picked me up by the waist, carried me like a doll. It was cold and hard and I didn't know what it was, but I didn't care.

I was amniotic — saline. Dead. Gone.

Flickering light woke me up. I was warm, too. My eyes focused: a fire. I was in a large cavern. The fire threw off steady heat, and I wanted to curl up into it like a piece of charcoal.

"Are you awake?" said someone—a woman's voice, and familiar.

I saw no sign of the tiny light. I had imagined it. I was sure I had imagined it.

My voice was barely a crackle. I was so hungry I couldn't even feel it. I just knew it.

A puddle of still water was in a hole in front of me. I dropped my face into it. I drank so fast that I vomited the water back into the water, but I kept drinking anyway.

I had trouble lifting my head out of the puddle, but I did it to gasp between gulps.

"Food?" said someone. She helped me lift my head from the water, and she placed soft meat in my mouth.

I swallowed. I was afraid I was going to choke, but I couldn't stop swallowing. I was so hungry.

"Don't hurt yourself," she said. She patted me gently on the back.

I looked up. I was looking at myself.

"I know," she said. "I remember what I thought. Am I Maia? Am I you?" she said, speaking where I could not. "Yes, it's me. But I'm you from the future. Kind of. Time here is...well, you'll see it for yourself."

"What?" I said.

"Do I really sound like that? You sound like an old, old woman, yet we're so young. You sound sick. Got something to show you," she said.

9

She turned sideways and pointed at her stomach. "Look at this." Her stomach bulged, like an infection. The skin was taut around the bulge.

Oh, my reflection was pregnant. Months pregnant, from the look of her.

"How did that..." I tried to speak, but I couldn't.

"Wait a bit. I'll help you a while longer, but then I have to go. I wish I could stay, but...it's too dangerous with the baby, and I don't really know how to take care of you here. Look, I'll tell you everything. You can't believe how wonderful it is to have someone to talk to that understands me. I've been silent down here for I don't even know how long. I was ripped from stasis. I was asleep in the stars, and...then, I went underground."

"I know," I groaned.

She had a pile of meat behind her. She handed it to me in soft strips. It was cooked and soft and I ate it so fast I couldn't tell if it was good or bad.

"Of course you know, but there's more," she said.

"Obviously," I said. The baby.

"Rest up," she said. "I can wait another fire or two before I go. When we start running low on meat, though, I'll have to go. I know you'll survive. I don't know if I will."

"How do you know? If time doesn't work right..."

"We don't have the luxury of reason right now."

"Reason is not a luxury."

"Perhaps you are right."

"Don't do that."

"What?"

"Don't give in like that," I said. "I know what you're doing. That's my trick. I pretend to agree to prevent an argument."

"I'm glad you're feeling better."

"Where are we, Maia?"

"I don't know," she said. "There's no sign of the station, or anyone from the station."

"What do I do next?"

"I don't know if I can tell you or not. I don't know what the rules are," she said. "Get yourself ready." She said nothing else.

I wasn't ready. She walked away from the fire, into the darkness. She was gone a while. I wondered if she was coming back. She returned with snow cupped in her hands. She placed it in a rocky indentation in the ground, to melt it at our fire. She drank first. Then, I drank.

"Close your eyes, Maia," she said. "Rest while you can."

"What about you?"

"As long as we stay quiet we should be fine. Close your eyes, Maia. I'll keep watch for you."

I didn't argue. My belly was full. My throat didn't burn so much. My nose ran and I thought I was going to be running a fever soon, but there was nothing I could do about that.

I slept. I had a nightmare of unceasing darkness.

Maia was gone when I woke up. The fire was fresh. The meat was still there, in a pile.

Never trust yourself.

I refused to take comfort in knowing I had met myself. I was a scientist. I refused to believe my eyes alone after so much fear and hardship and unknown things. I needed to trust science and reason and test any hypothetical truth I encountered.

I ate what was left. I crawled up to sitting. I thought I might be able to stand, if I concentrated. I was better. I was stronger. I still had a fire.

Where did the other Maia get the wood?

I looked closer. The wood was shaped like gnarled body parts. I could make out two monstrous palms with sharp claws, of wood. Bits of legs and things looked like organs, knotted up like knobs of pine.

I squinted out to the edges of my firelight. I moved cautiously over the stones.

This pile must have been where she had gotten the wood. I saw what appeared to be a pile of limbs, there. I saw these living limbs and organs, all piled up, all of wood and bent and mangled like vines grown into bipedal locomotion, never carved. It reminded me of the rubbish bin behind the botanist's lab.

I tried to pick up one of the pieces there. It was attached to the larger structure. The vines grew in these monstrous shapes.

I could not get anything loose. I walked around, to the edges of the cave plant. It was circular, like a leafless shrubbery. At its highest, it was no taller than my waist.

My fire died down, and I had harvested no more sticks. How could I, without a cutting tool or genuine strength of limb? I knew it was happening. I sat near the fire, watching the embers smolder. I was afraid to fall back into darkness. There was nothing I could do without abandoning this warm shelter.

I closed my eyes; then, I opened my eyes.

There was a light, after the embers.

The limbs of the strange bush surrounded a funnel of the lights. I heard no voices in the dark. I could barely see the limbs. I could barely see at all, except I knew there was light here.

I walked around the cavern, searching for the way up and down.

The death rot still stank. The way to the top, then, could be past the body I had found in the dark, when I had crawled underground.

I picked my way cautiously through the hallways, toward the stink of death.

I found the body. My feet kicked up against sticky damp and bones. I passed beyond the stench, through the cave, and up to the sliver of light at the rocky maw. I peered through the crevice. The sun was warm in my face. The ground was clear of snow. Small grasses, green as springtime, crept along the chalk wall.

I walked carefully down, searching for my suit. I tried to retrace my path, with no sign on the ground that I had passed this way, scraping my knees and elbows on the rocks beneath the snow, trailing pink where snow froze my blood. A tree grew near where I thought I had fallen into this place, but there had been no tree then. I found my discarded parts along the way. I found bits of glass and the heavy bulk of my suit in a patch of red flowers where my umbilicals extended out from the roots of the tree. The carbonates had cracked in long, long neglect. Decades of sun and wind and rain had devastated these hardy, space-worthy fibers. I ran my hands along the fractured seams. Tiny worms had burrowed into the foams—planted tiny eggs. I wiped the larva off of my hands along the grassy ground.

I sniffed at the flowers. They smelled safe. I ate one. I waited a while, unsure how long it took for it to reach my stomach, even as I tried to count down the seconds. I ate another flower, and another. I chewed on the stems. I collected grass blades and ate those, too. I considered eating the worms, but I had never eaten insects before and I wasn't sure if I could bring myself to it. I thought about the body in the hall, and wondered which would be first.

Probably bugs.

I sat in the shade of the tree. I held still and let the sun warm me. Light spilled on my face.

A sunset. A sunrise. I was warm, then cold, then warm again. I had no idea what to do next. Rescue seemed impossible if I had no comprehension of where I was or how I had gotten there. If I was lost, so too would be the ones searching for me.

Slow, quiet terror gnawed on me from the inside of my hunger and thirst.

No taller than my knees, four legs like a dog or a cat and the torso of a small babe with two arms; six limbs, like an insect made of flesh. It walked around a corner, then, not seeing me with its wide, childlike eyes, it turned another corner and was gone.

I stood up. I walked toward the creature. I peered down the hall where the creature had gone. The grasses faded into sand. The walls were stones and bricks mortared together as if by limestone cements. I saw the strange, small creature. It had turned over a rock on the ground. It gathered up the insects there. Some it ate raw, silently, with no joy in its face. Some it shoved into a small, dirty pouch around its neck.

"Hello?" I said.

The creature turned to me. It looked me in the face with human eyes. It bolted down the hall, around a corner, and away.

"Hello?" I shouted.

It had crafted a pouch of some kind. It had made a tool and used it. I had never seen its like. I assumed it was an alien of some sort.

I went back to my tree. I sat under the tree again, thumping my fingers on the carapace of my ruined suit.

Birds were singing.

Curious, this strange way the seasons had turned. I followed my remembered trail to the cave. I was always, at heart, a scientist. I wanted to try again.

I went just inside the cave's maw, where I could still see the light of the outside world. I returned to the world. Nothing of the warm sun and grass had changed. I stopped to eat more of the grass. It was better than handfuls of sand. Back into the darkness, I passed beyond the sight of light.

"Wait," I said to no one. I sniffed the air.

No dead body.

I felt around the ground with my feet, shuffling into the cave, sniffing. I had expected the cave to remain the same.

I saw the ghostlight again, spilling up in a silent fountain from the ground. This remained, only and forever, in the center of the bush of mangled wooden limbs like discarded marionettes.

I stepped out to darkness, nightfall, and an inscrutable season neither warm nor cold. I looked up at the stars and could not place the map of them without the processors that were currently riddled with decay and worm eggs under the tree where I had arrived.

I picked my way down to where my suit was. I found a rotten stump. I found a stain of carbonates, cracked to dust and caked in a smear in the sand. I sat on the stump and wept.

MAZE

There was no rescue. There was no understanding. I was alone, and I could not reach a soul back on the station. After so many years in the maze, all the names and faces are behind a gauze, and to remember is like clutching butterflies with feathers. I had a life I knew, and friends, and I knew where I would wake up and sleep for every day of my life until I arrived in this strange place. I think my mother's name was Julie. This is why I named my daughter Julie: so I would never forget my mother's face, my mother's name. I wept until I did not have the strength to weep.

I would have died like this. But I didn't die. I had left a trail in the ground, familiar to the sort of person who knows how to read the footprints in the sand.

Saitan would find my footprints in the sand and follow them away from his own path to the cave until he found me.

I was one of the lucky newcomers. Nothing really bad had happened to me before I was found.

I lay down with my head resting on the lost curve of a shoulder—
the last recognizable piece of my suit that hadn't been infested with bugs
or seeds. I closed my eyes and tried not to think about the ghostlights.
When my eyes opened, it was light out. A man sat on a rock, ruddy brown
skin and smiling with filthy teeth.

He said something I didn't understand.

I said, "Who are you?"

He said something else I couldn't place. He offered me something
that looked like meat. He gestured for me to eat it. I did. He had a water
skin, too. He drank from it. Then he offered it to me. He placed both
hands upon his chest. "Saitan," he said

"I assume that's your name," I said. I tried it on my tongue, but broke
the word. I drank from the waterskin. The water was foul and stained with
the flavor of bitter leather. I couldn't get enough of it.

He repeated his name, pointing at himself, while I drank his water. He
urged me to speak it. I tried until I got it right. Then, he pointed at me.

I pointed at myself. "Maia," I said. I pointed at him. "Saitan?"

He clapped once. He pulled a spear from the grass. He picked up
a large stick with a stone strapped to the end like a hammer from beside the spear. He walked over to a strange bump of rock and poked
at it. The stone was actually soft as mud. Then, the man pointed at a
place where a small puddle of damp against the stones had been splattered a little, into something resembling an elephant-sized bird's foot,
though much of the shape had dissipated.

He spoke. I shook my head. "I can't understand you," I said.

He pointed his spear to the cave. He wrapped strips of dry leaves
around the stone on a stick. He lit the strips of leaves on fire. He gestured
to me to follow him.

"Maia," he said.

I followed him into the ground. I held his hand in the dark. I had
been afraid so long, I did not have the energy to be afraid of him.

I didn't know this right away, but I learned it. Saitan pointed at the ground. A shape in the sand could have been footprints.

Saitan followed a monster into the cave. He followed the monster through the cave. He emerged behind the monster into a new season every time he emerged. First snow, then spring, then summer, then bitter autumn.

A simple enough path.

I followed him. He lit his torch. He led me down. He walked me past the strange bush with the ghostlights. He walked me around a corner, where the footsteps of the monster led him. We descended a while, maybe an hour. Then, the cave turned sharply up and we climbed up with it. We emerged in moments, in light.

It was as bitter cold as when I had first arrived, though it wasn't snowy. I shivered. I frowned. The man pulled me close to him. He smiled. He spoke to me, though I did not know his words, and I was not afraid of him. He was not touching me meaningfully. He was just warming me up. He ran his hands up and down my arm and breathed his odorous breath upon the side of my head. He smacked at my arms, laughing heartily, and making jokes I couldn't understand.

We walked a trail down from the cave, around a corner, and through long halls on the path of some creature with large, bird-like feet.

We passed a smear of blood that used to be a small bird, as big as a chicken.

Saitan stopped and cut at what remained of the bird.

We walked, he and I, a circle around the cave, then down the cave, witnessing this mystery of time.

We learned enough to speak together, though we didn't know the right words.

We followed something large and dangerous. We followed it because he wanted to destroy it and bring its head to a young woman he loved, among his people, near the water.

Where are your people, Saitan?

Back that way, past a lake, and where the lake used to be. He showed me by running his fingers through a puddle, beyond the puddle, and by running his fingers around to show me where a puddle had been.

And a beautiful girl, with blonde hair—like mine, he runs his hands through my hair—and he doesn't want me to be alone. He will take me back with him when he finds his monster, kills it, and takes its head home.

He showed me the tracks when the weather was damp and the air was full of rain. *Look*, he said, *we're catching up to the monster.*

He spoke a language I had never heard. It resembled nothing to me. I could barely comprehend the basic phonemes.

Time folded into a mystery of days and nights and seasons changing in moments. How long was it like this, with Saitan?

Women have a clock inside them that measures out their days. It couldn't have been long, I thought. It couldn't have been long at all, even if it seemed long.

Monsters.

Mazes are full of monsters. The small dogmen, like malformed children, I've mentioned the minotaurs. Saitan ran one off and killed another with his spear. We ate its flesh raw and cooked and dried. I have seen the strange gargoyles turn to stone beneath my very eyes, moving only when no one can see them. I have hidden from trolls; I have dissected their corpses. I have run fingers through the thick, bitter sap that passes for their blood.

There was a time when there were no trolls in the maze, hunting men, I think, and a time when the trolls did not know we were even dangerous, or edible. Then, one day, there were trolls, roaming the halls alone and in packs. Are they natives here, or are they like us, far from home?

Cavemen wander the halls with clenched fists and biting animal maws. They throw stones and howl like monkeys. They live in caves along a cliff far from here, where our strong men patrol to beat them back when the cavemen wander from their halls too close to ours.

Seasons spent learning to speak to each other. Talking of how to reach his home, through this hall and that hall—he marked them with his spear, but the markings died. I had to remember the maps he carved into the rocks.

He brought me food. He asked nothing of me. I looked at him sleeping under the tree, in broad daylight. I wondered what would happen to me if he were to be killed by one of the monsters here.

People need each other. Saitan walked these halls to return to the woman he loved.

Without my daughter, Julie, I think I would have died.

In the cave, Saitan snuffed the torch out. He pressed into my arm. He pulled me close and wrapped his hand over my mouth to keep me from screaming. *Shh...*

I heard the footfalls, steady as stones.

A flash in the dark—a moving shadow against ghostlight—and Saitan held me and hushed me.

Like a dead tree and a lizard and a man, it poked and prodded so carefully upon the bush of the ghostlight.

We watched it, Saitan and me, prodding the branches and the fountain of light like a gardener. Under the long, spindly fingers—talons?—of the monster, the bush seemed to expand a little and tremble with ecstasy.

We waited. It moved on, down and down the cave, beyond our light.

We waited longer.

Saitan let go. He ran his hand along my hair. He whispered something in my ear. *Don't fear.*

He gathered his weapons. He walked ahead into the room lit by ghostlight and the bush. He handed me the torch. (He made torches every spring from the branches of the tree and the skin of animals he hunted in the spring. The tiny dogmen taste like rancid pork. The birds have been generally greasy and bland.)

I won't let it hurt you, he said to me. I don't know what he said, but I'm pretty sure that's what he said.

He pointed. He waved for me to follow him with the torchlight.

I followed him down.

We made another trip into the cave and out again. Winter, now. Bitter cold, and snow on the ground, piled up in heaps against the maze walls where the shadows mute the sunlight's passage through the sky. Saitan poured snow into his water skin. He was a native of this place, and he had a container for water, weapons, the knowledge of torches.

The tree was still there, all these times. Rising and falling, I wondered if it was the same tree or generations of a tree. I wondered but I had no laboratory tools or ways of making any here. I wish I could have climbed the tree, looked out over the stone walls, and seen the maze spread out before me. I wanted to get distance from the maze, to measure these hallways and twisting stone paths. Plants grew where they could, and there were none in deep winter, but naked stumps. If I tried to climb, Saitan stopped me. I was too afraid of the place to challenge his unspoken command. The best I could do to measure anything was take Saitan's spear and grind a notch in the tree. We came around again—autumn—and the notch was gone. I never saw any sign of Saitan's cuttings for his torches.

Saitan cut again and again into the dirty bricks, marking the path to take to his village to teach me the way.

I ran my finger over sand to repeat what I had learned. I touched the walls before he could carve into them.

I learned as best I could.

The monster never bent its skull around to us. It did not reach a claw out to slice our necks.

Not yet.

Saitan waited to be certain of a killing blow. He couldn't take chances with such a deadly creature, with such terrible claws, and me beside him.

I was frightened of it. I was holding my breath. I was afraid to raise my arm to stop Saitan when he moved away from me. He lurked around in the darkness with the brickbat in his hand. He sought his opening to attack, there at the edge of light.

He found none. The monster dissipated into darkness after the gardening was done.

Julie, my daughter, I taught her of blood, because I thought it was how to understand what it meant—what the underground meant—about our world and our place inside of it.

It was my hypothesis, though I could not truly test it with my current facilities, if I could even remember how to use any real tools by now.

I did the best I could to teach Julie, though. I placed a piece of bread—a small piece—in a basket where no insects or mice could reach it. I placed an equally small piece in a different basket. I showed Julie. I took blood from a bird and poured it onto just one of the bits of bread—but only a little, just enough to put a spot of blood on the bread.

"Tell me, Julie," I said, "which one of these pieces of bread will be the first to grow mold."

"They both will, if you don't eat them," she said. She was clapping her hands after an insect. She was listening to me, but she was chasing an insect.

"Don't eat either one, Julie. I'm teaching you about blood and about the things you cannot see inside of blood. Why you must wash yourself if you are dirty with strange things."

"They'll both grow mold."

"They will? Which one will grow the mold faster?"

"They both will together."

"Well, leave the bread here and we'll check it tomorrow morning, and every morning, and see which one is moldier."

"It's a waste of bread. Enyo Gyoja won't like it. Geraldine will yell."

"Enyo Gyoja has forgotten more things than we could possibly do to anger him, and Geraldine won't yell as long as we don't tell her anything."

The blood, of course, sprouted fungal blooms and wriggling maggots. The other was merely stale.

"Julie, don't forget to wash yourself if there is blood. Boil water before drinking it. Rinse your hands before eating.

"Please, Julie, listen to your mother. I know other people do things differently, but they aren't like us.

"That's right, beautiful one, it is because we are scientists. We study the natural world, and prove things empirically. We don't just believe anything, like the children throwing vulture feathers into fire."

Moldy bread, with every cavity of yeast inside a cell for the pupae of plant and animal: fungus and worm. This is the maze, to me. And the blood of the maze? Julie?

Julie isn't listening to me anymore. She's gone off to play with the other children.

We were in the snow. The tree had dwindled down to a sapling, whether from old age or winding back from age, I do not know. We couldn't pluck from its branches, for it had so few branches. I don't know how trees grow here, and I cannot assume.

I longed for the comforts of the station. My body ached with the maze life's endless travel to no destination. Space was so inhospitable to life that traveling there meant the careful engineering of paradise.

Here, Saitan smiled patiently. He held my hand while I picked my way around a stone.

Will you hurry, Saitan? Will you finish your task and take me where I may rest a while?

A little farther, he said. He held my hand and smiled. I didn't want to return to his village. I wanted to stay here forever, just behind the monster. For in its wake, we were safer than if we settled in its path.

Saitan said the village was in its path.

We can't live like this forever. I can't.

Saitan didn't hear me. He looked up at the muted sunlight past the clouds and caught snowflakes in his open palm. It looked like a ghostlight. It melted into his vinyl palms.

He led me back to the cave.

We saw the beast—it ignored us—climbing the rocks toward the cave. It didn't walk up a trail, like us. It latched its claws onto the stones and climbed directly up to the gap in the wall.

Saitan considered the cliff like he was going to try jumping it. He shook his head to himself. Then he led me on, again, out of the cold, into the darkness, then, into the comforts of autumn.

When will you kill it, Saitan?

When I know I can kill it.

How do you know if you can kill it?

When it is alone, its back is to us, and it is making enough noise to hide my approach.

(He turned his back to me, waved his arms around, and crumpled his bare feet in the gravel. That is how he spoke to me.)

Do it faster, Saitan.

(This is how I speak to him: I threw up at his feet. I was sick. I was getting worse. Every day I puked. My head ached all the time. I was exhausted all the time. My body felt all wrong—all wrong.)

Oh, Maia, I'm so sorry. I had no idea. Let us rest a while, in the summer.

No, kill your monster and take me to your village where I can rest a while, in all seasons, and I'm not walking all the time, day and night afraid of all these mysteries.

He nodded. He ran his hands through my hair. He kissed my forehead. I let him kiss me, there.

We entered the cavern. Saitan did not light our torch this time. We climbed into the darkness. Our eyes adjusted to the ghostlight glow.

The monster was there, a jagged silhouette against the bush of fountain light. It tore apart the bushes, now—resorting them?—into geometric shapes I didn't understand. The lights splattered up like a fountain, pulsing in the adjustments like pain. The air hummed with the pain of the adjustment

The monster stuck a hand into the glow to pluck out a single ghostlight. It held it in its palm like a fresh egg. I almost expected the monster to pull it close and rock it like a doll, the way it moved so carefully with the fragile light.

Saitan placed me in a spot, deliberately, with his hands on my hips to move me there, and planted me still as a tree.

Saitan handed me his spear and his empty torch. He peeled his stony hammer from his back without a sound. He took a deep breath—jumped. He struck with an animal howl.

The monster took the blow to the head. It bent over forward, throwing the tiny light up into the darkness and away. The monster crawled a little. It turned its head to its destroyer.

Saitan swung again.

Was it a monster, Saitan? Was it a killer of men? It looked pathetic, crawling on the ground.

Saitan sweated like rain. The adrenaline glow poured from his back, making him glisten in the ghostlight. He lifted the stone hammer again. He smashed it again. Saitan lifted the brickbat again, victorious.

My hand hurt. I held the spear tightly enough to hurt my hand.

The monster fell. It touched the bush. It pulled upon the geometric shapes.

The strange bush moved, not the beast: hands upon hands and legs upon legs, rising up, spindly, spider-style. The ghostlight streamed from it like a rocket flare.

Saitan stepped backward, the brickbat in front of him.

The bush stood on dozens of legs. Saitan swung his brickbat, but it was torn away by dozens of hands. Then, his arm was bleeding.

Saitan ran toward me, keening.

I was a tree.

The bush, with its fountain of light, stepped forward and raised a wall of talons.

I held so still.

Saitan ripped the spear from my hands. He pushed me back, back, back. He was shouting something. He was swinging the spear, jumping and dodging around the cavern, and the bush after him.

*Please...*A light in the darkness, a voice shouting from light, from all ghostlight. *Please, help me...*

"How can we help you?" I said.

Saitan was bleeding. His hands were covered in blood. The bush—the light—circled him.

Put-me-in-your-lung-put-me-in-your-lung-put-me-in-your-lung...

"But you're so big, and my lungs are so small."

Saitan was pulling on my arm, but he wasn't strong enough to pull me. He fell to one knee. He was weeping, I could see that he was bleeding all over his chest and stomach. I thought an entrail had fallen loose, whipping around like an umbilical cord.

"Can you help us?"

Please-help-me-please-help-me-please-help-me...

"I want to. But, you have to help us. My friend is hurt. He's going to die. He wants to help you."

Saitan couldn't scream. His blood was all over me. I was still. I was a tree. I was in shock. I was in a dream. I thought how I was going to have to wash the blood off before it caused an infection.

The bush collapsed into shards of glass. The fountain of light fell upon Saitan. His skin boiled with lesions and explosions and he screamed. His hand let go of mine. I backed away.

Then, Saitan divided like a cell. There were two Saitans: one dead, one living.

The light had fallen into Saitan, and his eyes were light.

The new Saitan picked up something from the fallen bits of bush. (A cape to cover his nakedness?) He did not notice me.

I poked the new Saitan with the butt of the spear.

"Are you...are you all right?"

Saitan cut at his own corpse, peeling meat from bones with finger-nails, eating meat raw. He ignored me.

I looked closer. Instead of Saitan's black, curling hair, this Saitan had leaf buds along his head and spine—green, green. This Saitan had feet like the base of a tree—like the monster we had killed. They looked like wooden hooves.

I backed up. I backed up and backed up until I was in darkness.

The creature of light, broken free of the bush, bent down over the broken monster and touched its head with light. It, too, divided in twain. One devoured the other far faster than Saitan ever could. But, this monster was not a frightening thing. It stood up and stretched. It turned its eyes to me. I curled into a fetal ball.

The monster walked with its huge tree legs over the ground, grinding the gravel into the stones. It bent down over me with the groan of trees in wind.

It placed a hand upon my head, gently. I looked up into his eyes. He lifted me up in his arms and carried me down into the deep, deep darkness.

Once there, he placed a hand upon my stomach, gently. I looked down.

A light shone there, where I had never noticed before because of Saitan's fires.

I was pregnant.

With the creature in front of me, leading me out and turning his head to make sure I was still with him, I walked out of the darkness.

The creature built a fire from the cast away wooden bones of the wooden body that Saitan had destroyed. I did not see the source of the spark. It could build fires. Listen, trolls know how to build fires. Do monstrous things know that?

I saw Saitan's mangled corpse, there.

I saw myself, collapsed into exhaustion, not far from the corpse.

The monster picked up my collapsed other self. It carried her limp body while I watched. It placed her near the fire.

And the light in the air that called to me...*Put-me-in-your-lung*...

"I will help you," I said. I knew exactly what to do, but I couldn't say exactly how I knew.

I plucked the ghostlight from the air. I cupped it in my palms like a dandelion seed. I held it over my prone, broken, unconscious body.

I believed, right then, that this was the only way to save my life from these monsters. I placed the light onto my skin. I watched it fall into my womb. It had wanted a lung, but what did these monsters know of human anatomy?

Then the monster left me there, without a word.

I pulled the meat from dead Saitan's pack. I listened closely for the sound of the satyr Saitan's wooden hooves clomping like sandals on the rocks. I was afraid of him, wherever he was.

I melted snow. I touched my face and wondered what I should say, this time.

When she woke up, I did not smile or caress her cheek. I said, to her, "You're doomed. You're doomed. It's better for you if you just starve to death here."

That's all I said.

I left her some of Saitan's meat, but barely enough to last a day. I did not listen to her questions. I did not show her my stomach.

Because I am a scientist. Because I must doubt. Because I must test.

5: End

I suspect, Julie, that you are Saitan's daughter, somewhere in the maze.

Here, you are the child of light, placed not inside a lung, but in a womb. Your light kept me safe when Saitan died.

I walked the maze a long time, carrying you inside of me. I had to try to remember the way that Saitan had shown me. I failed. I followed the circling of birds, because I believed that birds would know where things were safe, and where things could be eaten. I climbed walls to see the sky and watch for birds.

I ran from minotaurs. I ran from gargoyles. I ran and I ran. My feet bled in the path behind me until they hardened. I ate roots and gravel and sucked dew off shady rocks.

I found a harpy, wounded and flying alone, a small creature with the face of a woman and the body of a bird. I beat the wounded creature with a rock until it died. I ate it raw, face and breast and all. It made me sick unto the edge of death.

When Ascalon and Joseph found me, they were patrolling a long trail to protect the village and hunt for meat. They clapped their hands at me and spoke kind words. They took me back to their village where no one knew my language, or believed me when I told them I had come from a station in the sky. Maia Station became my name.

I never told anyone about Saitan. I never left the village again.

I know what's out there, among the stone halls. I know what is under the earth. Now, I just want to rest, with you, my daughter. I can abide here as long as I have you.

How horrible it was, to see Saitan there. I wanted to scream when I saw him. I knew him right away. He was unmistakable, even if he was young enough to be my child. I said his name, and he looked up and I pretended it was a happy accident that a word I knew was also that little one's name.

Saitan played with the other little ones, and stole his grandmother's idols for toys. Aia waddled after her boy, screaming at his back. And he ran, and he laughed, and he lived and lived.

Travelers, all of us, hurtling through time in a machine of bone and skin. Blood is our time; time is our blood.

Once, when he was a young boy, Saitan and his friend, the bastard caveman child, brought me a dead stone cow. They thought it would make me laugh, because everyone laughed at it. The stone cow had fallen in a heap of rock after the herd had been turned back, and the boys had claimed the best part. They couldn't bring all of it, only pieces. It was the skull and the neck. Saitan, a boy barely older than my own daughter, placed his hand into the mouth of the cow. He pushed it through until it jutted from the neck, and his hand aged a hundred years. It was wrinkled and hoary and horrible. He wiggled his fingers and pulled them back through, and his hand returned to youth.

Time is blood; blood is time.

There are bacteria all through our bodies we aren't even aware of. Sometimes our blood cells push them back. Sometimes the bacteria outlive us and flourish upon our desiccating bones, and generations of the bacteria pass from generation to generation and smear all over everything we touch or taste.

I don't think the bacteria inside of me, or the tiny little cells of my blood, know why they do what they do, or what happened to the colonies lost in the catastrophe when my daughter was born, or what will happen when I fall into age and fall still.

My daughter's name is Julie Station.

I touch her hair and wonder what evil I have wrought.

Leukocytes infect infections. Bacteria never know.

My beautiful cuckoo is more important to me than my own life. I want her to continue to live. I want her to have a long time and to have daughters of her own.

If the light ever finds me again, I know I will do whatever it wants.

I will give my daughter anything she wants.

The satyr Saitan is out there, roaming the tesseracts of the maze, growing old—perhaps very old, like a tree, with leaves growing from his head and wooden hooves.

My daughter dances in the winter. She wears the vulture feathers. She cackles and crows and laughs. She sings the vulture songs with the other children. She circles the flame. She throws her feathers into the fire. We cheer for her.

You're so beautiful.

I'll never tell a soul about you, Julie.

I'll speak so softly, you'll never wake up from your dreams, beautiful one.

Jenny
Ghost

1: Breathe Deep

My name is Joseph.

I know exactly when Parks and I passed from my known world to this one, in the maze, but I do not comprehend what happened. The other ones know less than us. Parks, listen, I'm so sorry. It's my fault. It isn't anyone's fault, but it might as well be mine. I thought you were beautiful. I drank tequila at the reunion and I caught your eyes and heard your voice, and you lingered inside of me stronger than the tequila.

You didn't know when you and I shook hands at our ten-year reunion. We exchanged business cards. Parks, the line of your neck, where your blonde hair descended, captured my eyes. Your smile remained long after your face had faded into the crowd.

What the hell did we say to each other? Stupid things like, "Hello! How have you been? What have you been doing?"

We were so cheerful, then. Texas wasn't so bad. The flu didn't hit us so hard, and we were all young and healthy, so we were fine. Our graduating class was fine. Someone had died of cancer, sure. Someone had cancer, and I was cornered at a table with him for nearly an hour, splitting tequilas and miserable that I was stuck there and miserable that I couldn't do a goddamn thing but buy another round. But, the flu? The federal collapse? They were just big news to us, at the edges of our neighborhoods, and we didn't even talk about it, really. We were private school kids with jobs and good families. It was the poor that were really dragged to shit, and they weren't us.

What did we talk about, Parks? We talked about how you weren't wearing cowboy boots anymore, like you were in high school. You weren't defined by boots, anymore. "You remember those? God, I don't even remember those."

You were wearing red heels.

"How could I forget your boots?"

"I wish I could remember anything about you like that."

"Not a thing?"

"Seriously, did you even go to my high school? I don't believe it. I don't remember you. Are you one of those guys that goes to reunions just to make everyone feel awkward?"

"We ran in different circles. I wasn't on any women's sports teams. Come on, how often have you ever spoken to a tuba player in your life?"

"Oh, my God, do you still play?" she said. "You've had ten years to practice. You have to be extremely good by now." There's a twinkle in her eye. "Can you play that song about the elephant?"

"I'm the best tuba player that ever was, as long as I don't have to prove it." I played in high school for a year. No one else thought the tuba was cool. I went back to saxophone. I haven't touched an instrument since I graduated.

Parks, you laughed. It wasn't funny, but you laughed anyway. Parks, you swirled your beer in your hand, as if you were accustomed to cocktails and the need to keep them mixed. "Do you get tired of meeting people's husbands and wives?"

"They seem nice. I bet they're all axe murderers."

We walked together, then, to the bar for another drink. We wound up at a table with someone whose husband returned, and she got up to dance with him and we were alone.

If someone was missing from the reunion, mostly no one asked. What's the point? The crazy stuff was all years ago, and things were going to get better. There were pictures lined up along a wall. There were cards to sign. I ignored them all. I wanted everyone I had known to be young and carefree and wandering from one house party to another on the stumbling road to good colleges, good jobs, and normal lives.

What did we talk about, Parks? I can't even remember. I just know that if we had never spoken, then—and don't ask me how I know, because I don't know that—that if we'd never spoken, none of this would have happened to you. It would have only happened to me.

And the light saw Parks Rogers inside of me.

Are you even listening? Someday, Parks, you'll listen to me when I'm telling you this story. Yi listens to me, I know.

My name is Jenny.

I was in a city inside of a city inside of a city. In the shadows there, I slept. I knew only my name—nothing else—and nothing, and nothing else for a very long time. I slid from behind a shadow and a shadow. I saw you sleeping here.

Put me in your lung.

Breathe deep.

Listen, I was trying to sleep; the squatters from the abandoned edges of the apartment complex had been smashing bottles in the open-air stairwells. They wanted people to think a car had been broken into.

The squatters wanted someone to open a door, to check on their car, to get mugged, and their apartment robbed.

One of my neighbors fired a gun into the night—probably out a window, into the woods, aiming at no one. We were respectable people who had been living in a nice neighborhood. I heard the squatters laughing and running back to the abandoned edges of our apartment complex.

Finally, I thought I could get some sleep.

I was trying to sleep.

But, I couldn't sleep. I saw something above my bed.

A spark flittered in the air, but not quite a spark, above my head as if the luminosity of a weak light bulb had escaped from the filament and glass.

I was in bed. I was tired. I had just gotten back from my high school reunion. I was lying down to sleep.

I considered the light and wondered if another lightning bug had slipped into my apartment. They did that sometimes. The safety light outside my door called them there, and when I opened my door, they slipped inside. The lightning bugs flew around and flashed their lovelorn longing across my dark apartment until the cats hunted them down.

I looked up at the puff of light over my bed, and I wondered if it was some kind of lightning bug, and if my cats would be diving through the sky after it. I wondered if the cats would go for a drink after their meal and ooze the glowing fluids into their water dish from their mouths.

This spark in the air was not a lightning bug. It was puffy, like a dustball of light. I didn't know what it was.

I sat up in bed. I heard something whispering, like a dust voice. I couldn't make it out.

Then, I knew exactly what it was. This glowing thing dancing near the ceiling of my bedroom, trying to get my attention, was a ghost.

I said, "I can't hear you."

I listened closer. I let my ear lean toward the puff of light. It was no larger than my palm. The puff was in my bedroom in the dark, flitting about my ceiling and whispering something. I'm sure it was whispering something.

I wasn't afraid because the puff of dust said to me, when I heard it at last, *Fear not...fear not...fear not...*

I reached a hand out. I cupped the glowing ball of dusty light in my hand. I pulled it close to my face. I looked down and knew it was a woman in my hand, though I had no evidence either way. I just knew this puff of light was a woman.

"I am not afraid," I said. "Who are you?"

Jenny...help me...help me...

"I'll help you. How do I help you?"

I was mostly naked. I had boxer shorts on. I had a bachelor apartment with my sheets languishing in the washer, awaiting the day I finally moved them over to the drier and back onto the bed. I had just gotten back from my ten-year high school reunion. I had done two more shots of tequila in my kitchen before going to my naked mattress in my boxer shorts. I used a comforter folded into a taco shell to keep the uncomfortable mattress liner from my sweaty skin. Cats tumbled at my feet until settling with me on the bed in nests of their own shedding hair. My last thought before losing consciousness was about vacuuming my mattress in the morning. I was ruining my comforter doing this so many nights with the cats. Then, I woke up. I saw the light, like a glowing lure in the dark.

"How do I help you?"

Put me in your lung.

I wanted to help her. I thought of swallowing the light, but I knew that wouldn't work. That would not take her to my lung, but to my stomach, and the light would be destroyed. I thought about my nose, and snorting the light like cocaine, but I worried it would go straight through my skull, into my brain instead. I wondered if light could make its way through tissue and bone. I wondered if I could just push the bulb of speaking, dusky light into my side.

Ghosts walk through walls, don't they? Ghosts fall through the air like dust mites of ectoplasmic nothing.

I placed the glowing ball of light against my right side. I pushed it into me, between my ribs. I felt a lump of energy, like a heavy stone, nestled between my lung and my rib.

Breathe deep...

I inhaled. It hurt. God, it hurt. I inhaled. I felt a crack in my rib. I had a broken stone inside of my chest. I couldn't breathe any deeper. I wanted to scream.

Deeper...

I kept inhaling. I expanded my lungs until I couldn't and then I expanded more. I couldn't see my stomach past my chest. I couldn't move my neck. God, it hurt.

Deeper...

I was pregnant in my chest with glowing light.

I darted my eyes down at the side that hurt like being broken open, and I was unafraid. I knew the bubbles would fall free of me, and a woman would be born naked and trembling. Her name would be Jenny, and she would always be so grateful for this thing I had done for her, breathing her ghost back to life.

I was not afraid. Nightmares terrify you. The same thing happens in a dream, and it is nothing but a moment in the mind drifting in and out of deep sleep.

And in and out of sleep, and in and out of pain; I fell into a memory of Parks Rogers, or did it fall into me when Jenny Ghost was pulled from my side?

Before the light came to me in the night, I had returned from my ten-year high school reunion. My classmates and I had been at this big downtown bar with a large patio in the middle of skyscrapers and trees. We were from a private school, so we weren't too big for just a bar downtown.

A girl I knew in high school as just some girl in cowboy boots was still single like me. We talked—probably for the first time in our lives—and I realized that I could fall in love with her as easily as breathing.

Parks and I exchanged business cards. We wandered off into the crowd. We wandered back together. We had a drink, at a quiet table, off by ourselves.

I was thinking about Parks Rogers from my ten-year reunion—about what Parks Rogers would think about this ghost woman—when I saw Jenny Ghost fall out of my chest.

Parks would probably call an ambulance, rush for medical assistance.

My skin fell loose and itchy where it had been broken by the bubble of the ghost. A huge broken blister oozed stinking puss across my chest, down into my comforter, and into the mattress—all ruined.

It hurt. God, it hurt.

A small woman was on my bedroom floor, named Jenny Ghost. She did not look up at me, yet.

Jenny Ghost gasped for air as if she hadn't breathed in centuries. I was surprised that she was dark-skinned, deeply African. I had assumed she would be born white like me, but she had skin as black as Nile river water.

The black suit I had worn to the reunion had been abandoned in a drunken heap near the bed. She had landed on it. She pulled it over herself like wrinkled curtains. My suit didn't fit the tiny woman, but she held it all over herself. In the black suit, in the dark bedroom, I had to squint to see where her skin ended and the suit began.

My bones came back together, but still they ached. I didn't think I'd be going to the gym in the morning. My skin pulled back together, but I knew I'd have an itch where the skin seams merged.

"Jenny?" I said. "Are you all right?"

She looked up at me in the dark. The whites of her eyes stood out like beacons in her dark face. I held my breath. She was beautiful and wild-eyed. She was short for a woman and young for a ghost. She had a thin dusting of black hair on her head, but no eyebrows. Her nearly-nude skull descended down her neck in an elegant curve to her collarbone, the rest hidden in the black suit.

Parks wasn't her name, and I had never even thought to learn her real name. Jenny, at least, had told me her real name.

Jenny Ghost was on my floor, born of my side. I couldn't think of how to explain this to Parks Rogers. There was nothing to say, and nothing to believe.

"Jenny Ghost," I said. "You were a ghost, weren't you? Are you all right now?"

"I'm fine," said Jenny Ghost. She stood up. She was more than four feet tall, but not five. She wasn't a midget or a child. "Go to sleep," she said.

Then, Jenny Ghost walked to the bedroom door. She didn't look back. She took my suit—and my blood and the air of my lungs—and she opened my bedroom door and closed it behind her.

I was too sore to chase after her. I touched my side and wondered if I had broken a rib, or merely bruised it. I felt put together wrong. I needed time to heal.

I spent three days in bed, calling in sick at work, staggering into an empty kitchen to drink water before staggering back to bed. I took my comforter to the dry cleaner and finally replaced my sheets.

It was all just a dream. I had injured myself in my sleep, while drunk. I'd had a bad dream about a ghost.

On the third day, I felt better.

I called Parks Rogers. We talked about the last movie we had seen. We were just trying to talk about anything, so we talked about movies.

None of the theaters were open, anymore, with California as bad as it was. We were limited to the odd foreign films at art museums, or whatever local things people were doing—documentaries and poorly made amateur films. Nothing good new was being made. State lines were all we had left, and who would cross them with gas prices so high?

Art museums hung on, showing films and helping us pretend like things are still okay, and things were going to get better.

"Things will get better. They are getting better," said Parks, on the phone. "I mean, we're doing all right, aren't we? It's not like we're in California."

"I know, right?" I said. "We're lucky, here. We still have normal lives."

"Right. We still do normal things. We talk on phones. We go on dates. You did call me to go on a date, right?"

"Uh... Yeah. Do you want to go out? On a date?"

"Yeah," she said. "I'd like that. Yeah."

I heard the sounds of things moving and cats clattering around the apartment. I heard rough rummaging in the pantry. I closed my eyes and tried to sleep. It was all just a dream. It was a cat. It was a cat on a shelf it wasn't supposed to be on.

I had called Parks Rogers to go see a foreign film. I had gone back to work, and I had told myself I had just had a cold. I wasn't injured. It was like nothing had happened to my chest.

My suit was missing. Had I taken it to the cleaners? They'd lost my clothes before. One of the dry cleaning ladies had been killed with a ski pole through her chest because a homeless guy had wanted clean clothes.

Had the dry cleaners gotten robbed again?

Had my suit been kicked underneath something in my messy apartment?

2: Don't Be Afraid

The next time I saw Jenny Ghost, she was in my kitchen, rummaging in my pantry for peanuts. She was still holding my abandoned suit around her like robes. I imagine she hadn't left my little apartment. I had a living room, an attached office area, a bathroom with a full tub—I paid extra for the full tub, but I only ever showered—and a bedroom. Jenny hid from me during the day—where, I don't know—and came out at night to rummage for food in the dark.

I had found the remains of her cravings in the morning, though I saw nothing but her trash for days. I didn't want to think about what was eating my saltines, fruit, and raw pasta.

I woke up to use the restroom, and I quietly padded out, barefoot, before I went into the bathroom, because I heard sounds. I saw her dark shape in the kitchen, moving around in darkness by my pantry, rummaging for peanuts. The light switch was next to me, near the bathroom door. I flipped it on. Jenny Ghost froze, an open jar of peanuts in her hand. She hid her prize in the rumples of the suit and looked at me with a blank face.

"I bet you haven't eaten decent food in a while," I said. "Want me to make you some eggs and toast? When women spend the night, I usually make them eggs and toast. Maybe some pancakes?"

Jenny put the peanut jar, unclosed, back into the pantry, and the lid next to it.

"Don't be afraid," I said. "I'm not afraid of you, am I? Look, sit down at the table. I have to pee, and I'll come back and make you a decent meal. You don't have to rummage for peanuts. You can sit down with me, and relax, and we can talk about anything you want to talk about. Okay?"

She said nothing. She stepped to my little dining area gingerly, with the hem of my suit pants smothering everything but her toes. She was within arm's reach of me, now. She looked at me like an animal looking at its own reflection. I gestured to the chair. She sat down.

She smiled, and she had a beautiful white smile. I guessed her age between sixteen and thirty-four. She was a beautiful, small woman, naked under a black suit that was far too big for her, and the jacket opened between her small, dark breasts, and the suit pants had to be constantly tugged and held by hands that scrunched up rolled sleeves to grip anything at all.

"A woman hasn't been here for a long time," she said.

I blinked. That was the first thing she had said to me since she was born. Of all the things to say, I had never imagined it would be that.

"No one has, lately," I said. "I don't even have that many friends."

"Your possessions are in heaps as if they aren't yours."

"The cats like to knock over my stuff. You sound like my mother."

"What is a mother?"

I pointed at the restroom. "You know some things but not some others, and that puzzles me. I'll be back in a sec. Don't hide. I won't hurt you. I want to help you if I can."

I went to the bathroom. I washed my hands quickly. I was worried that she would run off. I came out and she was still sitting at the kitchen table. She stared at her hands.

"I'm going to scramble you some eggs, unless you want pancakes. Eggs are easier."

She didn't say anything. I cooked her some eggs and toast. I placed butter and jelly on the table, and ketchup and hot sauce. I didn't know what she'd do next.

I put the food out in front of her, hot.

I pulled silverware out of the drawer. She had already begun to eat the eggs with her fingers. She stopped to suck the ketchup like a bottle of slow soda.

Why should I stop her? I'd already given up on that suit she wore like a bathrobe. I didn't want to criticize her. The last girl had left me because I was always so critical. I let Jenny Ghost eat. I didn't say anything to her at all. I waited for her to want to speak.

"Are you always this quiet?" she said.

"I don't know what you mean. Is there anything you'd like to talk about?"

She didn't say anything else. She stood up. Her dirty hands dripped egg from her fingertips. I was surprised she didn't lick her hands clean like one of my cats. She walked into the bathroom. I waited a moment, expecting the sounds of a toilet flushing. I heard nothing. I heard nothing for some time.

I walked toward the open bathroom door. I averted my eyes. I knocked on the doorjamb. "Are you all right in there?" I said.

Again, I heard nothing.

"I'm coming in, okay?" I stepped through the door, with my eyes at my feet. I turned on the bathroom light—she had not turned it on when she had stepped into the bathroom. At first I thought she wasn't there.

I looked around.

She was in the dry bathtub. She had her eyes closed. She slept. A cat nuzzled against her chest, purring. The suit lapels had fallen open around the cat. Her breasts, in full, with one of my cats nestled between them. She was short enough that the tub didn't cramp her. It fit her like a coffin.

I stared a long time—probably too long.

She began to snore.

I turned away from her. I turned off the lights. I left her with the cat.

In the morning, I couldn't find either her or that cat. I looked under the bed. I looked in cupboards. I looked in closets and behind furniture. I couldn't find Jenny Ghost anywhere. I couldn't find my cat anywhere.

I worried about her. Of course I did. But, I went to work. I came home. I didn't see her. What sounds I heard in the night were probably cats. It was probably just a dream. Cats were getting into the pantry, eating too much food, and stealing anything they could break into.

I was pretty sure Jenny wasn't real.

When the time came to meet Parks Rogers for a movie and dinner and drinks, I did not hesitate.

Fort Worth was a lost metropolis. Empty houses huddled against sky-scrapers that were mostly drying up and falling over like dead flowers. Train tracks had gone green and wild in the absence of trains. I didn't know why there weren't any people there anymore like there used to be, because all the bad stuff wasn't so bad here. Dallas was worse, but Dallas has always been worse.

I tried to take the highways into the city as long as I could. The state mostly kept the highways up, so folks could drive past Fort Worth and keep driving. From the high bridges of the Interstate, you could look down and pretend the city was like it had always been. The buildings looked the same as they always had, to me, if I ignored the broken win-dows and the way acidic rain had eaten at the paint like turpentine.

Parks Rogers still lived there. I did, too. Bars hung on downtown, where folks liked to remember the way things used to be and pretend like it wasn't so bad. Squatters weren't downtown, mostly. Security was tight everywhere, where there was money. A squatter was better off at the edges of town, where wild dogs could be caught in snares for food and collapsing buildings were only one or two stories.

I was early. I went up to the top of a building that used to be a roaring twenties whorehouse before it became just a bar. I took a seat on the balcony. I ordered a whiskey on the rocks. I watched the ice melt before Parks arrived. I measured her punctuality with the taste of water in my whiskey.

She was late enough to reach plain water. I had to order another whiskey, and it was a little watery when she finally arrived. I saw her walk through the door with a beer in her hand. She scanned the crowd.

I stood up. I raised my glass at her. She smiled and walked over to me. She was tall and thin and blonde, and her teeth were whiter and straighter than mine. She wore jeans and a polo shirt. I don't think I'd ever been on a first date with a girl who wore jeans and a polo shirt before. She was cleaner than I was. She was from a cleaner part of the world than I, who worked with lawyers and miners and the ones who fled for the coast, who were all folksy and one handshake away from mineral-stained palms. She worked in high-end retail and interstate shipping, web-designers and advertisers, and the kind of people who shopped in the gated malls. She walked over to me and said hello.

"I realized something, Parks," I said, instead of hello. We shook hands. She had smooth hands. They felt cold. The fingers were thin. I wondered how a tennis player could have hands like that. My hand must have felt like an inelegant clump of clay in her palm.

"What did you say?" She sat down across from me.

"I said that I realized something, Parks. I don't actually know your name. I only know your nickname. Unless Parks is your real name, in which case I'm just an ass."

"Karen, but call me Parks."

"Karen?"

"Do you want to know why everybody calls me 'Parks'?"

"I'm just glad I actually know your real name, but, yes."

"My dad called me that when I was a kid because I was too much of a tomboy to go by Karen. I hate my name. Parks was my Dad's thing. I don't know where he got it. I think it was because I liked going to state parks a lot. I think it's a better name for me than Karen. Why does everybody call you Joseph instead of Joe or Joey?"

"Joey is a whiny criminal's name, and when I introduce myself as 'Joe,' most people start calling me 'Jeff' or 'Jim.' I figure I'll just introduce myself as Joseph and let people call me whatever they want. Most people stick with Joseph."

"I'm going to call you Joey, now, Joey."

Who gave Jenny Ghost her name, if not a mother?

"If it makes you happy. But, if you call me Joey, I will steal your purse and complain about what's in it. That's what 'Joeys' do."

"That reminds me," she said. "I always tell a joke when I meet someone. I don't want you to laugh unless you really think it's funny. This is important. Humor is important, you know."

"Humor is serious business. You're right about that."

I'd never heard Jenny Ghost laugh.

"Okay, so listen. This is important. What has four legs and one arm?"

Had I seen her smile? I think I saw her smile.

"I don't know."

"Think about it a minute," she said. "See if you can figure it out." She played with her drink. Whenever she was thinking, she swirled her drink.

A sudden laugh, I think, like the kind of laugh a schizophrenic would have, that starts and stops like a machine gun. I didn't want Jenny to laugh, because I think it would scare me.

"I don't know," I said. "An elephant?"

"Nope. A very happy pit bull."

I blinked. I shook my head. "Okay."

"You don't think it's funny?"

I wondered if Jenny would eat a cat if I ran out of food. I wondered if she was real enough to eat a cat. I wondered if she was real enough to even pet one. Parks, do you think a ghost-made-flesh can pet a cat?

"I don't get the joke," I said. "Wait, I think I get it. Okay. That's kind of funny."

"But it's not really, really funny?"

"I don't really know any jokes. Honestly, I only know a couple, and all of them are dumb knock-knock jokes."

Did you ever hear the one about the ghost that wants you to put her in your lung?

"Tell me one."

"They're really stupid."

She said *breathe deep.*

"Tell me one," said Parks. "I don't care if it's stupid."

"Okay. Knock knock."

"Who's there?"

Jenny Ghost.

"Elvis Presley," I said.

"Elvis Presley, who?"

I don't know who she is. I don't know what she is. I just know that she is exactly what she is, and I can't make sense of her.

"You haven't heard of Elvis Presley? I'm the King! I'm Elvis frikkin' Presley!"

Parks blinked. She made a strange, warped expression with her clenched lips. She nodded slowly, as if to appease a madman.

"Our senses of humor are clearly incompatible," she said.

"Clearly. We can finish our drinks and go home, wise in our knowledge that this will never work out."

I don't know anything about her. I think I might be crazy. This sort of thing doesn't happen.

"Wise, yes. Drink, yes."

We paused for our drinks. I mirrored Parks' gesture of stirring the unstirrable with my own beverage, because I thought it might help her feel comfortable if I mimicked her body language. I wanted her to be comfortable with me. I wanted Jenny Ghost to be comfortable with me.

"Tell me about tennis, and I'll tell you if I think it's funny," I said.

She grimaced at the end of a gulp. "Don't we have some weird movie to catch?"

"Probably," I said. "I miss real movie theaters. I watch things online, at work, but it's not the same."

"We should start a drive-in movie club. If we get enough people together, we can hire security. That's what we do for the tennis club."

I frowned in faux sincerity. "That's not very funny," I said. "I told you I would tell you, and I am always honest about these things. Not funny."

Parks laughed, and it was mostly a pity laugh, but it was an honest pity laugh.

We talked more that night than we had at the reunion—than we had in high school. We talked about high school, and about how all the days have gone since. Things weren't so bad in Texas. We didn't have bad things to talk about.

At the end of the night, I had been taught the basic rules of tennis and Internet marketing. I had taught her the ins and outs of mineral rights and international oil and natural gas markets. I don't think either one of us had any clue what the other had really taught us beyond the basics by the end of the night.

We resolved to meet again, for lunch, later that week.

We hugged. Her blonde hair smelled like strawberries and cigar smoke. I hoped she liked how I smelled. I certainly liked how she smelled.

I went home, alone, to the shadow woman in the black suit hiding in my apartment. I couldn't imagine explaining Jenny Ghost to someone like Parks Rogers, who played tennis by night and did Internet marketing by day, and in between listened to iPods and drank beer and warmed the hearts of all men with her beautiful presence.

In my apartment, I made scrambled eggs. I placed them on the table. I put a fork and spoon next to the eggs.

Jenny Ghost emerged from her hiding place behind a couch. She sat down at the table.

"You were gone a long time," I said.

"You were gone, too."

"I had a date."

She reached her fingers into the eggs.

I held up a hand. "Wait," I said. I picked up the fork and used it to stab at the clumps of eggs. "If you use one of these, your hands will stay clean. Try." I lifted the fork with the egg up to her mouth for her to eat.

She bit down hard on the metal fork. She grimaced at it. Then, she slid the eggs off the fork that was in my hands. She looked at me with blank eyes—a mysterious, mercurial emptiness, glowing out from all that smooth, dark skin.

I put the fork down on the table. She picked it up carefully, holding it more like a delicate club than a sturdy utensil.

"Have you ever used silverware before?"

"I don't know," she said.

"I want to ask you a question," I said. I chose my words carefully. I spoke slowly, gently. "About before you came to me."

Jenny said nothing. She kept eating her eggs, with silverware. If she had trouble getting egg onto the fork, she used her fingers to push the egg onto the fork. Parks, did you ever volunteer at a homeless shelter? Did you ever work among the mentally disturbed? I wonder if you'd buy her clothes, wash her face, and teach her how to tie shoes and walk among the rest of us.

I didn't know what to do, so I stalled with questions.

"Where were you before you came to me in the night?" I said.

"I was in the shadows, before."

"What does that mean?"

"It means I was in the shadows."

"What kind of shadows, exactly?"

She paused, as if to think, but her face never changed. Then, she spoke. "There's a city inside of a city inside of a city. In the shadows, there I slept. I knew only my name, nothing else. I slid from behind the walls and saw you sleeping."

She kept eating. When she was done, she stretched her arms over her head. The jacket fell away from her breasts, and I couldn't help but look. She saw me looking at her torso. She peeled the jacket off and threw it onto the table, on top of the dirty dishes.

"Where were you, before?" she said.

"What do you mean?"

"Before I found you, where were you?"

"I was living in another place," I said. "Houston. Before that, I lived in a different part of this city, with my parents. I moved here, to this apartment, two years ago. I work here, for an oil company."

She neither blinked nor yawned nor smiled nor frowned. She was a statue of black marble with wrinkled cloth pants of black.

"Joseph, from Houston," she said. She held very still.

I stood up. I reached out a hand to her face. She was motionless under my palm. I stopped my hands at her neck.

I had strong hands, from weightlifting before work. I touched her neck. Her face didn't change. I clenched a little. I was experimenting with her blank face. I didn't want to choke her. I just wanted to test her.

In a dream, nothing scares you. In a nightmare, even simple gestures fill you with unspeakable dread. I was in a dream, unafraid. Parks, you know I couldn't do this if she didn't want this. You were there, in the tower at the heart of the maze. You know what it means to the creature in my kitchen.

I was choking Jenny Ghost.

Her face never even flinched. Her lips parted and struggled for air a little, but her eyes showed no pain, no fear.

Outside, the squatters were drunk and wild, throwing bottles again and taunting us inside of our apartments. The sound of them stomping up and down the stairs, and the glass breaking, crept into my head. A bottle smashed against my door. Then, a fist pounded on it. Someone shouted at me to come out and play.

I stopped. Jenny was neither happy nor sad to breathe again. I was dreaming—I had to be—but I felt in control of my own dreams.

I went to bed. I closed the door to my bedroom. I heard a gunshot. I heard a man screaming. I heard a siren in the distance, but it didn't come here. It disappeared as urgently as it had arrived. I heard one of my neighbors—the government worker, with the dachshunds—shout out to the complex that they were gone, now, and we could all get some sleep. Someone shouted a thank-you from a third-story window.

I wished management would do something about the squatters, but they probably didn't because if we chased off one set of squatters we'd only get another, and they might be worse than the ones that came before. At least our squatters were only bad when they were drunk, and they couldn't do it much with whatever homemade mash they converted into their own personal poison. Once a week—maybe twice—and the rest of the time it was fine.

Things weren't as bad there as they could have been. There were just too many apartments. At least rent was cheaper than ever.

In the morning, I took a shower. I went to work. I came home.

I wonder, if I had killed Jenny Ghost and thrown her body out of my apartment to the dangerous men, if then I could have taken the suit to the cleaners and called it all just a vivid dream to haunt my memory. It was all just a dream, Parks.

I was wrong about her name, and about what she was. Enyo Gyoja would help me understand this another day, far into the future, when I live in the maze.

Jenny was not her name.

The way Enyo Gyoja says it, and the rest of the people of the maze say it, is more like this: *Djinni.*

Parks drove a small Toyota hybrid. She owned some gigantic four-bedroom nightmare on an empty block. A pack of dogs had moved into one of the houses. She fed the wild dogs when she could. Dogs chased off squatters.

I knew what she meant when she said she preferred dogs. I carried a knife when I went from my car to my apartment, strapped against my ribs like a gun. I moved fast, too, especially after dark. I'd move out, into a gated community with at least a couple security guards, like Parks', but I preferred to rent until things got better in the cities. I didn't want to pay taxes to the state that ignored the new value of things. It wasn't so bad, after all, where I was.

Everyone said things would get better, soon.

South, to the Gulf Coast, is where people went after my company bought up all their mineral rights. They sought a better life near the ocean's easy shipping lanes and cheap tidal power.

Parks came to pick me up. We took her car. She picked me up from work, and she drove me into her neighborhood to a patio café cut into a huge, empty grocery store. They served lemonade and beer. The owner was a Bavarian folk musician. He had dozens of jukeboxes, all broken, that he swore he could fix, but they were never fixed for long. He wanted to fill the huge grocery store with broken jukeboxes. He wanted to fix them and hear how different music sounded from different machines.

We lounged on benches in the shadow of twisted sequoias. We sipped limo—half beer, half sprite—as if we were in a biergarten in Europe.

We talked about nothing important and we drank our limo.

Then, we went to a movie in the art museum. We were lucky to get a good deal on tickets from a scalper in the parking lot. We didn't care what was showing. We didn't even bother to watch the film. We went into the theater together, holding hands. We sat down in the last row, underneath the projector's window. We kissed there, the moment the room darkened. We kissed for a long time. We stopped to breathe and watch the movie, and we laughed because we had no idea what was happening on the screen, or what language they were speaking, or what old, black and white reality the director struggled to convey with his harsh lens.

I found my eyes drawn to the dark places in the room, where the projected light passed through the air—where it struck floating bits of dust and filled the air above me with mysterious illusions.

"I want to see where you live," she said.

I have a roommate. She's a squatter, kind of, but I haven't chased her off. I want to help her if I can, but I don't know how, and I'm not even completely sure she's real. "I have to work tomorrow," I said.

"Me too."

"We should call it a night," she said.

I want you to come to my apartment because if you see her, I know I'm not crazy. If you don't, then I know I'm crazy.

"I don't think the night cares if we call it or not. It always tends to show up. Who keeps calling it? The only party crasher I hate more is morning."

"We shouldn't, though," she said. "I'm crazy. I've had too much to drink. We shouldn't rush this."

"You're right."

"Why not try tomorrow night?"

"That would be rushing, wouldn't it? I'll think about it," I said.

"I'll come over, but we won't do anything," she said. "We'll just hang out, you know. I mean, that's what I want to do. I want to see how you live."

"Oh."

"Because it's too soon."

"It is. Come over, and we'll hang out. We'll make dinner together."

"After ten years, is being an adult everything you thought it would be when we were in high school?"

"Yes."

"It's lonelier than I expected, I admit it. I never expected it to be so lonely."

"People died. A lot of people died. We were lucky to be away from the worst of it. We shouldn't complain. Besides, in high school and college, we were surrounded by friends. We made friends without trying. Now, if it wasn't for work..."

"I can come by after tennis club. You can show me your CD collection, and I'll laugh at how quaint it is to collect CDs and not even own an old iPod."

I went home to the mysterious dark woman in my house. She was waiting for me, on the couch. She hadn't bothered to put the suit jacket back on. She came to me, when I walked in. She placed her hands on my shoulders. She leaned in close to me, as if she were going to kiss me. I felt the tips of her nipples against my shirt.

She didn't kiss me. She smelled me. She smelled my lips, my face, my neck, and all the places Parks' hands had been in my hair.

"If she comes over tomorrow, she can't run into you like this. Maybe you should leave. Put some clothes on, and get away from here. You can go find the squatters and stay with them a while."

"I will leave," she said. She stepped back from me. She walked into my office area and bent down behind a couch and she was gone into the shadows, a darkness hidden in the darkness.

I followed after her. I looked down upon her in her dark hiding place. "I don't know what you are. Are you a ghost?"

"I'm Jenny." Her teeth flashed white like a Cheshire Cat when she spoke. A smile? Was she baring her teeth?

"Right," I said. "What was it like before you were here?"

"It was a shadow world, but it was as real as this shadow world. What was it like here, before I was here?"

"Lonely," I said. "It still is. I like having someone here, even if you're completely fucking haunted. You're going to have to get professional help. Maybe I am, too, for dreaming of you. Are you real?"

"Nothing is real," she said.

She had a fork in her hand, held in a fist like a knife. She ran the fork through one of the cats' fur. It purred under the sharp tines. The cat purred and let the tines scratch it all over, roughly.

The next day at work, I read through the contracts I needed to read. I went to a meeting about a party we were going to throw for the people who would be signing the contracts after we were done with them, as a kind of goodbye gesture for them. They were all leaving for the coast.

I got an email from Parks. Her tennis club was canceled because of the rain and she was going to just go for a jog on a treadmill. She wanted to come over to my apartment, because she didn't want to be lonely.

I hadn't known it was raining.

I left my cubicle. I went two floors down so I could access a window that wasn't locked away behind a lawyer's door. I looked out at the city, the empty streets and the emptying skyline, and the few people left holding everything together. The roads spread out before me in their ragged grid, below the rain.

I thought—and this memory haunts me now that it has become a literal truth—I thought—listen—how my city was all a huge maze, with those streets twisting this way and that way, and all the lost people wandering the alleys between the failing buildings.

I drove home. Jenny was nowhere in sight. I shouted out to her to remain hidden because someone was coming over, and she wouldn't want to see another woman in the apartment. "At the very least, put a shirt on, Jenny."

I cleaned, aimlessly. I vacuumed cat hair. I cleaned the litter box. I took the trash out. I banged the dumpster before I threw the trash in the can to warn the raccoons and cats that another bag was coming. I had my knife in my hand when I did this, the whole time. I was ready to fight, and I wanted anyone who might have been looking to know it.

I was walking back when I saw Parks' Toyota pulling into a spot near my apartment. We said hello with a friendly kiss. I offered her the grand tour of the building.

The stairwell was there.

The dangerous people lived over that way. Sometimes they came over to raise hell until someone shot at them. It was usually that guy there, who worked for the state government, but I didn't know what he did. I was grateful that he was there to shoot his gun. I didn't have a gun.

I never walked around that corner, because the buildings were all abandoned over that way a long time.

Those neighbors were the couple that fought all the time at the top of their lungs, unless they were fucking at the top of their lungs. They were to be avoided. They were ashamed to make eye contact with any of their neighbors. We knew too much.

"I'm sure they're very nice people."

"My one-bedroom apartment is right here. I live alone with my cats. Wait—" I stopped Parks in her tracks. My hands were around her waist. I wanted to tell her.

"What is it?"

"I have to tell you something important."

"What?"

"In my apartment..."

I want to speak. I want to tell her that a squatter snuck in, and she's kind of crazy, but she isn't violent, so I don't know what to do. I can't tell her. I want her to walk in like it's nothing. I want her to see nothing. It's all a dream, and nothing else.

"What is it?"

"I don't just have, like, two cats."

"Okay. You have, like, three cats."

"No."

"How many cats do you have?"

"Seven."

"How many?"

"I have seven cats. Listen, I find them. If they seem friendly to people, I take them in. No one else will. I know it's a lot of cats, but I keep their box clean, and if I didn't take them in, who would? I don't bother naming them. I let them out if they want to go. I let them in if they come back. I feed them, and take them all to the vet once a year to get them fixed."

"Wait," she said. "Seven cats?"

"I know..."

"That's a lot of cats."

"I know," I said. "I've had nine before, but they wander off."

"You're a crazy cat guy. Is that what you needed to tell me?"

"Probably."

"Okay," she said. She smirked at me. "At least you couldn't possibly have any rats."

That isn't what I wanted to tell her.

Jenny Ghost was an intruder. She was an unwanted houseguest overstaying her welcome. She had taken my blood and my air and my food and my black suit, and she had refused to give me any answers. She was just a squatter. I'd call her one. I'd howl at her and throw her out. Parks would help. Then, we'd bond, together, over what we had done, chasing out the crazy intruder.

Dreams and nightmares: peeling an orange takes on the significance of death itself in a nightmare; peeling back a skull is as casual as peeling an orange in a dream.

I opened the door. I let Parks in first, praying silently to myself that my unexpected houseguest was at least wearing clothes. I didn't know what to expect.

I felt the knife under my shoulder, where it rested. I had to stop myself from reaching for it when I opened the door. I didn't want Parks to worry. I was ready to pull the knife and get Parks' help chasing away the woman who had fallen from my lung in the night. If there was a ghost here, at all, which I wasn't sure about. It couldn't be real. If it was, I had to act like I didn't know about it.

I was nervous, but I was not afraid.

Parks took two small steps into the apartment. She stopped. Her breath caught.

Jenny stood in the middle of the room, on top of a table, nude head to foot. Her growling head and lean, black body shivered with a violence I had never seen in her.

Parks hesitated there, in my open door. "What the...?" Parks held still, looking up at the short woman on top of a table, nude and trembling.

Jenny's white teeth were larger than her head. She frothed at the mouth.

One of my cats ran off out the door. I didn't move to stop the animal. I didn't move at all.

Djinni—I will call her what she really is, now—jumped with an open mouth for Parks. Djinni landed on Parks' long neck. Djinni bit. Parks collapsed under her attacker. I saw the blood. Djinni looked at me with her beautiful, empty eyes while she bit into Parks' neck.

Parks crumpled like a doll. Djinni didn't unclamp her teeth. She dragged Parks toward the bathroom.

I couldn't stop anything.

I had the nerve to follow, but not the power to stop what was happening in front of my eyes.

Dreams and nightmares bubbled like cauldrons inside of my head. Somewhere, a cat was screaming. Four of my cats followed us, yowling and hissing. Parks' supine body and Djinni's naked back disappeared into the bathroom, with my cats.

I reached the bathroom door. I peered inside. I saw Parks' eyes. They were alive, in terrible pain. Djinni was pushing herself, feet first, into the sink's drain, with Parks' limp body in tow like stunned prey in a cat's mouth.

Djinni slithered into the pipe somehow. I don't know how that's even possible, to bend time and space like that, to fit two grown women—one small and dark, one tall and white—into a small sink.

I reached out a hand, gently. My hand trembled. I touched Djinni's naked shoulder. I squeezed. "Please, stop...please...My god..."

Parks' blood had spilled down to the floor, where her dragging feet spread it everywhere. Blood ruined her clothes and dripped onto my bath mat and smeared where her long legs painted it. Djinni's mouth was full of blood. The terrible white teeth, now as large as her head, were stained with red blood.

Djinni didn't stop. I didn't want to stop her. I wanted to stop her. I touched her back. I clung to her. It was all I could do.

The sink opened for us three. Like some kind of snake, the sink rose up, widened its mouth and wrapped over us, or, we shrank, spilled head over heels like water, and tumbled into the sink. I don't know which. I remember both.

The pipes pressed against my skin. I didn't fit. It was musty and damp. It was full of small maggots that wiggled toward the fresh air on both ends of the sink, that were smashed into my body, my face, my ears, nose and mouth. I clung to Djinni's body. I felt the cats moving around my ankles, all screaming into the maggots.

I felt Djinni's body covered in slime under my palm. I lost my grip. Terror broke through the numb. I screamed.

I grabbed for Parks. I had my hand on her ankle for a time. I heard her moan a little, like crying. Her ankle felt cold and slick with blood.

I stayed with Parks as long as I could.

We were moving forward. I don't know where we were going. I squeezed my body through the slick pipes of my sink. I hung on. The metal warped around me. It altered the shape of my skull, my ribs, my limbs. I felt bent up, like a soda can.

Maggots moved between the metal and my skin. They had a song, now. I listened to the hum of maggots, like songbird cicadas.

Since the spark in the air, this was the first time I had been afraid.

I lost hold of Parks' leg. I scrambled after it. I shoved myself down the pipes with wriggling and will. I listened for the sounds of my cats screaming, but I couldn't hear them anymore over the maggot song.

The maggots poured over me. I banged my hand on something metal and cold. I curled my flesh around it like a snake. It hurt to do that. I kept pushing and pushing through the tiny maggots.

After my legs, I felt the pipes returning to their place in the world, all small and thin and caked with lime and wet, disgusting fixtures of old toothpaste, shaving cream, and hair and tiny maggots.

I scrambled forward because I didn't want the shrinking pipes to crush me. They must have crushed the cats.

The maggots hummed their cicada whistle. I felt their little wriggling bodies reverberate against my skin with the hum. The song filled my mouth and nose and ears because I had maggots there, wriggling around the open places in my head.

The pipes shriveled up behind me. I couldn't move fast enough. The shrinking pipes pushed me forward. I traveled a long, long time this way, but it wasn't long at all. A thousand years. A moment. A bending tesseract I'll never comprehend.

I was born into darkness, caked in rotted lime and humming maggots wriggling over my skin and under my skin and all smashed dead. I was in a long, dark place. I spat the maggots out of my mouth. I shook them out of my ears and scraped at them with my filthy fingernails. My stomach turned, at last, with room to erupt.

My eyes adjusted. I saw past sewer grating to sunlight. I grabbed at the bars and was surprised by the feel of calcified stone instead of steel. The bars were made of rocks, not metal. I pulled myself up to the top of the grate to look outside at the sky, the sun. I saw a blue sky, cloudless and blue, like a perfect summer day. I pulled and pushed the heavy stone grate until it swung open with a loud clang. I pulled myself out of the hole in the ground.

My body ached with spent adrenaline, and bent up, beat up flesh and bone.

When my eyes focused in the sunlight, I moaned in fear at what I saw before me. I was too afraid to scream. I held my breath.

I gazed upon a barren pueblo city, a rocky, empty ruin. I was on a hill above the endless, endless, endless maze.

Joseph's
Maze

1: Shadow City

Doorways and windows and rooftops and furniture inside; that is how I knew I looked upon a city on a hill, though I did not know the builders. Apparently there were enemies that longed to tear this empty city down enough to justify the defensive walls wrapped around the buildings.

The defending walls, ruined now, were all full of holes. I saw the maze beyond the city, through the crumbled places, though I did not recognize what the maze was except for more walls. The city was on a hill. Through a large enough hole, I saw over the maze walls, too.

I still don't comprehend the maze. I still don't comprehend the city. There is no anthropology here .

In the city, sienna-colored sandstone blocks piled into square-roofed houses in ordered rows that had eroded into ruins. How long would the city stand against wind? Rotten wood doors hung open to broken tables and chairs, and everything was as decrepit as antiques left to fester.

I sat on a dusty road, smothered in the dirty, maggoty scrapings of the pipes. I had the city in front of me, rising up to the top of the hill, where a castle grew out of the stones, even as all the buildings had begun their long, slow collapse back down the hill.. At the top of the hill, a jagged jumble of towers reached above these sandstone pueblos. The castle looked like a yucca made of granite bricks, shooting towers out in bending angles and jumbles around a center tower that peaked like a flower growing into the twisted crenellations of a castle.

I stood up, alone in an empty city. Dust walked the streets in the bending breezes. I looked around for any sign of life.

I saw little drops of dampness in the dirt, like blood. I knew it was blood. It had to be blood. It had to be her blood. Someone had to save her.

The blood drops dribbled toward the nearest wall, to run in shadows up the hill. Then, the blood walked up the street, toward the huge, yucca-shaped castle. I followed the blood to the castle at the center of this strange city.

I touched the blood on the side of the sandstone walls. The blood climbed directly up a wall, smearing the white granite, as if Parks had been carried by a giant spider, and not a creature of hands and feet.

I tried to find the door to the castle, so I could climb inside and crawl up to the top of the tower to find them.

Sweat beaded on my neck. It was both fear sweat and heat sweat. I had stepped into a realm of summer, and I was dressed for a breezy spring night.

I realized, in the proverbial flash, that I was not in possession of any water whatsoever, and I had no idea how to find water. I also had no food in my pockets. I had some breath mints. I put one under my tongue so I could feel something in my mouth. It pulled water from my cheeks while I sucked on it. It made me feel less hot, less thirsty. I followed the white granite wall.

The castle spread like an endless cathedral. It must have been as big as a football field inside, with palace rooms and towering ceilings.

What looked like windows were high above my head, but they were shaped in strange bends and whorls, as if they had melted out of the shape of windows, or grown into them. If I'd had a rope and grappling hook, I could have investigated them.

Also, I thought to myself, if I'd had any idea how to use a rope and grappling hook, to go with this hypothetical possession, I could have investigated the windows. I was in far beyond my abilities. I read mining contracts all day long. I worked out in an air-conditioned gymnasium on machines. I ate microwaveable food and drank water in fancy clear bottles that I bought from fancy, clear refrigerated machines. I had the ceramic knife under my shoulder that I had honestly hoped never to use, and I had no skill or training with it. I leaned against the wall. I slid down it. I was breathing hard, hyperventilating.

I was so scared.

I grabbed my legs and pulled my head in to my knees.

I was so scared.

I tried to breath.

(*Breathe deep*, she had said.)

I blacked out. I don't know how long it was.

My clothes were filthy. I leaned against the castle wall, close to what appeared to be a door in the center of my field of vision.

I flicked off a gently humming maggot that still clung to the smeared sink filth all over my chest, crawling around and singing. I leaned against the wall. I looked at the castle door, dangling slightly open and creaking when the breeze blew over it.

I panicked.

I ran back toward the blood trail. I ran as fast as I could down the road that wound down the hill between all these empty houses. I threw myself upon the grating. I bruised my fingers yanking open the sewer and dove in. I clawed all around me for the way home in that dark place. I prayed to a God I had ignored since I was old enough to make up my own mind about it. I had never encountered anything that had required a faith in God until the spark in my bedroom had pulled a woman from my side who had become a monster. I scraped my fingers raw searching the underground sewer for the secret hole or switch that led to my familiar world. I prayed to God to help me. I don't know how long I looked. When I stopped, I was still in an empty sewer that continued on in both directions. There was only the faintest trickle of water. I was thirsty. The water looked brackish and green. I knew it would make me sick. I wondered if I could collect enough of it, if I could boil it somehow. I thought I should start a fire and boil the water.

I wanted the nightmare to end. I wanted to go back to my office and read contracts, and notate the contracts in the computer system, and hang out in the break room, and tell lawyer jokes to lawyers. I could do nothing for Parks. I had to save myself, and it was all I wanted to do.

I climbed out of the sewer. The nearest house, built like a pueblo, had nothing that might ignite, but it had a clay pot that wasn't completely broken. I used my hands to fill the pot up with water as best I could until my patience and my trembling hands—I was so thirsty—made it so hard not to lick my hands clean of the filthy green water. In another house, I found old furniture, as dry as newspapers and brittle. I piled the broken wood up.

I placed the pot with the water on the firewood.

I had no way to start a blaze. I had no matches. I had no flint.

I pulled my knife out. My blade was ceramic, not metal. I had nothing to make a spark. Not even my hilt was metal.

I didn't panic. I took a deep breath.

Then, before I could talk myself out of it, I drank the water from the sewer. It tasted like rotten eggs, dirt, and something else indescribably awful. I choked down the urge to puke. I expected that this water was going to make me horribly ill—possibly kill me. I did not drink enough to quench my thirst. I couldn't.

I slipped into a house. I climbed up to the second story. All the rooms were empty of furniture. One of the rooms had holes in the floor that peered down into another empty room. I chose a room that seemed to have the sturdiest floor, one with a window that looked out over the sewer grate.

MAZE

I listened to the silence of the empty city—a big, terrible empty like I had never heard before in the cities of my life. Between breezes, there was no sound.

I was missing meetings. I imagined the way things must have looked, with me up and gone in the middle of the night and all that blood.

I had fallen in with squatters, wandering from city to city, scavenging for food like coyotes. I imagined the police talking to my boss, my co-workers, and everyone so surprised to learn I was gone in a trail of blood. I was missing, and so much of her blood...

Shadows leaned down to sleep with the sun. Moonlight and starlight came to this strange, empty world. I recognized no constellations. I slept, too, for a time.

I heard something.

I clenched my fist over the knife's hilt.

My ears strained, and I thought I heard the crackle and hiss of a fire. I sniffed the air, and I smelled the smoke and the cooking. It was a large fire, and meat was burning.

I unsheathed my ceramic knife. I walked cautiously—quietly—toward the sounds. I moved away from the castle, down the hill to where it was nearly flat through the streets of the empty city. I walked toward a wall. Even in the moonlight and starlight, the pillar of smoke was visible above the dilapidated wall where the hill descended sharply into the maze. I heard sing-song grunting. A man's voice sounded like the singing hurt his throat.

At the edge of the city, a desiccated wall separated the city from the hillside between the maze and the ruins. A giant flame burned there, on the sloping hill, with thin branches piled high and what looked to be rope or vine and stones arranged to level the ground below the burning mound.

A figure danced around the flame. I couldn't make out any details. He had a long coat that fluttered behind his wild flailing. He had wild hair and a long staff. He had sandals that lifted him high off the ground. I didn't know how he could dance with those sandals. He was dancing too wildly to notice me creeping toward him from the shadows of the city beyond the broken wall.

I nudged myself into a crack in the mortaring, wide enough to let me pass through sideways.

A bonfire as big as a funeral pyre, with wood piled in heaps to match the height of the broken wall, burned with a heat and light I could feel from where I stood.

I saw the shadows at the top of the burning pyre.

Two bodies, larger and smaller, dead and burning.

The dancing man sang a painful song with a scratchy voice. I don't know if the song had lyrics or if it was only a sound. I didn't speak the language.

I could make out the shape of burning bodies. It could have been two. It could have been Parks and Djinni, both.

The man's huge jacket, like the kind gunslingers wore, was held together by leathery patches and ragged cloth. It moved behind him like a cape. He was naked beneath it, lean and glistening. He danced wildly. He waved his staff around; little metal loops jangled at the top of the staff. He was dancing, but it was not dancing, for it had no order or balance or pattern. He moved to the sound of his own mournful voice.

Beyond him, the fire illuminated the empty space where the sloping hillside beyond the wall descended into the stone walls of the maze. The weeds along the hill looked like they might catch fire. The air was dry enough for a grass fire. In the dark, I couldn't tell if the grass was dry enough.

I kept my knife ready, held with the blade concealed along my arm. I found a larger gap in the wall, where I could climb through the breech.

I didn't know if it was Parks there, or Djinni, or anyone burning.

My shoes scraped against the edge of the wall. I did not know how to walk in silence.

The man froze. He turned to find the noise.

I saw his face. I dove back behind the broken wall, into the city.

Was I right to call him a man? His mouth and chin looked like an ape's with canine teeth and a beastly, jutting maw.

I clenched the knife hard.

I backed away, ready with my knife. He paused at the gap in the stones. He caught my eyes. He growled. He sounded like an animal.

I stepped back.

"Please stop!" I shouted. "I won't hurt you!"

The man swung his staff through the wall. It struck me on my shoulder, hard. I clenched my teeth.

I swung the knife against the staff, but I couldn't stop the man. He jumped through a large gap in the wall. He had terrible eyes.

I grabbed at the staff. I missed. I caught it. I pulled on it. The man pulled back hard. I didn't let go.

He didn't let go. He had the staff in both of his hands, and he pulled hard. He snarled something at me, garbled through the beastly maw and teeth. I didn't know if it was language. I had my knife in my other hand, but I hadn't used it but to try to block a little. I pushed the knife toward the man. I swiped at his body but missed. I swiped at the arms and the staff. I drew blood through the coat sleeves. He released his staff with one of his hands. He snatched my knife hand in his powerful fist. He kicked at me with his wooden sandals. He shoved the two wooden slats at my legs. I stepped back from him. I didn't have the balance to kick back during the onslaught. I backpedaled, taking painful kicks to my legs. I held onto the staff and the knife, trying not to be too badly kicked.

I pulled hard with both arms when the man was kicking me. I tried to pull him off balance with his legs kicking. It worked. He fell forward, his glistening, sweaty chest bouncing off of mine. His beast face, all contorted in violence, flew into mine. His teeth snapped like he was going to bite me.

I kneed him in the groin. It did nothing.

I wrestled to get my knife free, to tear the staff away. I pushed at the beast man. He was too strong. He had momentum. He kept falling into me. I backpedaled, getting kicked again. I stepped backward into the deserted streets. I tripped on my own feet like a fool. I fell onto my back. I lost hold of the staff.

I'm lucky I kept hold of the knife. He pulled.

The beast man stood over me, with his weapon free and me on my back below him. He barked and growled.

I saw my death. Even the squatters near my apartment would steal before they killed—would negotiate. Here, death was a hawk upon a sleeping hare. There, in that face, I saw death: an animal hidden in the skin of a man.

The man smacked me with his staff. It hurt more than anything I had ever known. I curled into a fetal ball with my knife hand clutched in his stony palm. I tried to protect my head, my bones.

The beast man threw my knife hand down. He lifted the staff over his head and struck me once, very hard, on the wrist that held the knife. I couldn't believe I didn't lose my grip. He struck me again, with both of his hands swinging the staff, on my skull. The pain was muted by my empty hand, where I clutched at myself.

I didn't want to die.

I lunged at him with the knife. His hands were over his head to swing wildly with his staff. I lunged low. I had the knife in my hand. I wrapped my arms around him.

I got him in the gut. I got him again in the gut. I swung around to get him in the back, too, inside of his coat. I stabbed him again in the back, spilling blood along the inner lining of suede and cloth.

Again.

I held him with one arm. Pain shivered through his body. Blood wept. Quivering in pain, making wild faces, he screamed.

I stabbed him in the side. I stabbed him again, in the throat. I stabbed him high on his back, through his duster. I felt my blade glance off a rib. I found his spine. I found the soft places next to his spine. I dug the blade deeper into a hole I had already cut in his stomach. I cut him again, higher, in the back of his neck. I cut him again and again, everywhere I could, until I was all that held him up.

The beast man was limp, completely, leaning against me and bleeding on me.

I stepped back from the him. I let him lean into death, gently, as if he was greeting his own shadow with a kiss. I left him there, in the streets of the empty city, in the growing darkness.

I plucked the staff from the ground because I wanted another weapon in hand. I went searching for his fire, but I could barely walk to do it. I leaned on the staff. My body was a field of bruises. I had killed the beast man, but I hadn't won the fight.

The fire burned strong, though the beast man who had danced around it was dead.

I looked down the hill to the maze beyond the city. A million curves of brick and stone tangled through the hills, as far as the night horizon allowed me to see. I walked around the fire. The bodies were burnt beyond recognition. I knew they didn't have the faces of beasts, but that was all I knew. Neither one looked like Parks or Djinni. The child was too small. The woman too large for Djinni but too short for Parks. The fire burned them down to greasy ash. I whispered a quick prayer to God, ashes to ashes and dust to dust, whoever these bodies may be.

I don't know why he attacked me.

I don't know anything.

I'll never know.

Djinni brought me to this place, this time. That's all I know.

2: Life is Eternal. Go to Sleep.

People stumble into the maze, I know, from all over the world and time. Most of them die right away. They starve. They get killed and eaten by the monsters. I was lucky to be alive.

I'll tell you what I think the maze is. It's like the Bermuda Triangle, but it's not that at all. It's where things go when their dreams are too powerful to contain inside their heads, but that's not it, either. It's a place indifferent to us. We fall inside in our ways, unknown to us.

Then, we do the best we can.

I made my way slowly back toward the dark city, where the body lay in the street. I rummaged through his coat for any kind of pockets, or water. I found nothing. I unwrapped the coat from his body because I thought I could eat the leather where it wasn't that bloody.

I went to the nearest empty building. The door was gone. Inside, all the furniture had been smashed.

I leaned into an empty corner. I closed my eyes.

In the morning, would I have the strength to open the sewer grate and drink more of the filthy water there? My arms felt pulped and swollen. My throat was cracked and dry. I couldn't imagine lifting the grate, climbing down into the sewer, drinking the foul liquid, and climbing out again. I couldn't imagine surviving another day.

I slept in the numbing kind of pain, so strong the body mutes itself away from everything felt and thought. I thought of nothing.

I saw the shadow in the dark. I was asleep, and I saw the shadow. It loomed over me.

"Jenny?" I said.

She touched my ankle, where I had touched hers.

"Please, Jenny...please, help me..."

She came close to me, in the dark. She was smelling me, from toe to head.

I closed my eyes. "I think I'm going to die," I said.

"Not yet," said Djinni.

"Where's Parks?"

"What is Parks?"

"The woman you took. You bit her neck. You dragged her away like you were going to eat her."

"She's always here."

"Help me, Jenny," I said. "Please...What do you want from us?"

"I will help you," she said.

"I think I'm going to die, Jenny..."

She touched my arm. "Life is eternal. Go to sleep."

I obeyed.

What gauze boundaries did I cross in sleep? I don't know. I'll never know. Nothing works the way I think it should. Was it a hallucination, there, when I closed my eyes and opened them again?

A family of dark Djinni sat down to a meal in the house, but all as intangible as shadows, to me. A shadow of a table hovered over the ground at their knees and they squatted around it, all female. On the table, a raw beast man, oozing blood, his dead eyes like skinned grapes staring at me.

The family of Djinni turned as one to me. They cocked their heads.

One of them, on the other side of the table from me, shoved a knife into her eye. Behind her eye, a light like Jenny Ghost drifted like a dandelion seed down to the dead beast man's body. It took seed, rumbling.

Put me in your lung...

The nearest one to me had turned her head around like an owl to look at me. She leaned over me and placed a hand upon my ankle, and it was Jenny grabbing my ankle, dragging me back into the sewers. Then, I saw the rest. All the Djinni were my Jenny Ghost, with other lungs to birth them. The rocks and sand grinding into my back felt real. When I awoke, I felt the little scabs there, and the grime in my clothes.

My name is Djinni...

I closed my eyes. I was terrified. Was it real? Was it a dream?

I heard screaming, and it was so terrible. It was Parks, and she was screaming, and she was far away, and I couldn't save her.

Today, I think that any dream that does not wash away when I open my eyes is not a dream at all. All remembered things are real. All felt, remembered things are real.

Vultures' laughter yanked me from the shadows. The sun had risen. I had been sleeping in a sewer. Was sewer the right word? There were grates of stone, not steel. The walls did not appear carved. They seemed found, not built. The water flowed, but here on the top of the hill I could not think of a source above ground.

Nothing makes sense. I'll call it a sewer. I think water flowed from one world to another. I think water flowed through tesseracts, indifferent to the way time doesn't always work like it's supposed to work.

I saw the body the vultures had swarmed around, but it was too small to be the man I had killed. It was some large animal, I thought, like a dog.

A rock clattered on the stones beside the birds. Then, another. Then, three rocks of different sizes flew through the air and landed directly on birds.

Birds jeered and shouted. Smaller ones flew off.

The vultures spread their wings and hissed like cats.

More rocks flew through the air. I heard women's voices shouting at the birds. I turned to look, but couldn't see the throwers of the rocks between the houses. I don't know what the women were saying. I didn't care. I hobbled into the nearest open door. I huddled into a corner. I held my breath.

A woman tracked my steps through the sandy streets into the house. She carried a large rock with one hand on her shoulder like a shot-put. I looked up at her. I didn't move. She had a human face, but she was so filthy I couldn't tell what her ethnicity was. She had strips of strange leather wrapped all over her, body dirtier than her, like clothing.

I slowly lifted my ceramic knife and the dead man's staff. I held them in the air between us. I tried to move my legs to stand up, but I couldn't stand up. I was too weak.

I started to cry.

She smiled. She was missing teeth. She said something calming. She did not lower her rock. She called out to the others. Another woman arrived. This one was the tallest woman I had ever seen. She was taller than I was by at least a foot. Her limbs were meaty and long, like a basketball player's. She knelt at my feet. She gently reached for the weapons I held up. She spoke soothingly.

I said, "I don't understand you." It sounded more like a croak, with my throat so painfully dry.

I lowered the staff. I did not let go of it. I pretended my knife was a glass of water. I gestured with my hand at my mouth. I mimicked drinking. "I'm so thirsty."

The woman with the rock pointed at my weapons. She waved them down, toward the ground with her free hand. The tall one had taken a wad of leather from her back. She shook it. It sloshed with liquid. She held it out to me. She spoke soothingly. She wanted me to put my weapons on the ground, too, with her eyes and hands.

I did, but I kept them close to me.

It was water. It tasted hot and stale and bitter. I drank as much as I could stomach. Then, I drank some more. I drank until I thought I was going to throw up.

The giant woman placed her hands over mine. She took the water skin from me and handed it back to her friend.

The giant woman helped me to my feet. She touched her chest. "Aia," she said. "Aia." She touched my shoulders, and looked at me expectantly.

"Joseph?" I said.

"Yjusf?"

I nodded. I pointed at her. "Eye-uh?"

The woman with the stone was named Yi. She didn't try to pronounce my name.

She smiled and clapped her hands. Behind me, Aia gathered the weapons from the ground where I had left them. I shivered at her, behind me, holding weapons. What could I do that wouldn't get me killed?

In the street, near the body of the monstrous thing, a third woman stood over the corpse. She could have been the small woman's sister. She had a long wooden pole, and she had lashed the arms and legs around the pole.

It was a six-limbed thing, like a centaur, with a human torso and an animal body. It had been mauled by birds, but it still had the face of a baby, with puckered infant cheeks. It had two hands like a child's. Its skin merged seamlessly with some kind of dog-like beast, with wiry hairs and padded dog feet and a dog's shaggy tail.

Food, I assumed. My stomach rumbled at the thought of food, but it also turned a little at the thought of eating that strange, rotten thing.

The two short women managed to heft the creature on the pole between them.

Yi picked up my knife slipped it not into its holster, but into the holster's strap across my back, where I could not reach it easily. The staff, I was given to help me walk.

Aia kept her arms around me. She helped me walk .

I tried to stop. I tried to point to the tower. I heard the screaming there. They looked, with a frown, to the towers at the top of the hill, but did not wish to stop.

I said, though I knew they wouldn't understand me, "Jenny?" I said, "Jenny took my friend. Do you know of a... thing named Jenny?"

"Djinni?" said one of the small women. Her eyes widened. "Djinni?" She pointed up toward the palace.

This stopped them. This made them look toward the sound of screaming.

"Jenny, yes." I gestured at my side and tried to explain how she had come to me, and grown from my side, and taken my friend to the tower. I waved my hands around. "She has my friend. We have to save her!"

I do not know what was understood and what wasn't. I know their eyes clouded with fear. I know they led me away from the castle.

We climbed down the naked hill, where bricks of the ruined city wall had tumbled with bits of broken furniture and all sorts of strange bones and old fire pits. I took my first, fateful steps into the maze.

I lost sight of the horizon, then. The breeze died. The ground was littered with the erosion of the walls, though the walls still stood.

More people were there, at the edge of the place where the city wall eroded down a hillside into the maze. Dozens of people of all shapes and sizes and colors had stone and bone and wood and leather huts. They lived there. They told me their names and tried to say mine.

(You know their names. Here we are, and we are one of them. Many were born here, and some found themselves here, and all will die here, in the maze.)

I saw our future when I saw them living near the wall.

They were dirty, as if they had been born of the maze bricks, like birds emerging from eggs. Their clothes were in tatters worse than any squatter. I recognized pieces of clothing: part of a wool skirt, and what remained of leather jackets, and burlap, and even some boots that had been re-soled roughly with stone or wood. I saw plenty of bits of clothing I couldn't recognize, torn and fixed and torn and fixed until they were more patch than shape. I didn't count their number, but there appeared to be more than two dozen people—men, women, children.

Faces and names, faces and names. I spent the day sitting on a rock with them, accepting their food and drink and learning names. I learned the word for drink and the word for food. I learned how they squatted over grates, and how they celebrated the return of a successful man who had snared birds with nets or a woman who had gathered soft roots that tasted like raw rhubarb.

We tried words against each other. No languages sprouted between us, yet. Food and drink. Sky and ground. A face, a name, and a wall of babbled sounds.

We heard Parks Rogers in the castle tower. I knew it was her. I can still hear her screaming sometimes, if I listen to my memories, or I'm lying down to sleep.

God, she was screaming.

The screams, again. Why didn't these people save her? Couldn't they hear her screaming? Eyes turned nervously skyward at the distant screams magnified by the silence all around us.

Parks Rogers, I could have fallen in love with you as easily as breathing, and now my nightmare has consumed you into a nightmare worse than mine.

If you had just stopped screaming, I could have forgotten you. If you had stopped screaming, I could have lived among the tribe, then, with only a distant anguish where you were torn into this place and lost in a trail of blood. Would it have been better or worse for you? Would you have chosen for me to come for you, to try to save you when there was no balm for my sins, no happy ending for us, and no homecoming?

The screams, again. The native people here turned their eyes to the tower, then most looked away, back to what they were doing. A boy—Wang Xin was his name—shielded his eyes from the sun and gazed up. Then, he turned to me, and I knew that he knew it was all my fault. The eyes of the child looked to me as cold as blame.

Aia, Yi, Enyo Gyoja, Jon, Regina, Ascalon, were all there, looking sadly up to the tower. This is the life where death is always close. The screams would fade eventually. How many lives would be spent to save someone they didn't know from a danger that could kill them all?

Injuries were serious, here, where cuts infected and bones didn't mend straight, and no opiates calmed the nerves in the night. If it was bad, and there were screams like that, then it was only a matter of blood and time.

But Wang Xin, the boy who had come to this maze like I had, found among the halls as a child, remembering nothing of his arrival but a bicycle and a fall, he looked at me like he knew. He took a long drink of water. He looked right at me. The screams were being ignored. He wasn't ignoring them. He was waiting for me to do something. I was trying to ignore them, but I couldn't ignore screams like that, yet. Then, Wang Xin looked me in the face. He drank, again, and looked me in the face. He knew that I was a sinner. He could see my guilt and shame.

I would save you, Parks, because I loved you and it was my fault this happened to you.

God, your screams Parks.

God, you were screaming.

The two Asian-looking women took the dead body away, toward a small fire. I was right about what they were going to do with the body. Women with sharpened stones butchered the flesh with practiced hands. Organs were thrown into a large stone bowl. The body was carved into chunks and skewered on sticks.

I was led to an old man. He sat on a rock. He had a smile on his face that exposed all the empty spaces in his rotten teeth. He held a staff and wore a green cape of leaves. He mopped sweat away with green leaves. He looked at me, expectantly.

I didn't know what he wanted me to do. I tried shaking his hand. He looked at it, indifferent to it.

He said something to me, then, that sounded pleased with me. I don't know what he said.

The giant woman said something to him, and I only recognized one word: *Djinni.*

His smile disappeared. The old man nodded.

I pointed at myself. "Joseph," I said. I did it again.

The old man pointed at me. "Jesiff."

I nodded. I pointed at him. I cocked my head.

He nodded. He pointed at himself. "Enyo Gyoja," he said.

I repeated it back to him, and he smiled and nodded, but I knew I was saying it wrong.

I pointed up, past the giant woman, and past the maze, toward the castle and the tower that we could still see looming above us. "Parks," I said. "Jenny and Parks."

"Paks-Jinnimpaks?"

I shook my head. I thought a moment. I sat down on the ground in front of the old man. I picked up a rock from the ground. "Joseph," I said. I placed the rock on my head. I, then, put the rock on the ground. I picked up another rock. "Parks," I said. I put it on the ground beside the rock I had named for myself. I picked up another rock. I held it up. "Jenny," I said. I placed it on the ground beside the other two.

"Djinni," said the old man. He nodded. He leaned over. He picked up the rock that I had named Parks, and the rock that I had named Jenny. He lifted them up and gestured toward the tower. "Djinni Parks?" He held them up one at a time as he spoke.

I think he understood, then, though I could not explain exactly what he understood. I had no way to explain to him, yet, how I had come to this place.

Aia sat down next to me. She ran a hand through my hair. She pulled at my clothes, as if she were trying to figure out how they stayed on my body. I don't believe she had ever seen buttons before, or a belt. Everyone here used leather lashes to keep the rags on, as far as I could tell, and hooks and eyes made of bone and leather were the best they had. No one used buttons.

I pulled at one of my buttons. I opened the top of my shirt. I closed it again. Aia laughed and clapped her hands.

She immediately pulled me off the ground and led me to the others so I could demonstrate the buttons to everyone.

I was determined not to show anyone the zipper in my slacks, or the teeth of my cotton belt.

This was a permanent encampment, here, on this side of the empty city's hill. I would soon know it like a home. People didn't live in pueblo houses. They probably didn't even know what such a thing was. They lived in lean-tos, pressed against the sturdiest section of the city walls, where they could defend themselves against intruders better, as I would see soon enough. A single sheet of leather formed a roof from wall to ground. Below the huts, people slept in heaps, clustered together. Large sacks of various leather origins contained all the belongings, piled in heaps. Dried out bladders filled with feathers were pillows and furniture. Children ran naked, singing and smacking at each other with tiny fists and stones.

Aia took me to her hut. I sprawled on a large, soft pelt. I placed my head on a leathery pillow, gently.

I closed my eyes.

In my sleep, someone took my shirt and pants. Someone rubbed oily lard all over my bruises. I woke to the horrible smell and all that dusty leather. It was night when I awoke. It was dark. Aia had pressed against me, innocently. She breathed on my shoulder. Her body heat warmed my naked chill.

I was lying in the middle of a strange, dangerous place in my boxer shorts.

I fell back into sleep.

I peeled away from Aia. I saw a young man, Ascalon, wearing my pants, belt and all, playing with children. Yi wore my shirt over her leathers.

I scraped my fingernails over the fat rubbed into my bruises. I flicked it off my nails. I looked around at the people here, laid out on the ground or leaning against the walls of the maze, waking up from sleep.

They looked like a pack of murderous cannibals. They reeked of blood rot and death rot and unwashed skin.

I thought about how I was going to die if I did not become like them, and kill like them, and eat what they ate, and follow vultures to dead meat for my next meal.

I also thought of Parks.

Other people woke up. The skin of the dead creature was stretched out and scraped for drying.

A lone bird flew overhead, though it was too high up for me to know what it was. I assumed it was a vulture searching for the dead.

Enyo Gyoja led me past empty spider webs and ant mounds, down a hill of fallen rocks that led us to the many entrances of the maze. I followed Enyo Gyoja deeper into the maze, dread hanging in my stomach like a fallen brick. Enyo Gyoja seemed to know where he led me.

Sounds faded in the bending stones, then bounced back again. It sounded like ghosts. It frightened me, but I stayed with Enyo Gyoja.

We turned a corner, to a place where water poured out from a wall, as if like magic, spilled down to the ground, and fanned out over the dirt. The stream wasn't even an inch deep. Men and women were here, gathering water in skins and lingering on fallen bricks. Children ran and played around the edges, singing and clapping and laughing. They are whom I heard when we walked near to this place, not ghosts.

Some of the men held brickbats and spears and watched the edges of our group.

By then it was mid-morning, and I felt the sunburn all over my white body. I felt my skin drying and crinkling. I wondered when the blisters would set in. I wondered if the sun would be enough to kill me, as dehydrated as I was.

We rested by the water. My skin burned, unused to sunlight. I tried to find shade. Yi rubbed lard all over my red, painfully sunburned skin. I had blisters bubbling up all over. She cooed at me, soothingly.

"Yi," I said. Tears filled my eyes. "Yi, please don't." I pushed at her hands.

"Sh, Jusiff," she said. "Sh, Jusiff." She pushed back. She had strong hands. She was trying to help me—to heal me. "Sh, Joseph."

I pressed my hands against the rocks. I clutched. I tried not to howl under her touch. I held my breath. I clenched my teeth. Tears leaked out from my eyes like screams clenched into tiny diamonds.

Many years have passed, and pain is no longer so unfamiliar. This is a hard place. There are no doctors here. There are no dentists. Our food fights with better weapons than ours—talon, horn, and fang. I have scars now, and skin cured by years of sunlight. Mosquitoes break their beaks on my calloused hands and feet, then I eat the ones I catch on my skin— smash them and lick them up.

In only a day, I learned how to say water, and food, and to communicate where and how I was in excruciating pain. I learned the word for sun, and sunburn. I taught them to say shirt and pants. I tried to teach them the word maze, but they had difficulty understanding something too large to be pointed.

When all our water skins were filled and we had rested, one of the men called back to us. We all stood very still. All their heads turned toward the sound at once, like my cats did toward buzzing fireflies. Something moved, with thick footfalls in a lumbering sort of gallop.

(I know it now: a herd of minotaurs. Feet like walking apes, with monkey-like hairs up their straight-backed torsos to the long-snouted, carnivorous faces and bull horns. We called them minotaurs, like the Greeks, because—I assume—a Grecian stumbled into the maze.)

Without a word, the group quickly gathered up all it possessed and fell back from the water, away from the sound of something coming.

Yi stayed with me, strong hand gripping my arm. She led me away, quickly.

We returned to the village at the edge of the abandoned city. Enyo Gyoja pointed up at the tower. "Djinni?" he said, to me.

"Parks and Djinni," I said.

He shook his head and kicked at the dirt with his sandal. He mumbled something under his breath that might as well have been *That's just awful, I tell you, just awful, but there's nothing we can do about it.*

This place is my home, even now. It's yours, too, Parks, forever.

There's nothing to say that you don't already know.

Some of the men—five besides Enyo Gyoja and me—had taken up position with spears and brickbats fashioned from broken furniture and tree branches of mysterious origin and broken stones at a narrow place in the road between the palace and the encampment.

(That one, over there. The one where we hide on the other side when stone cows come for the plants. It's narrow, there, and we can close it down from both sides without getting trampled.)

The men had thrown up barricades around the door of the castle. Piles of rocks were behind the men.

They were grim-looking, those men. They spoke little. They guarded the narrow place in the street that led up the hill to the palace.

Stones and sticks and leather walls were getting piled up around the edges.

(We stay here, in this place, because we can defend it. I figured that one out when I saw the kids knocking over huts and stealing the walls to frame the gaps where bricks did not defend us. We wanted to keep the creatures that were coming for us landing at the strongest point. The little dog centaurs weren't intuitive creatures, so it wasn't hard to outsmart them. Not like the cavemen, who can think a little, and perhaps communicate with each other with their hideous faces.)

I heard the scream in the distance again, like something I was hallucinating, like a bird keening. Then I heard something that wasn't human.

I walked toward the barricades. I pulled my knife from its hilt. I took a spear from the boy, Wang Xin, urging him to give it to me. When he realized what I wanted, he released it from his hands. I re-sheathed my knife, wondering to myself why I had taken it out in the first place.

The men didn't stop me when I reached their barricade.

They had set up two long walls of wood and leather and bone, parallel to each other but angled in the corridor between two pueblo huts. Anything running downhill would run into the alley, where it would get skewered.

I saw blood on the ground, but I didn't think it was human blood. Up the hill, I heard nothing. I didn't even hear the people behind me setting up barricades. I made my way to the castle at the top. I tugged open the giant, smooth wooden door by its own knobby bark-like protuberances.

I didn't expect to survive this. I wanted to die instead of living like a wild thing. I had slept through your screams like a wild thing. Parks, she was there. Listen, never sleep while the people you love are in danger. Do you hear me? Never, never sleep when the people you love are screaming in pain. God, forgive me that. She still won't.

I pushed my way inside.

3: Shadow Palace

The doors shut behind me. What little light that slipped in from the melted-looking windows high overhead could not illuminate the giant space.

I used my new spear like a blind man's walking stick and moved ahead. I turned to the right and moved forward until my spear found a hole in the floor, too misshapen to be intentional. I maneuvered around the hole in the floor carefully. I found another wall. I stumbled in the dark, looking for stairs.

I found a strange obstruction in the center of the room. It seemed to feel like a stone pedestal, with armrests and a small chair back. It felt like a chair. I tested the sturdiness of it with my hand. It was attached to the floor—a part of the castle, not a piece of furniture.

I felt around the chair for any sign of traps or danger. I found nothing.

I sat down. I took a drink from the water skin. I couldn't even see enough to find the door back out to the empty city.

I strained my eyes for any sign of light. I strained my ears for any sound of life.

Then—right then—I saw the shadows move. Darkness inside of darkness, like blackness against midnight stones. I gasped. I screamed a little—not even brave enough for a scream, I was.

Shadows moved.

I closed my eyes.

This was a nightmare. I was too afraid to move. I held my breath as long as I could. I breathed as quietly as I could.

I whimpered when I tried to speak, to call for help.

The shadows moved.

(*I was in a city inside of a city inside of a city. In the shadows there, I slept. I knew only my name—nothing else—and nothing, and nothing else for a very long time. I slid from behind a shadow and a shadow. I saw you sleeping here.*)

When my fear passed down into a numb, manageable hum, I did the impossible.

I opened my eyes. I watched a long time, still too afraid to move.

The shadows were having a party.

The shadows were almost shaped like people in the darkness. They said nothing. I recognized women in ballroom gowns and men in top hats and tails, moving like shadow puppets. I recognized bowing and men kissing the women's palms. I recognized dancing, though I heard no music.

A servant of darkness carried a tray of black wine. The shadows plucked glasses from the tray. The shadows toasted in silence, and some of them seemed to be dancing more wildly than the others, in the middle of the floor, without partners to slow them down.

I stood up from the throne. I still saw the shadows.

I wondered if I would be able to see them in all the buildings, now that I knew what to look for in the night, in the places where no moonlight spilled.

(I couldn't, but I still look for them in the dark where I am now.)

I prodded at one of them with my spear. It was as if nothing was there, before my eyes. An older man, fat and with a long mustache, waggled his chins at a much taller woman who hunched over to listen. She touched the man's arm. She bent over and kissed him. She moved through the blade of my spear like it wasn't there.

My heart pounded in my throat. I took four steps before I remembered about the hole in the ground. I jammed my spear into the ground, again, using it like a walking stick. The shadows ignored me. They passed through me like ghosts. They grew in number. I could not make out individuals among so many dark shapes.

I found, again, the hole in the ground. I found, again, the walls that had confused me.

I found a door. I didn't know where it led. I shoved it open and jumped through, with the shadowy tendrils behind me, lifting the hair on my neck. Fog-like shadows reached for me, urged me to join the party.

Sunlight melted all the shadows as if they were never there.

I had returned to the empty city of savages in the center of the sprawling maze. I stumbled out before the barricades. The men jumped to their feet. They shouted ferociously.

I shouted at them not to hurt me.

Rocks flew over the barricades. They flew over my head. I turned and saw the thing that was struck by the rocks. It was small, barely a foot high.

It had four legs, like a dog's, and two arms and a bald, round head like a baby. It had teeth jutting from its mouth like some kind of ogre.

The rocks smashed it in the head and knocked it over.

Yi jumped over the barricade with two men. She ran to me and yanked me back from the fight.

Two men swung brickbats and smashed the thing that crawled down the outside of the door like a spider.

The other men didn't seem to notice the shadows.

Yi walked me back to the hut where I had convalesced. The idols there must have been considered helpful. Enyo Gyoja came in as soon as I lay down. "Djinni?" he said to me.

I shook my head. "I couldn't find her," I said, sadly. "I couldn't find the stairs up."

He seemed to understand my tone. He nodded sadly. One of the men brought the hideous thing into the hut. He held it up for Enyo Gyoja by its dog-like hind leg.

"Paks?" he said, pointing at it.

"No," I said. "I don't know what that is." I sat up. I pointed at the hideous thing and shook my head. "We aren't going to eat it, are we?"

The creature was taken off. I didn't want to think about where it was going and what I had been eating already, these days.

"I have to go back," I said. "In the morning, I have to go back and find Parks."

Enyo blinked. He shrugged. He left me there, with Yi.

I imagined that monstrous little thing running through the darkness and the shadows, frothing at its tiny mouth, waiting for any leg to pass before it.

I stayed inside again. When I heard screams, I ignored them, for now.

Night, and the people of the empty city returned to their huts. Aia, the giant woman, returned to this hut. She pressed her body into mine, and together we beat back the chill of the dark.

Whether I heard them or imagined them, the occasional screams in the night mocked my prayers.

I fell in and out of nightmares. I woke up screaming. Aia clenched her arms around me too tightly when I screamed, and it made it worse. She muttered threats into my ear.

Often, the pain of my skin against the gravel woke me. I adjusted. I fell back into another nightmare until pain woke me again.

In the morning, Yi came to me. She rubbed lard all over my old injuries, scraping away the sand and flecks of dead, dried, burnt skin. Another woman came to me, much older than Yi.

She placed her hands on my body in a way I couldn't recognize. She pressed her palms against the sides of my ribs, around my neck, and over my hips where they met my torso. Then, she left in mystery.

When she returned, she had the long cowboy coat of the monstrous man I had killed. She wrapped it over my body as if I were part of their tribe. She lashed it closed using the many sharp teeth of the thing that had followed me from the castle.

The old woman had slashed the leather where I kept my knife under my shoulder. She pulled the hilt of the blade through, so I could reach it quickly. She understood the importance of weapons.

It was daylight.

I ate the meat that I was given and tried not to think of the origin.

Enyo Gyoja came to me. He smiled with his solitary tooth. "An-Paks? Djinni?"

I sighed. I nodded at the tiny old man.

He led me to the cookfire. He urged me to sit down on a stone. He removed my shoes and socks. My shoes, he placed back on my pale, white feet. My socks, he stuck onto the ends of sticks. Then, he smeared fatty oils and greases all over my socks from a small bladder full of grease. He stuffed the socks with leaves.

I watched him do this, clueless as to the meaning.

He smothered my socks in this grease. He wrapped leather lashes over one of the sticks. He gently placed it over my shoulder like a rifle. He stuck the other stick with my greasy sock into the morning's cook fire until the lard-covered sock caught the flame. It burned, steady and calm. He handed it to me.

"Djinni An-Paks," he said, like a punctuation mark.

I had light now. The people there watched me take the light on my sock. They did nothing to stop me, said nothing to me at all. They just watched; interested or not, I could not tell.

I held up my torch in the air, and I held my knife in my other hand. I stepped past the barricade. I entered the castle, armed with light.

I held in my mind an image of the place as I had explored it in the night, with the different walls and hallways and empty places in the floor.

When I opened the door, I saw none of these things. I saw only a long, long hallway, and the holes were merely missing tiles that fell an inch into the ground. I saw a chair at the end of the hallway. I saw various buttresses along the inner walls. What I had thought were hallways was just the maze of the buttresses and the gaps in their mortaring where a man could walk through the broken, wilted places in the walls.

I walked straight toward the chair. Like a tiny throne, the chair held the center of this room. The sturdy thing grew up from the floor; it had armrests and a back, as if designed to tower over a dwarf in majesty. When I sat in it, I felt the armrests pressing against my hips. I towered over the stone back.

A shiver went up my spine: Djinni was only just above four feet tall. Was this her throne? Had she spent so many years waiting here, in the darkness and shadows?

I did not see the trap door below my feet, yet.

Beyond the chair, I saw sprawling spirals of staircases. The many stairways twisted like mangled helixes around each other. I looked up above at the way the stairwells unraveled and traveled up to the different towers.

I couldn't tell which stairway led to Djinni, and to Parks.

I guessed.

I climbed up and up the stairs until my legs ached. There were no railings, only stairs. I so much as stumbled slightly, I'd fall fifty feet straight down. Fortunately, despite their strange, sprawling patterns like some kind of cacti of stairs, the actual treads were smooth and even stones.

I stopped to rest my aching, burnt body before crossing over past the dark place where the stairs reached beyond the ceiling. I didn't know what to expect, beyond. I drank from the water skin. I tried to hold very still so my sunburnt legs and back would stop screaming. I was glad I had the leather shirt between my second torch and my skin. If that splintered wood had been rubbing against my naked back, the pain would have been crippling instead of the manageable excruciation I felt over my sunburn there.

I looked at my knife and considered how it would feel to stab Jenny Ghost with it. I couldn't imagine cutting her face.

I couldn't imagine stabbing her in the chest, where a cat had so recently slept in peace. I could probably stab her in the gut. It would be soft, and slow, and very painful. I couldn't imagine cutting her throat—or anyone's throat. I couldn't imagine stabbing her in her beautiful, terrible face.

My hands remembered the way the monstrous man had felt below my knife. I didn't want to think about the feeling of jamming a knife into soft flesh until it hit the bone.

My first torch had become too gentle. I sheathed my knife and unstrapped the second torch. I did not try to light it, yet. When I ran out of light, I would have to stumble on in the dark without a spear to guide me.

I tried to hurry up the stairs, beyond the ceiling, to where the passage narrowed into a bending tower's tunnel. I walked against a wall. The stairs hugged the sides of the tower. The center was open, tumbling freefall around the oddly bending angles and elbows of this tower.

After what seemed a very long time, I pressed my second torch against the first and hoped the fire would catch between them.

I climbed very slowly, then. I was getting tired.

There were no railings here, either. The stairs spiraled upward endlessly. I leaned against the wall with one hand. The first torch was nearly embers. The other would not burn forever. I climbed, my breath ragged and my feet heavier with each step. I prayed to God to keep my fire burning long enough.

If I was near the top, I could just walk in the dark, and it wouldn't matter that I was out of light. There would be windows in the tower, wouldn't there? I recalled seeing windows. There would be something like windows. There would be light at the top.

The tower twisted and bent higher and higher.

At the top of this tower, the stairs ended at a stone ladder that jutted up sharply to a trap door.

I opened the trap door. I climbed up to the top of the tower.

I climbed up into a large, dark room.

The first thing I saw was the tiny throne. I had climbed back up to the main room that I had left far below me. I climbed out of a trap door disguised with thin tiles in the stones just in front of the throne. I dropped down and looked at where I had climbed and the tangled maze of stairs. I came up, into the throne room.

Did I curse? Did I moan? No, I did none of these things. I was amazed at what I had just witnessed. I was amazed the stairway had led me back to where I had begun. I had never seen anything like that.

My last sock had nearly burnt through. My legs had no more stairs in them. I closed the trap door so I wouldn't accidentally fall into it if the darkness returned. I sat down on the throne. I believed, right then, that all the stairs led the same way, to the same place. I was in a maze, and a city of shadows. Why shouldn't the stairs lead to Djinni's empty throne?

I sought out the trap door in the floor again. I couldn't open it the same way it had opened, from below. The hidden hinges did not bend that way. Instead, I scrabbled at the stones with my fingernails. I flung the door open in the direction that it would open.

From the hole in the ground, I heard a chittering sound, like some kind of insect. I gazed down into the trap door from whence I had climbed. I saw clouds. I saw birds. I saw sky. Maggots, like the ones from my portalling here, lined the walls of the hole, chittering gently in the soft beginning of their song.

Sunlight poured in from this open door.

I felt gravity pulling at me, the wrong way and the right way both at once.

I flung the trap door closed. The loss of sunlight thrust me back into the darkness of my fading socks. I panicked.

I bolted for the front door.

I stepped outside, into late afternoon. I walked as quickly as I could toward the village.

Then, I saw the village walls were up. I saw the killing zone in the center, where there was a slight gap to invite a monster's charge. I saw the fighting.

When I stepped into the street, they were already fighting, though I never heard a thing from inside. There were so many of them. More fell from the sky above, gliding down on wings that disappeared into their bodies once they struck the ground.

One of the men had fallen, his face a chewed side of meat. A handful of the terrible little beasts danced on the limp body. Other men swung wildly at the monsters. Brickbats sent them soaring. Spears crashed them over like battering rams. I threw my torches at the ones on the dead man. I pulled my knife out. I dove into the mess as if I were brave.

More dropped down, gliding like leaves down from the high towers overhead.

The monstrous babes had carnivorous teeth and too many legs. They howled and bit and wanted to kill us all, though they were only strong in waves of teeth. Alone, they were as weak as children.

I snagged one by the neck. I yanked my knife across its guts. I grabbed another. It bit me and wouldn't let go. I stabbed it in the eye. It had a baby's eyes. It wilted limply when it died. It had broken my skin, but the hot blood running down my sunburn hurt worse than the bite.

I felt like I had just killed a puppy.

Then, all the monsters fled. They galloped like wobbling puppies through the empty streets on their little legs. Some had four, some had five, and some had more than I could count in a glance. They babbled like children with something in their mouths. The giant teeth made their babbling awkward.

I clutched at the deeper incision on my hand, where I was bleeding in spurts. I thought about bleeding to death, but it did not strike me deeply. I was beyond fear of death.

I waited for the women to come out of their hiding places. They stroked our hair. They mourned their dead man deeply. They did not treat him like meat. They placed him on a rooftop and gave him to the vultures and ravens and crows. They wept below the building. They threw dust and ash all over their bodies and knelt in the dust and ash and wept.

I watched with a cold detachment. The men who had survived, and whose wounds were not too severe, remained at the barricade. Enyo Gyoja touched my arm. He pulled me back toward the castle. He pointed up the castle, to the towers. He pointed down at the ground below us. Then, he pointed sideways, at the doors around us. He led me to a building beside us and opened the door. When he stepped through, he pointed up to one of the towers.

I nodded. He handed me a new torch, wrapped in animal furs smeared with lard. I walked with Enyo Gyoja to the fire, where the beasts we had killed were waiting for the women to return from the funeral. Small birds darted toward the bodies and nipped their shares. Vultures seemed to be avoiding the fire.

Enyo Gyoja smacked at the ground with his stick. He ran toward the dead bodies and shouted, waving his stick. The birds flew off. He shouted at the children. They shouted back. Enyo and the children threw rocks at each other.

(The children had been waiting for birds to come so that they could be hit with rocks, killed, and eaten. Enyo was angry they weren't being vigilant.)

Enyo harrumphed like a weary grandfather, though none of those children were his.

He lit my new torch in the fire. It burned with a heavy, animal stink. It smelled better than my socks had. He led me to the barricade. He pointed to the side walls, between the buttresses.

I went inside and went straight for the side walls. I opened the first door I found. I should not have been surprised by what I saw. This door led to a door on the other side of the throne room, though my view of my own back was hidden by the buttresses. I decided I would just wander aimlessly through all the doors until I found the one I needed.

I wandered a long time. I entered one door after another. I entered new throne rooms that looked exactly the same as the last.

What else could I do?

My torch died. I didn't bother to run anymore. I didn't flee the sight of all those shadow creatures wandering through the halls.

They ignored me. I ignored them. I kept my hands on the wall. I kept an image in my mind of the shape of the room. For some reason, I still trusted my mind and the room to remain mostly the same. I exited rooms in darkness and turned to the right. I didn't know if I was winding along the same path again and again. I didn't know what would happen.

The shadow people provided no clue. They danced to silent music and gossiped about shadows and ate and drank dark things.

I finally gave up and thought of finding the throne again. I thought of finding my way outside by starting at the throne.

I stepped into the hall. I guessed a distance that felt like it might be the center. I turned in a direction I thought would lead me to the throne. I banged into a wall. I turned the other way. I walked carefully.

I tried to use the shadows to orient myself. They were in a ballroom, and I was in an empty room. At the center of their room, and mine, would be the throne.

I followed the crowd around the center. I found the throne.

I saw the king there, and his shadow was not tall. He had a staff in one hand, long, like a shepherd's, but with a circle at the top instead of a hook, and small, dark things jangled from the hook. It looked like the shadow of the staff that I had given to Enyo Gyoja. The king had a long cloak that spilled a motley darkness all over the throne. He had no crown, but kings don't always wear crowns.

I couldn't see the throne, but I knew by the king's shadow that it was there. I sat down, on top of the shadow of the king.

I closed my eyes. I drank from the water skin. I thought about Parks and about the way Djinni had taken her, along the side of the building instead of the front door.

I had no illusions about my ability to climb up the side of a building.

I opened my eyes. The shadows had lined up along the sides of the room, as if they were waiting for someone to enter the hall.

I looked at the door. I expected a shadow to come.

The doors opened. Moonlight poured into the hall. How long had I been sitting on that throne?

Djinni stood there, in the moonlight, larger than I had remembered her.

"You're looking for me," she said. "I know."

I stood up. I fumbled for my knife.

"You want to kill me?"

"I want to find Parks. I want to find her alive. I want to take her home to Texas."

"You promised that you would help me."

She slammed the door shut. I ran toward the door. I opened it. I saw her standing in the street.

"Where did you take Parks?" I shouted.

She ignored me. She walked to the ground where blood had congealed in the dirt. A swarm of gnats clustered over the blood, slurping at it. She had killed all the men guarding the castle in the night. Their bodies were torn open. She drank their blood like the largest of the flies.

She bent over, her nude backside splayed open to me. She slurped up the blood like a dog in the moonlight. Even smothered in the blood of the men who had helped me, I could not deny the deep twists and turns of her nude body.

"How can I help you, if you hurt the people I care about?"

She stood up.

She entered the castle of shadows, and her dark skin was just another shadow among the shadows there. Hers was the shadow with white teeth. Hers was the shadow with blood caked on her hands, and her mouth and neck.

I stepped into the darkness behind her. I left the door open. It didn't provide much light in the darkness.

I thought about opening the trap door to bring more light into the darkness, as if from windows. I just had to be careful not to fall. I opened the trap door. I gazed down at the sky and felt the strange twist of gravity, as if I were looking out a window and the floor below me was a wall and the room fought its own re-orientation.

Djinni sat next to the trap door. "Above the city, above the city, and all above the city," she said. She twisted her body around to enter the trap door backward. She kept her hands gripping the edge of the door so she wouldn't fall. She let her body drop down, over the side. I jutted my hands out and grabbed at her.

"What are you doing?" I shouted. I spread my body out on the floor and stuck my head out the window below me, trying to see what she was doing.

Djinni dangled there, like wet laundry.

"You promised you would help me," she said.

I looked all around me, there, at the maze disappearing over the horizons like a stone forest.

Djinni growled. She yanked on the ledge and jumped upward, toward me.

I flinched and stumbled back into the throne room. I expected her to come jumping out after me.

She did not come.

I leaned back over the edge of the door, where it became a window. I saw no sign of her, there.

I closed the door. I lay next to it, in the darkness, feeling all the forces of nature sigh back into something comfortable. I opened the trap door, again, and I gently edged my feet out. I gripped at the floor and the ledge of the window. Blood rose in my ears. I heard the song of fear inside of me. The shifting gravities brought nausea. I didn't stop. I awkwardly crawled out the window. I tried to find purchase with my feet. The stones were smooth and offered me none. I tried to pull myself up. Adrenaline burned into my muscles. I tried so hard to pull myself up. I got my head up over the edge. I saw inside the tower. I didn't pay attention to the details inside. I darted my eyes around for something to grab.

Djinni shoved her arms below my shoulders and hugged me into her naked body. She pulled me through the window, into the tower room.

My hands and arms shivered after the terrified exertion of my muscles. Djinni placed me gently on the floor. I scooted backward, toward the wall.

The room was as big as a bedroom. It wasn't empty, like the throne room had been. This room had a stone slab that resembled a bed, a chair, and a desk, and dozens of trees, like bonsai trees, all over the walls.

Two naked feet on the bed were pale and unmoving.

I stood up slowly. Djinni stood still, waiting for me, with a blank face. She stroked one of the bonsai trees' leaves as if it were a cat. I half-expected the tree to purr and lean into her fingers.

The body on the bed was Parks. She was naked and pale and her eyes were closed. I saw her bare chest moving up and down slowly in sleep. A bonsai tree was between her splayed legs. The tree grew from inside of her. The roots dug into her body. The tree had tiny blood-colored fruits.

I leaned in closer. The fruits, no larger than small pebbles, had moving, milky shapes below the red skin, like kicking miniature fetuses.

"What did you do to her?"

Djinni touched my arm. "She isn't enough," she said. She touched my hair, gently.

I let her touch my hair.

"Will she survive?" I asked.

Djinni pressed her body into mine. She leaned into my ear. "She isn't enough," she whispered, like sex.

"I don't want to hurt you," I said. "I don't want to hurt anyone."

I should have been screaming. I should have been fighting. I should have been trying to yank the tree out of Parks. I should have done so many things.

I couldn't do anything. I let her lay me down next to Parks. I let what remained of my underwear be torn off and the leathers across my chest to be yanked off. I let Djinni straddle me. I let my body respond.

I didn't move much. I was a dead fish for her. I heard the wet sounds of flesh. I wanted to close my eyes.

I looked beside me, at Parks, sleeping comatose there, with the scars on her neck where Djinni had bitten her, and the tree sticking out from between her legs like a lamprey, and such pale, bloodless skin.

I screamed instead of moaning.

I don't know what Djinni wanted from me. I never did. I don't understand how her mind works, or if it works at all. I felt the skin of her that had been born of my own skin. I felt the whole room shake with the sensations of this moment.

I lifted a hand up to her throat. I lifted another. I squeezed.

She didn't stop me. She gasped for air. Her body shivered in what—I assume—was some kind of orgasm. She didn't stop me at all from choking her.

I kept squeezing her neck. Her eyes rolled back in her head. Her mouth opened. She grabbed at my arms like bliss. The light inside of her died.

I came inside of her. Her eyes rolled back in her head like dying, with her jutting tongue and her grasping hands, choking.

I held her over me. I held still. Waves of sensation rippled slowly through my spent body. She was limp, but still warm.

I let her fall backward, to the ground.

She was dead.

Her stomach was not dead. It rumbled with convulsions. Then, it grew like a boil. Then, it was more like a balloon full of water. Her dark skin liquefied in the stretch. She was larger than a pregnant woman.

Horrible, amorphous shapes convulsed beneath her thinning skin, all red and white now, like blood. Her stomach bulged and grew and bulged and grew until it was three times her size, filling the room. Her dark skin thinned into a sick white, then a sick, fleshy pink. She was all stomach now.

Her flesh peeled open like a flower. Tiny embryos spilled out from her, only vaguely human. Some had dog bodies with baby hands and feet. Some had the heads of deer or cattle. Some were bird-like—or bat-like—and flapped uselessly in the pooling fluids and blood. Two heads, eight arms, animal pieces jammed on like mad science, and none of them identifiable as a human—moving like animals, not people. Fish tails and serpent hair and tentacles and insect bits and crustacean faces mingled with pink, fleshy skin—and worst of all: infant-like wails, moans, burbles.

The light of her—I couldn't see it, but I knew it was there—tumbled into the shadows, down the stairwell, and I don't know where she went after that.

This was a nightmare.

It smelled terrible, like a birthing chamber and a slaughterhouse.

I watched all those writhing shapes on the ground, my ugly children.

The horrible creatures skittering like baby spiders, fighting for purchase of foot or claw or worse.

They began to mewl and chitter. They began to chew on Djinni's body. They began to lick, with whatever horrible tongues they had spilling from mouths that ran frontways, sideways, and—worst of all—perfectly normally human with little baby teeth and little baby lips and little baby tongues, slurping up the pink puss blood fluids like mother's milk.

I watched. I watched them chomp on bone and slurp up marrow. I watched them turn on each other, next. I watched my horrible children tumble away into the strange passageways of the castle, devouring each other as they tumbled. I watched the living eat the dead. I watched the living drag the dead away into the cracks in the walls and the shadowed places of the tower room.

I waited a long time.

I touched Parks' face. She murmured nonsense dream sounds.

I touched the tree growing out from her. I tugged it, gently. It had grown in firmly. I moved around her body, carefully eyeing the monsters that lingered in the corners of the room. My remaining children ignored me. They licked the gore off their own bodies. A crab-like child slithered a long tongue, like a snake, across the shell of its back. It seemed to be the only one eyeing me at all, with a fourth stalk of eye.

I grabbed the tree in Parks' body. I tugged. It was in tight. I felt the groan and snap of the roots inside of her. I pulled a little harder. Her legs convulsed. Her arms twitched and flailed around like a madwoman's. Her eyes remained closed. Her face was calm as sleep.

I pulled harder. The little tree bent and cracked. Berries and leaves trembled and fell to the filthy floor. Bits of root structure peeled away. Blood spurted out from her.

I kept pulling.

The roots snapped a little at a time. Then, blood lubricated the roots. I yanked harder. It came loose. It looked like a demented carrot, all sickly brown and covered in blood and feasting on blood like one of the monster children all over the floor.

I threw the tree, berries and all, to the crustacean child. It snapped it from the air with its tongue like a frog snatching a moth. It chewed aimlessly. The shell of the crab hardened like wood. The face thickened.

Parks was bleeding. I had nothing to stop the blood. Her eyes opened slowly. Her face twisted as the pain came to her. She screamed in agony.

I pressed my hand into her bleeding. I held it there, trying to stop the blood with just my hands.

MAZE

My monster children lurked around my ankles, licking up what I could not stop. The crab child whipped its tongue out again and snatched up a smaller, imp-like thing.

Parks' hand pressed over mine. She held it there. I fumbled for anything cloth, anything bandage. I had the jacket. I pressed it over our hands. I moved mine. I moved hers.

She screamed, and trembled, and whipped her hair around.

The blood slowed. The screaming and writhing slowed. The pain remained. She breathed in gasps and spurts. She wept.

I helped her to her feet. She leaned into my arm. She couldn't speak, yet. We opened the trap door. I didn't know where it would lead from here. We stepped down. We climbed down a stairwell. I gazed down at the long stairs. I closed the door over my head. I opened it. I pushed her up into the throne room. I climbed up after her. I sat her on the throne, in the slanting light from the open doorway.

Enyo Gyoja stood alone below the arch. His sandals clacked on the stones. His staff prodded the darkness before him. He stripped his cloak from his body. He wrapped it over Parks' shoulders. He pulled her to her feet.

Yi came, with tears running down her face and Aia holding her up by her arm. Others were there, men and women, all filthy and wearing leather and rags, carrying brickbats and spears and looking at us.

They led Parks and me into the empty city. They led us past the broken wall. They led us into the halls of stone and better barricades.

Gangrene spread up Parks' stomach and neck. Mushrooms sprouted like warts from her legs. They were red and white and milky, like the berries. We fought them with fire. We burned them off of her. We poured boiling hot water over her, even if it made her scream.

Aia took her and me deep into the maze, to a weeping willow that grew among the halls of stone as if it had ripped open the bricks below it. We chipped away the bark of the willow. We boiled it into tea and filled Parks' weak mouth with the tea. We stayed with the willow tree, hiding her in its shadow, until she survived and the mushrooms stopped growing and the gangrene faded from her body.

4: The Best Life We Can

You lived a few years, Parks, but your legs were always weak. You never bore a child to any man. You couldn't run with the hunters. You carried water, but you couldn't carry much.

You never spoke to anyone.

(Except once, near your end. You said, to me, in English, "I'll never forgive you for this.")

Then, the plague came back and filled your legs with mushrooms. The fungus spread up your stomach and up to your face. Then, you died. We placed you on this wall, here. We used your body as bait for birds.

I'm sorry, Parks. I wish things could have been different. I wish that saving you meant a happier life.

Yi's husband had died. She blamed me for his death, for I had brought the Djinni to life in my lung, and the woman I had arrived with had given birth to the things that killed him. When I tried to comfort her, she broke my wrist and spat on me. Aia set the bone for me. It hurt.

By then, I spoke enough of the language of the maze to talk about what had happened.

I had been plucked from the world of men. I was stuck here now, like all the rest of them, in this ancient maze. The monstrous man I had killed had also come here; he was not a human, but something older and wilder, before humans. He had found two outcasts in the empty city and killed them both. He had stolen the clothes that had been stolen from Enyo by the man and the woman who had been outcast.

Djinni was one of the many monsters of this place, and one of the worst. My will was not strong enough to defeat her before she could defeat me and fill the maze with the monstrous children.

How did all these people get here? Most of them were born here. My children would be born here.

MAZE

Fort Worth was a dream in the night. I had no way of explaining the journey here, the things I had faced.

We had encountered an alien, if you want to call her that, for truly she was alien to us. We had fallen through the wormhole, if you want to call it that, for truly there were worms. We had slipped between the fabrics of realities we didn't understand, and Parks, you were there, with me, for truly none of this pain and misery was real.

We lived here, in the maze.

We made the best lives for ourselves that we could.

What else could we do?

When I learned to speak better, Enyo told me about the castle...and Djinni.

The castle is dying, but it is still a living thing, made of stone. It is not time that flows through the castle's veins, but it is like time, though we do not understand it.

There are creatures made of living stones that look like cows. They eat rocks around the roots of plants. They lumber in a huge herd. I have seen these stone cows with my own eyes. I have felt the rumbling earth when their heavy stone bodies lumber nearby. I have touched their stone faces with my own hand.

I have seen the gargoyles creeping. When they know they are seen, they turn to stone—real stone. They're easy to kill because you just have to place your weapon carefully while they're stone, and then look away.

I believe Enyo Gyoja about the castle, now. I have asked him to explain my passage here, with the Djinni, and the singing worms in my sink. Enyo Gyoja does not tell me anything about that. He says that knowledge is outside of the maze, and the maze is all he has ever known. He says that I will never find a way back to where I was, and I should make the best life for myself here.

For three long years, I found nothing but pain and misery in the maze.

When my third summer rolled to an end, I expected nothing else but that, until death.

Then, I found a home here.

Yi came to me one night. She was weeping.

She cleaved to me, in her sadness.

My skin was bronzed from sunlight, by then, my body hardened from the hunts through the halls. Winter crept over the walls like a tidal wave, spilling cold wind and tumbling clouds and flecks of snow. We both needed more warmth.

Yi came to me one night. She was weeping.

She cleaved to me, in her sadness.

Parks (are you listening to me?) and all of the lost people, do you know of this? Not love. Never love. We leaned into each other, my world stolen from me, and her love stolen from her. We pressed our wounds together and made the best life we could.

Yi came to me one night. She was weeping.

She cleaved to me, in her sadness.

She bore me a son in spring. I named him Gokliya because he yawned a lot, and I remember once reading that the great Indian Chief, Geronimo, had been named Gokliya before he led his people to war. I had always thought it would make a good name for a son, though I had known that no woman in Texas would have allowed such a name for a boy who ought to be called "Christopher," or "Jonathon," or "Michael."

Yi came to me one night. She was weeping.

I cleaved to her, in my sadness.

I named our first son Gokliya. Yi liked the name. He looked like both of us: her high cheekbones, with my green eyes; her golden skin, with my heavy bones; her soft lips, with my booming voice.

Yi came to me one night. She was weeping.

We cleaved to each other.

Parks, are winters any easier for you? Winters are terrible here. Spring and summer are better.

We have plenty of maggots, growing among bushes that taste like crunchy berries in spring. In summer, we make wine from the petals of the weeds that grow along the hill.

There are more wonders in the maze than I could ever find or enumerate to you. The most wondrous of all are my three surviving children.

We made a life here, Parks. I made a life here.

We made the best life we could in this terrible place.

Wang Xin's
Maze

1: In Water's Eye

There was a light. It called to me. It was in a bucket of water. I was so lonely, and the light told me that it would help me, because I was so lonely. I placed my head in the water, to see the light better.

My name is Wang Xin.

The light, when I saw it, wasn't holding still in the water I had displaced with my head. I blinked, but it didn't matter. The light touched my eye.

I saw my whole life before me, and though years have passed, I haven't forgotten.

I had thought the light was sent by my mother. It had a woman's voice and came from far away, like I had.

I found a broken bicycle in the maze, but I wasn't supposed to find anything. Is my memory of what I saw in the water's eye fading at last? I wasn't supposed to find this bicycle. I was supposed to find nothing but footprints.

I tracked strange footprints through the snow—they could have been human, with strange moccasins—away from the broken bicycle. I turned six corners. I walked down a long corridor. The tracks entered a cave in the side of a small hill full of caves and caves and other openings.

The maze continued underground, I knew, but the dark was home to terrible things, and Enyo Gyoja said never to go underground.

Normally, no one would never willingly step into a cave, but there were footprints, and a person had walked away from a bicycle and into the cave. I had to go down and see if the person was still alive to take home to the village. I had to do it quietly so I wouldn't call up the cavemen, with their beastly maws and inhuman howls, or the worse things that hunt in darkness.

I did not like doing this, because I knew what I would find, but I was supposed to investigate deeper. I remembered from the water's eye that I was supposed to go down to the bloodstain beyond the light of the cave entrance, and to investigate the predator's strange tracks.

Perhaps, like the bicycle, things would be different from what I had seen, and the person would still be alive, terrified and scrambling through the darkness. I didn't know what I'd do then. Would I kill him, to preserve the vision in the water's eye?

Fortunately, this decision was not to be.

I found the blood three steps inside the shadows, where light still reached from the cave's maw. The blood had crystallized in the freezing cold. I knew what frozen blood felt like between my toes, by then, and I only looked at it a moment. There was a lot of blood. I investigated the predator's tracks. I couldn't identify the beast, though I knew its tracks from the vision of things to come. It looked like a tree was walking on the ground. Hard stones were scattered in heaps around the mess; they seemed to melt the closer they were to the cave entrance. I didn't know what they were. I had known I wouldn't. I had to look, though. That is the nature of my life. I know the path I must walk before I walk it. This place holds little mystery for me, after all I saw in the water's eye.

Until the bicycle, I had faced no mystery.

I backed out of the cave quietly. I returned to the broken bicycle, confused. I scratched my head. I was not supposed to find a bicycle today. That is not what I remembered. Should I take the bicycle or leave it?

We were not supposed to have one, so I should leave it here. Yet, people would want it, so I should take it. Should I hide it? What if someone finds it and sees my tracks in the snow?

I must preserve what I have seen in the water's eye, after all. I will find my beautiful love on this long trail. I will find a wonderful place for our people to call our new home. But, how can a simple bicycle change the path ahead?

If another found it, they would wonder why I had left it behind.

I wouldn't want them to know about the pathways in my eyes if I did not have to tell them about it. I did not wish to be like Aia, prostrate before idols, casting pointless spells and curses upon our people, advising where advice was unwanted. I keep my unwanted knowledge to myself.

I never asked the watery Djinni to enter my eye. I never asked to see all the paths of my life, long ago. I'm not even sure it was a Djinni. I never asked Enyo Gyoja what it was. I never told anyone about it, and especially not him. I don't know what else to call what it was, and it seems to be what a Djinni might do if it were to enter my eye.

I was a boy, back then, new to the maze, and weeping because I longed for my mother. My face was dirty.

A man, the Mahometan Selah, who took me in for a time until his death, had dipped my head in the water, to wash my face. I was just a boy, and he was looking after me, then, and arguing with Aia all the time about the faith I should be following.

I didn't care about either of them. I just wanted to go home.

In the water, I saw a light, like a firefly. It wanted my lung, not my eye, but I did not control the bucket. Selah blessed the water for his god's sake, and poured the water over my head. The light in the water entered my right eye. It burned a vision there, like my life flashing before my eyes. But this was not the life that had passed, but the life that would be. I saw my whole life ahead of me, then, burned into my mind. I cannot forget it.

Until now, and a broken bicycle.

I scratched my head. I was not supposed to find a bicycle today. I had not seen one since I fell from one in my youth and landed in the maze. That was how I had found my place here. I had been riding my bicycle down a hill, and I had hit some sort of bump that threw me over the handlebars. When I landed I was not on a hill, anymore. I was in the maze.

I should take the bicycle to protect the knowledge of pathways in my eyes. If another were to find it, they would question me and wonder why I had left it behind.

I hefted the broken thing onto my shoulder and walked back to the camp, near the empty city. We stayed in our huts near the walls. Huts didn't collapse in snow like the square roofs did sometimes. Huts were easier to defend, because we could leave them quickly and go to our narrow places in the maze hallways. Huts were better for us. Enyo Gyoja showed us how to make them and explained everything to us. He was right.

Joseph took the bicycle from me the moment I returned. He tried to tell me what it was, but he said the wrong word. I told him the word I knew for it. He clapped. "Of course we'd know different words for them, Wang Xin. We spoke different languages. Listen, we'll call it a 'bicycle' because it is somewhere between our two words."

"I won't call it that," I said. "That's not what it is."

"Fine, don't." He tried to ride it, but the chain had snapped and the wheels were bent.

He asked me where I had found it.

I told him about the smear of blood in the cave.

"Xin," he said, "did you notice any sign of how the bicycle and the person on it could have gotten here? Did you see any sign of a portal or a doorway?"

"Of course not," I said. "If you wish to leave this maze, you will have to pass the door of blood and darkness. Death is our escape. It is our only escape. The person who brought this bicycle found a way out. Pity this person could not take their bicycle with them."

Joseph sighed. He bent over the broken chain and touched the gears. "No pity at all, Xin! The metal will make good tools, if we can find a way to break it all apart." Joseph began to tear at the bicycle with his hands. He struggled to break it into parts, metal bars and plastic ropes from the pneumatic brakes that could be used for tools and hunting and rubber tire loops that could be cut and sewn into warm clothes. He made no progress that I could see.

This would keep him busy for many paces of the sun, I knew. And, in all that time, he would neither kill something to eat nor carry water up from the little hole in the rock with the groups of women that went all day after the water. We could tinker all night long on a full belly, sipping warm water by the fire. We couldn't hunt in the dark. We couldn't gather water in the dark.

I hoped it would not keep him from his urge to travel soon.

The water-bearers went in one large group, and armed. Gokliya and Robert, Joseph's two sons, went with them. The boys gathered ice flowers. They plucked them at the root and bunched them up in baskets. We could make thread from the heart of the brittle ice stems, and we could eat the bittersweet petals.

Gokliya told me that Enyo Gyoja was worried that our sluice of fresh water might ice over some very cold night. Enyo Gyoja wanted me to go with the women and use my axe to chop back the ice. Enyo said it had happened before, but I don't remember it ever happening. Enyo said that our prey wouldn't come to the water if it was frozen over.

I thought he was foolish to worry about water when we were surrounded by snow, and every morning the snow fell, and every night the snow fell, and what little wind blew through the hallways blew snow around endlessly, piling up in shadowy corners and lingering in the shadows deep into spring. We were surrounded by ice, so let us not worry about water.

Blood was the rare drink in winter.

I went hunting again, alone. I carried a spear in one hand and my stone axe in the other. I had made the axe myself, out of obsidian I had pulled from an oddly-colored spot in a wall. I had chipped the rock into a wide axe edge and left a large knob on the back end for the leather lash to hold against the wood. I had wrapped the knob in four broken spears and strips of leather, to make the sturdy handle.

Our tools don't last. The damp eats the wood—even smoke-cured wood. We don't have many trees, and we have to make what wood we take last. We have to smoke them every chance we have.

I won't waste my axe on water.

When I first made the axe, I killed a caveman with it. I sliced into the monster's naked shoulder, and the gush of blood spewed out from an artery like a red geyser. He was dead before I jammed a spear into his gut with my other hand.

We gorged on the caveman's meat for a week.

I hunted. I found things to eat, and I killed them. I found things to use, and I took them.

The day I found the bicycle, I had also killed a manticore in the twilight. I chopped off the manticore's poison tail with my axe. I chopped off its infant-looking, puss-filled face. I carried the golden lump of fur home held out from my body by a golden paw, and the meat dripped its poison blood along my trail. My arms wearied. I carefully put the meat down, to keep any blood from touching me, and I tied its hind legs to my axe shaft, so I could carry it away from my body, blood spilling downward, not leaking toward me along the shaft.

We would have to let the manticore bleed for three days, until plague mushrooms sprouted from the wounds, before we could smoke the meat. We would have to hang it somewhere and keep it safe from vultures and crows while all the poison blood oozed into a smoldering puddle on the ground.

Even after we smoked the meat, eating it would be unpleasant. Our lips would numb. Our tongues would swell up. Our heads would ache. Our insides would twist and fart. But, we'd be full a while, and the manticore wouldn't be eating the rats the children caught in traps and baked over hot stones.

In the spring, I would have merely killed the manticore and walked away. Winter, even bad meat was better than none.

I would have to wash the poison from my weapons and my hands and clothes. I'd have to do it somewhere that it wouldn't pollute the water when I was done. I would use melted snow far away from the stream.

Snow crunched under my bare feet. Snow hid in the shadowy corners of the maze, and would remain long into spring.

I jammed my spear downward, in case something was hiding inside the piles of snow.

Snow held all the tracks and trails and signs of passage. I expected nothing from the Djinni's eye, but it took so little effort to look, and I was supposed to search the snow.

MAZE

Late winter was the best time of year to explore the maze and learn the trails. You could see where you'd been. You could follow where the way you walked picked up and dropped down in new places.

Wrap your feet in rags and leather to keep away the frostbite. Change your rags twice a day, and let the old ones dry hanging off your back. Carve new trails where the snow marks where you've been and tells you what creatures have walked there since the last snowfall.

Gaius, an orphan, tried to eat the manticore on the second day, when no one was watching him. He was dead when we found him, with bloody strips of meat still hanging from his mouth. We placed him on the top of a small wall, barely longer than two arm lengths, in the middle of a larger passage, like an island in a stream.

Aia cried. She always cried for the dead, but this boy had been turning to her since his parents had died. Some comforted her. It wasn't really her fault that the boy was hungry and impatient. Gaius had been born in the maze, and he had been with us long enough to know better. "He did it on purpose," shouted Aia, "just to spite me!"

Most of us just watched the vultures.

Belm handed me a rock. She had a few in her hands. Joseph had a jagged gear from the bicycle in his. Enyo Gyoja looked held up his spear to urge us to wait until there were enough birds.

Almost everyone had bricks and rocks.

More birds landed. Enyo Gyoja dropped his staff to locate his own brick from the ground.

There was no signal. We had rocks. We lifted our hands. We threw them as hard as we could at the birds at the top of the wall. We ran around to the other side. Our rocks smacked three vultures to the ground. We had broken their wings or dazed their heads. We snatched them by their necks before they could escape. We snapped their necks.

We spit the vultures on the metal pieces of bicycle Joseph had snapped loose. We turned them over the fire.

They tasted better than manticore.

We split the vulture feathers among us equally. The feathers were shoved in between two leather skins, like the stuffing of blankets. We wore them in lumps all over our bodies, wherever we could get a few feathers to fit.

2: A Better Place

I never pray to Aia's gods like I'm supposed to, in the water's eye. I bow to them, because I remember that I am supposed to bow to them. I learn the words that Aia wishes me to learn. But, in my heart, I do not pray. I am angry at these tiny idols. I do not believe in them.

I know only one prayer.

Whatever gods are in this maze, may you suffer as we have suffered. May our prayers leave you ill and dying, as you have left us.

I do not tell others about the water's eye. If they knew their own suffering, they would try to avoid their futures. But, suffering comes for all of us, whether we know it or not. If I take the path away, I may be their hero for a time, but then I will confuse the paths in my eye, and I will not know anymore.

I know it is cruel to walk the boy, Gaius, to his own death, but I do not change the path before me. Imagine what it would be like for me, to see the maze like everyone else, as dangerous and full of mystery—me, who knows all the secrets of the water's eye.

I would rather let the boy die. I know the rest of us will survive a while and raise more children. The vultures we killed were food that kept more of us alive a while longer. Gaius did not die in vain.

I did one thing different when I brought the manticore home to dry. I touched Gaius' hair. I kissed his forehead like a father. He looked away from me when I did it, and ran away from me. Why wouldn't he run away from me, when I had just doomed him?

At least his sufferings are over. Plenty others continue to suffer, and the water's eye has shown me the path that will ease our winters in the maze.

Gokliya, for instance, will live beyond what my eyes see. For Gokliya is a true friend to me all the days of my life and a son to me when he marries the daughter of the woman I will love: for his sake, I should not change the path I see in the water's eye.

When I was a boy, I dipped my head in water. Selah helped me. He was yelling at Aia and washing a crying boy's face, and he did not notice the explosion of light in the water when I saw all paths before me. No one noticed anything but the yelling. The light entered my right eye, wordlessly. It filled my vision with my future, and fills it still.

I cannot forget it.

I close my eyes, and I can see my whole life shining before me.

I am glad I spend most of my time hunting. People do not always do what they are supposed to do when I am around.

For instance, Aia was supposed to bend her back to me the night Gaius died, just before I left with Joseph and Gokliya.

I remember this clearly, because I was looking forward to that moment—my first like it—for quite some time. I bowed to her gods like I was supposed to. When the time came for her to open for me, to make our son, she was surprised. She screamed and tried to stop me. I had to hold her by the throat. She was crying. Why was she crying? In the water's eye she was not crying. I told her it was fate. I told her—though I don't think I was supposed to—about the water's eye, and what I saw in the bucket of water and continue to see. I told her that she needed a son to care for her in her old age.

She said nothing to me. She wept. I placed a hand on her back. I told her that I had given her a son, who would live long after we were gone, and bear sons and daughters of his own to care for her gods.

Aia punched me. She threw her idols aside with one long sweep of her arm. She kicked at me. She kept kicking at me.

I ran from her. She was screaming at me. She was howling at the moon. I felt terrible, and I didn't know why. I don't understand why she did what she did.

People don't always do what they are supposed to do. I wish they would. I have seen the future for us all, and it is best to stay on this path. We are going to find a much better place, soon, where winter will not be as horrible as it is here, near the abandoned city, and our children will be safer from the dangers of the halls.

Enyo Gyoja wants to stay near the city, now that it is empty of the Djinni. He says this city was full of the awful Djinni once, but they are gone now, or they have wandered off, or perhaps they were never here. That is what he says. They are only one strange monster in the maze. They can't be eaten and they don't eat us. Why worry about them?

Enyo says they are the seeds of the castle—a living castle, like a giant, ancient, stone tree—that grows in ways we cannot comprehend and sends forth Djinni like dandelion seeds. Enyo Gyoja says that the castle is slowly dying, like an old tree full of winter plague, and good riddance to all the Djinni that used to grow there. The strange sap that flows through its veins is like time, but it is not quite time, and anyway it dries up, now, and nothing is like it used to be.

Wild things grow along the empty hillside, where we do not cultivate our few patches of the little screaming orange trees. Enyo says there used to be fields of crops there, long ago. Now there are maggot bushes in spring, growing flies and mosquitoes that plague us until the autumn chill kills them off, unless we and the birds eat the sweet maggots all up in time. There are dandelions in summer throwing seeds like snowflakes. There are the fallen stones waiting to reveal themselves in autumn, only to hide again in winter snows.

Then, of course, there's us.

Gokliya followed me. I knew he was following me. He didn't know how loud his footsteps were in all that snow. He had never learned to creep over the dry stones. He slogged through mud and snow. He breathed heavily. He made shuffling noises when his feet dragged on the ground. He was going to chase off prey if he did not learn to walk in snow like a hunter.

I waited for him around a dark corner. He stopped at the corner.

"Wang Xin, I think you are trying to trap me, again. I think you are waiting around this corner for me."

"Good for you, Gokliya. Yet, I can hear you coming, and I know you are following me. You will scare off our supper."

"They are right to fear us," he said. "We are mighty hunters."

"We are only mighty when we are quiet," I said. "I will show you how to walk quietly tomorrow. For now, walk with me, and see if you can mirror the amount of noise I make by yourself." I pointed to my feet, and the way I stepped on the balls instead of the heels, and the way I didn't put weight on my foot until I knew nothing was there to make sound. "Watch how I walk, where I step, and how I breathe. These stone walls throw strange echoes. We must control our echoes here, in the snow. We must watch for the stones hiding in the snow that can make us stumble."

I led the boy a different way. I knew all the ways here, so close to our home on the side of the hill. He did not know I was leading him home. We turned corner after corner in the stone passageways. We slipped through the gaps in the walls, where bricks had fallen. We listened to the sound of a single bird flapping wings in the sky—an owl, I think, with a hoot-hoot-hoot when it landed in a fluster of feathers and wings. I looked around, and listened, but I could not see the owl in the halls. I could only hear it.

Gokliya mimicked my footsteps. He walked on the balls of his feet, carefully. He tried to stay up on the rocky, exposed ground and places between snow and mud. He tried to open his mouth in a whorl and breathe with a wide, quiet throat. He tried to keep his leather leggings from rubbing against each other and making noise.

He couldn't do it naturally, of course. I exaggerated my movements so he could mimic me. We looked like fools.

The owl hoot-hooted behind us. Was it laughing at us? It took flight again. I saw the shadow against the sun. Night creatures flying and hunting in the daylight was a bad omen to me, a hunter.

When I was only a young boy, I rode a bicycle away from my parents. I fell. I found myself inside the maze, with no bicycle. I was found by a group of hunting men—all dead now—and taken to the encampment on the hill. We were only a handful of mouths to feed, and most of us were big enough to hunt and gather.

The only other people to come from somewhere else were Joseph, when I was a boy, and Parks with him. Parks is dead.

Now I am older, and our people have children. We have so many children. We have found a few more wandering men and women in the hallways, like Joseph. We took them all into our tribe. They, also, have children.

Gokliya is Joseph's eldest son. He is the oldest boy that has not yet built his own hut and taken a bride. He is still too young for that. His voice cracks sometimes. His body still grows.

We reached the edge of the empty city's hill around a corner and around a corner and down a hall. There, I knew Gokliya was mad at me. He had wanted to hunt with me, and I had led him back to the other children, playing on the hill near the huts that huddled up against the intact places of the old city's wall. I did not know what he was going to say, but I knew he was going to say something with an angry face, because I remembered what I had seen clearly. I didn't feel like fighting with him now.

I let him vent his anger. I did not listen to him. When he was done, I smacked his head. "Now is not the time for me to teach anyone how to hunt. Look around you, Gokliya. Do you not see how hungry everyone is?"

"But, I can help—"

"Not by chasing off our meat with your inexperienced steps. Go mind the water bearers. Walk the perimeters and watch for trouble. Practice what I taught you about walking. Be silent. Make no echoes."

"Xin, I want to hunt."

"Soon, Gokliya. Soon. I will be thirsty when I return. Boil water, snow, and ice together with willow bark and screaming orange rind and make me some tea. Until then, gather wood. Scour the safe trails to the trees and bushes with your brothers, and gather wood. Keep your ears peeled for danger. Carry spears and jagged stones. Gather wood, Gokliya. Wood is as important as hunting. Watch for me at nightfall. Have boiled water ready to warm my cold throat."

I left him at the edge of camp. I slipped into the stone maze as quietly as death. I ran faster than Gokliya could follow. I needed to make up for the time I had lost walking Gokliya home. I needed to get farther down the halls, always farther, where the water's eye revealed the trails I had to run to find the supper that I would kill, if I were to find supper—which I wasn't, this time, sadly. Still, I had to run. It was easier on a trail, alone, to follow the path of the water's eye. I only had to run, quiet and alone.

Owls hunted for rats late in the morning where I had been walking. There would be no meat here but the owl, and I didn't know how to catch an owl without a dead rat to bait it. I had to go farther and farther and follow what I knew from the water's eye.

I know that I will find the woman I love by following the path of the water's eye, and there will be a better life for all of us in the grove far from the empty city.

When I returned to the camp, I was happy, because today was the day that Joseph would choose to speak to Enyo Gyoja about the water.

Gokliya had forgotten to boil water for me, but I had known he would forget. I took some boiled water from the old widows, who smiled at me and touched my strong arms, and kissed my cheek with their toothless mouths. The water warmed my cold chest.

I went to Enyo Gyoja, on the stump in the center of our encampment. Joseph sat in the snow below Enyo, with Gokliya. Aia was there, too. She sat near Enyo's feet. She looked down at his feet, and her hands rested on the ground near them. She had been begging him for something. Whatever she had to say had been said before I arrived.

"Wang Xin, you did not catch anything today?" said Joseph.

"Not today. I will travel out farther tomorrow."

"Tell me, Wang Xin, do you wonder why we have wintered here all the days of your life?"

"Water. The fresh water here, never under ice, means we drink well and our prey wanders closer to the water in the winter, winding through the halls after fresh, flowing water."

"Yet, there is no prey."

"Not today. Tomorrow is another day."

Joseph frowned. "I have been thinking," he said. "I have been thinking, and I have talked to some of the others. I have talked to the ones from before I was here, like Aia."

Enyo tapped the jangling tip of his staff at Joseph's feet. "I am an old man. Every winter I survive, I am grateful," he said. "How long have you told others that wandering off alone is a quick way to find death? You would take this path for yourself?"

I smiled. Soon, I would walk the path toward my beloved wife, far away from these halls. No one consulted me about this. I tried to contain my smile. I couldn't.

Aia snorted at me. "I do not think it is the path of wisdom to chase water in the middle of winter. We must survive until spring. Then, we can search for new winter camps."

I could barely contain my excitement. My hands trembled. I had been waiting for this day a long time. I spoke with a calm voice, but it was hard to keep calm when I was so excited. "You would go hunting for water, when it is water we have? We have snow everywhere to melt down. We have water sweet as milk from the stream. We need meat, not drink!"

Joseph was surprised by me. He leaned back and eyed me up and down. "Wang Xin, you are correct," he said.

Aia shook her head. "If you start wandering, you'll get lost with everyone you take. How will you find your way home to us? If we do this, we must all travel together."

"No," I said. "No, Aia, if we all traveled together, we would be too slow, and too loud, and we would attract the things that hunt us."

She looked me in the face with an anger I had never seen in her. "Wang Xin, I would be pleased to see you wander off to your death. Go alone, if you wish it. Go alone and die out there." Aia turned her head to Gokliya. "But, Joseph, how could you take your son, Gokliya, who is almost a man. What would Yi say to that? What will Robert and Geraldine do if you do not return?"

"Gokliya comes with me because he, of all my children, wants to come with me. The other two wish to stay here, because they want to stay with their friends. I did not come to Enyo seeking permission. I came here to tell him. Please, Aia, watch over Robert and Geraldine until I return. Burn dandelions on your altars for Yi in the summer."

I had known what would happen, but I had never heard the words. The two things lined up in my mind: the water's eye, and Joseph's words.

People surprised me when they spoke. Sometimes their faces looked a little different. Sometimes I knew they weren't saying the right things, because their lips were not moving the right way. I thought of the bicycle I had found. I worried, then, if we would ever find my beloved.

I had been dreaming of this path my whole life, with longing.

I placed a hand upon Joseph's back. "I will take you to the edge of the paths I know, and together we can follow the streams that braid through the cracks in the walls until we find a better place."

Enyo placed his staff across his lap. He hunched down into his log, thoughtfully. "Wang Xin, our best hunter...if you go seeking winter camp, carry your best weapons. If you go, travel swift in the daylight. Keep a watch at night to listen for hunting things. Use the snow to shelter you against the snow. Return to us with much meat and better tidings. Wang Xin, I am too old to hunt in your place."

Joseph looked up at me. He nodded at me. I removed my hand from his back. Joseph took it from the air and shook it like a friend's. He wasn't supposed to do that.

Aia, pleading, bowed before Enyo and touched his sandals with her hands. "You wandered these halls all the days of your youth, Enyo Gyoja. Do you know of any other place like this one?"

"I was not here to see it, but I remember what I was told by the old men when I was very young. We never settled. We wandered, always, searching for a way home. Then, we found a home here."

We waited for Enyo to continue.

Gokliya spoke, at last. "What happened?"

"It was too long before this time we have. I do not remember what happened. Follow the water to its destination. But, do not merely do that. Walk beyond it. Find a place where we can set our camp beyond the water. Walk softly, Joseph. You are not a great hunter like Wang Xin."

Aia snarled at us. "You are fools! You're going to get yourselves killed!"

I was still angry at her. She should have been happy when I gave her a son to care for her in her old age. She was supposed to beg me for that son. Now, she was yelling at us for leading our people to a better place.

She was supposed to weep, and pray for our safe return. She was supposed to be weeping, not angry.

I struck Aia hard across her cheek. I'm not sorry I did it. She collapsed in a heap at Enyo's feet. She looked at me with anger and terror. I had struck her hard. She wept, at last, but it was all wrong, and her weeping was wrong but it was less wrong, because she was not yelling anymore.

Everyone around us was silent. They had watched me strike her as hard as I had. They had their mouths open, in horror. Not even Gokliya spoke.

I spoke. "All day I walked the trails I knew, as far as I could. I smelled snow in the air. I heard only the wind through the halls. We will go exploring. We will return when we can."

Aia's voice was calm, through her tears. "How dare you strike me. Go, now, and die with all the curses of all the gods upon your head. Die out there, and be devoured where no child of yours will remember your face, your name."

There wasn't enough moonlight that night for traveling, and it was bitter cold. We couldn't leave until daybreak.

Joseph was afraid that Aia would harm me. He invited me to his hut. In the water's eye, I had spent one more night with Aia, sleeping in her arms. I would have had to bind her hands to do that, and I didn't want to hurt her again.

She was supposed to be grateful to me, for her son.

I was confused, then. I didn't want the confusion. I wanted to find the woman, and the grove. I wanted the things I had seen in the water that had entered my eye, long ago.

That night, I joined Joseph with his children. I held the warm love glow of my future in my memory.

Joseph and his children kept their lean-to near the edges of the encampment, where we could hear night watchmen pacing with torches. Their hut was cruder than most because Yi's first husband had built it, and he was not a great craftsman, and Joseph was worse and could not easily repair anything. Leather and old cloth were wrapped around bones and sticks to build a long, rugged plank. This they had jammed against an intact place in the wall that used to surround the empty city. They had wrapped animal skins down the edges and around the openings on either side of the long, angular hut to make doorways.

Snow had accumulated against the triangular hut, catching on the rougher places in the roof in deep drifts around the jagged bones, insulating the sleepers against more snow, more cold.

I stayed with them that night. I was too excited to sleep. I was angry at Aia, but I couldn't hold it in my mind for long, because we were leaving soon, and my wife was out there, waiting for me.

Gokliya sat awake in the darkness, like I did. He had been checking his brickbat and spear for signs of damp rot. He had rubbed warm oil and tree sap over them. They glistened. He drifted off—as I did—with his back against the cool stone wall.

I dreamed of my wife catching birds in nets, with her delicate hands picking through the vines and her face beautiful lost in concentration. Gokliya and I awoke early, in our uncomfortable places. We had fallen against each other while sitting. When one of us woke up, the other did, as well. We stepped from the hut together. We stretched our stiff bodies in the cold morning air. Snow dropped slowly over the maze like dandelion seeds on a windless day. I couldn't see the castle spires through the early morning fog. I couldn't see the sun beyond the grey, though I felt the light of it in my eyes, pushing through the murky maze of cloud and fog and snow.

"Is your father awake?"

"Maybe."

"Wake him up."

Gokliya stuck the blunt end of a spear into the hut.

Crying—was it toddling Geraldine with her pudgy face and brown hair, or was it Bobby whose voice was gentle like a girl's, and he was so young, so soft? It sounded like the girl, but it could have been either one.

Joseph emerged, blinking into the daylight. He stretched. He pressed flasks of water against his skin to melt the ice that had grown inside. He took a brickbat from his son. He slipped it through loops in his clothes so it hung from his back.

"How much food do you have, Xin?"

"Not enough."

"I have some dried fruit I've hoarded since autumn. We'll have to hunt as we travel. We'll have to bring flint, too."

"I have flint."

Gokliya took a deep breath. He tried to stand tall, like a man among men. "Then we're ready?"

I smirked at the boy who would walk these dangerous halls with men. "You should stay behind, Gokliya. You should stay and take care of your brother and sister. It is the right thing for a man to do, to care for his family."

"Enyo Gyoja will see to them. The people will take care of them."

"You should stay behind. This is a dangerous thing."

"I will not be a coward. I want to go with you. I want to see more of the world than this."

Joseph touched his son's rough hair. "If we try to leave him behind, he'll just follow us. He learned to read tracks from you."

"In the snow, anyone can read tracks. Even you. Let's go. We shouldn't waste time."

"Just a moment, Xin."

Joseph leaned into his hut again. He reached his hands out to his crying children. He kissed Geraldine and Robert and told them to be brave, be strong, and look out for each other. "Listen to Aia and Enyo and any of the adults that help. Never forget your mother's face, or her name. I love you all so much."

Joseph told Gokliya to say goodbye to his brother and sister.

Gokliya didn't look at them. He snorted. He mumbled something resembling a goodbye.

Joseph knew his son was too tough for soft words. The boy needed to wear courage, not goodbye.

I scratched my head. "Are you done?"

"You have no children, Wang Xin. How can you understand what it means to tell your children goodbye?"

"I'm leaving now. We have to hurry while there's light to see. Come with me or not."

We went first to the source of the water, where it spilled from the wall in a stream that braided through the walls around it. We drank the icy water there and checked the depths of our water skins. We turned our eyes to stone halls that spread out before us, turning and turning and bending and bending. The maze of twisting halls and ancient stones made us take slow trails while the water cut straight through the cracks and broken places in the mortaring under walls and over roots. We traveled then, out to the edge of the paths our people knew among the ancient stone walls, where the river pressed against the edge of a cliff and stumbled down to a new stream that spread on and on, braiding through the halls of the ancient maze that continued across all horizons. We found a path to the bottom of the cliff. We walked softly past the cave mouths, alert for any sound or flickering shadow. We heard nothing but the babble of the stream. We saw nothing but snow and stream and the maze, the maze, and the endless maze.

We followed the stream that wandered aimlessly around its own maze of cracked mortaring, failed walls, and occasional tree roots worming holes in the stones. (We stopped to strip the bark, for it could be boiled and eaten, and the bitter buds of the leaves, as well.)

But, this was winter, still, and the water wasn't always water. It was often ice, hidden below the snow. We had to shove our spears through the mounds in the walls' shadows. When I tired of waiting for them to stumble through the snowdrifts, pounding their spears after ice, I went to the place I knew water would be found. I placed my spear tip there. I declared my discovery.

How could Aia have been so upset with me, when the water's eye had shown me all of these other things? Aia should have been grateful and happy. My spear found the ice where the water's eye had shown me the ice. I had given her a child that would comfort her in her old age. I would find my beloved bride upon this trail, and a better home for our people.

I cleared the snow away enough to show the water there, below the ice. We considered whether it looked strong enough to follow, or if we thought the water would drift away into a thin sliver and fade. When we decided it would fade—and I knew it would—we turned back to the path we had walked before, toward the braided river. We chose a new stream to follow through the halls.

Snow huddled in the corners where the sun never warmed enough to melt it. I imagined this snow might linger deep into the summer. A core of snow, in a deep corner, remained frozen for centuries.

Clouds rolled through in the corners of the day and shook light snow over us like little sneezes blowing dust.

The icy streams fanned out into thin strips of ice. We spent five days following failed threads and going back and picking which thread of ice looked stronger than the last.

They were frustrated by this.

I was calm. I did not join the arguments they had. I held a beautiful woman's face in my mind. I imagined what it must feel like to hold such a small, gentle woman in my arms when all my arms had known was tall, bony Aia, fighting until her angry surrender to my strength.

Joseph and Gokliya argued and argued. I left them to it and gathered bark and tree stems and rats and birds and anything else that could be eaten. We made bitter stews out of snow and my gathered things. Joseph and Gokliya did not argue about the streams as much when they were eating.

Finally, in a lull, Joseph wanted to climb over the walls to follow the water he had chosen. The brick walls on either side of us were only twice as tall as a man, and the passages were narrow enough that Gokliya could touch both walls with his hands spread. I asked Joseph how he planned to get us over the smooth sandstone bricks. He said we could help each other by boosting one person up, and then letting the person at the top reach down to heft the rest.

I didn't feel like explaining to Joseph why this idea of his was no good. In the water's eye, I explained the futility of Joseph's plan in depth, and we argued until we struck each other, and I knocked him bloody to the ground. I didn't feel angry enough to do such a thing. I didn't feel like telling him the truth. Here, among the stones, after all of Gokliya and Joseph's arguing, I wanted only to hear silence, again. I swallowed my pride, took a long drink of melted snow, and looked to Gokliya.

Gokliya's eyes were wide as bricks. He had probably never thought of going up and over a wall before in his life. He had always lived beneath them, never on top of them.

"Joseph, boost me up first. I'm stronger than both of you. I can pull you and Gokliya both to the top."

We did just that. Gokliya and Joseph planted their feet and linked arms to give me a boost to the top. I climbed up. I shouted down to them to hand me the equipment first. They handed it up to me a little at a time—spear, water skin, brickbat, bag of food. I dropped these things down on the icy finger of water that cut through the hall. I straddled the wall. I leaned over and reached down a hand to Gokliya. I pulled him up while Joseph boosted him. Then, Gokliya and I together reached down and pulled up Joseph. We sat there, straddling the wall, looking all around us at the walls jamming into each other and all the snow as far as the eye could see. I looked behind us and saw the crumbling towers of the castle at the center of the empty city, high on the hill above the cliffs. Smoke from the campfires where the humans lived left a black trail in the cool blue sky.

"Look," I said, "do you see how hard that was? Can you think of doing that all day long? If we had ropes, maybe, or ladders. Even then, look around you. If anything is hunting men, they can see us better on the top of walls than they can if we stay down, below the walls. We should only do this if we are desperate. We are not desperate. Let us climb down and do what we have been doing."

Joseph said nothing. Gokliya gazed around in wonder. Had he ever seen the maze from the top of a wall? Children usually did, but we discouraged them from it. We had to hide most of the time. We had to work together to hold back the things that hunted. We didn't want to stand out, alone on a wall. We put our dead on walls to draw creatures to us, to kill them.

On the other side, we walked in silence, following the paths that we thought would bend again toward the water and backtracking when we thought they wouldn't.

Soon after we climbed down from the wall, Gokliya sang while we walked, loudly enough that I knew he was taunting his father, but softly enough that he could pretend he was singing to himself.

> *Don't climb the wall,*
> *Don't climb the wall,*
> *What will happen if you fall?*
> *What will happen if you fall?*
> *You'll spend your life at a crawl,*
> *You'll spend your life at a crawl,*
> *You'll break your bones, break them all—*
> *You'll break your bones, break them all—*
> *And never stand or walk at all!*
> *And never stand or walk at all!*

I stopped, suddenly. I raised my hand. "Gokliya, be quiet."

He obeyed me.

Then, we all heard it. We held very still. We pressed our backs against a wall, into the shadows there. We looked all around us. Sound danced all over the stones. The source could have been anywhere.

The sound came from above.

A gigantic bird—wings as big as ten men—swooped through the air above us. It did not seem interested in us. Its wings were mostly feathers, but there was a greenness to the bird, as if it was also draped in leaves like Enyo. Its long beak ended in stems, and huge flowers sprouted from its glorious feet—talons and thorns, feathers and leaves.

As soon as we saw the giant creature, it was gone in a gust.

"What was that?" said Gokliya.

"I don't know," I said. "I don't know."

"It was a bird," said Gokliya. "I think."

"Do you think it will hurt anyone?" said Joseph.

"I don't know," I said. "Let's keep going. We should stay off the walls. Maybe it saw us. Maybe it was looking for us. We'll stay down below."

"Follow the water, then," said Joseph. "We'll take the turns we think we must. We'll do our best."

"We did."

I shuddered to think of the green bird soaring over the walls. I had not seen it in the water's eye.

We found a dead minotaur, covered in flies and reeking of death. We could not tell what had killed her. Buzzards hadn't found her, yet.

Gokliya didn't wait for us to tell him what to do. He scraped a bone knife over the body. He peeled back the skin, where the maggots rooted deep into the rotting tissue. He gathered the maggots in bunches, like wriggling berries. He dumped the maggots into an empty water skin. He kept digging for maggots in the rotten places of the flesh.

I smashed my stone axe through the beast's ribs and breastbone for the monster's heart. The axe tip chipped against the bone, but I couldn't worry about that. I used a spear tip that had fallen from the rotted leathers and damp wood of a spear to dig into the flesh and shove away all the smashed bones. I pulled out her heart. I divided it into three parts. We ate it raw.

Something had already taken the liver, along with most of the stomach and legs. Gokliya and Joseph dug through there, collecting maggots in the rotten gore.

Joseph pointed at the tracks around the body. "Anything nearby?"

I shook my head.

I didn't know what creature made those tracks. It had two feet, but very large ones that were knotted and knobby like chunks of wood. It had three huge toes, each as big as my arm, with claws at the tips. It had eaten its fill, then left.

"How many monsters do you see, Xin?"

"One, long gone. The rest of the minotaurs ran that way. Chasing or fleeing, I cannot see." The minotaur's blood had frozen into ice crystals. The body was kept in the cold, where the meat wasn't exposed. "We should take all the meat with us to collect maggots. We can rinse the rest of the meat in melted snow and cook it when we find something to burn."

"I'm glad you came with us, Xin."

"What will we do if the water takes us underground, Joseph? Would you follow the water into a cave?"

"Yes."

I would follow any trail that took me to my love, and our grove. I would brave any danger for her. I would do anything to keep her safe. I would crawl through caves and any number of strange new monsters to find her and bring her to our hut in the grove, where we will live a long life in peace and happiness together. "The water will not go underground for a long time, Joseph. Even then, we'll go back and find a good stream to follow, over land."

"What will we do if the strong water falls into the ground and there is no cave to follow it down? What will we do if the water disappears and we can no longer follow the frozen stream?"

"We will go back, and we will follow a different thread of the stream, Joseph. Listen, do not be afraid. We will find what we seek. I will cut the minotaur's legs if you cut the arms and head. We will take all we can carry. Gokliya, watch the halls. We are not the only scavengers here."

"Can I hold your axe, Xin?"

"Of course. Don't break it. I don't have many blows left with that cracked stone."

We turned a corner in the hall and found five paths like the spokes of a wheel bending away into the maze. Which path should we take? A week ago we would have stopped to discuss our path. This time, we did not think long. We moved toward them. We shuffled our eyes and ears around the five halls, and we thought—silently—all together about the icy stream we had abandoned behind us to choose the path that met the stream again. We wove through the maze, tracking the stream's straight paths. We did not need to speak about our path anymore.

Without a word spoken, or a glance shared, Joseph, Gokliya, and I picked the trail to follow.

We were right to pick that path. The ice stream curved into our hallway, edging along the side of the wall and straight ahead, as if the water were suddenly running toward something.

We walked uphill, following the stream that cut through the center of the hall. We plucked some ice flowers we found growing there and chewed on them, gingerly, breathing hard with open mouths to try to warm them. The petals melted on our tongues. They tasted different from the ice flowers near the castle—much, much worse. Gokliya spat his out. He chewed maggots to wipe the flavor from his tongue. He ate the white bodies and spit out the black heads.

We kept walking.

Snow fell hard the second week. We stopped to camp and wait for the sun to reemerge and melt down the white blanket that hid the stream from us.

Gokliya lost a tooth. He slipped it into his pack. He smiled and stuck his tongue in and out of the new gap in his face.

Joseph shook his head at his son. "Do not celebrate that. You will never grow another tooth to replace the one you lost. You aren't a baby anymore. When you lose a tooth, it is gone forever. Do you see all these gaps in my mouth? All of them gone and never growing back. Someday, we will be like Enyo, and we will only have a few green teeth to chew our meat. We will long for the days of our youth when teeth were as common as the petals of flowers, always growing back when they fell out. How old are you, Gokliya?"

"I'm twelve winters."

"You are all grown up now, Gokliya. Do not celebrate the decay of your body. You should be kind to the girls, and not tease them, for you shall marry one of them and pour your life into your children to spite your body's decay, and when you are old and you have no teeth, your children will chop up your supper into small bits and feed it to you."

"Father, I just want to be a hunter. Xin never married, and he is a mighty hunter. He is strong and brave. That is what I want."

"I am your father. Aren't I a good enough man to follow in life—I, who raised you up all your life and cared for you and your brother and sister?"

"Father..."

We waited. No one spoke for a long time. I checked our weapons for more signs of rot. I rubbed them down with leather. I did my best. The leather lashes on my axe were worn down. I tightened them as best as I could. The last brickbat's wood was nearly rotted through where the leather lashes met the stone and stick.

I didn't want to think of what would happen if we faced a foe with skin too hard to puncture with a spear, and only one brickbat that threatened to snap loose on the first swing.

We drank melted snow. We rubbed our cold, stiff limbs. We ate small mouthfuls of rancid minotaur meat. Ice flowers grew here, all through the snowy shadows of the halls. We were grateful for them. We bit down on the cold, oozing things and slurped the bitter sap of their leaves. Gokliya didn't spit them out, anymore. We ate any insects and flies we could catch with our hands.

We curved around a bend. There was no sign of the water. We had expected it to be there, but it wasn't. We walked down the curve a little farther. There was no sign of water, only stones and snow.

"Did we lose the stream, Joseph?"

"I don't know."

"Let us go back and see if we walked over it," I said. "This stream thins, and we seek a place where it grows."

"Do you think we should backtrack, Gokliya?"

"No, father." said Gokliya. "We should climb a wall and look around us, just once—carefully. Let us peer over the walls and see what we can see. Perhaps the stream grows beyond this wall. Sometimes they grow instead of dwindling. We shall climb and take a look. Then, if we cannot see any stream, we can backtrack and try again."

I frowned. The walls at our sides were both smooth, grey granite. Time had worn the edges down to nubs. Whatever mortaring there was couldn't hold them together if someone pushed them hard enough. We had seen the places in the walls where the mortaring had given in, where something had clattered against a wall, bricks everywhere, and usually bones beneath them, chewed down to the marrow.

I tested the wall with my spear. I nudged at it in spots, searching for the strongest place.

"Here, Gokliya. Your father's eyes are better than ours. We shall boost him up and help him back down again, carefully."

Gokliya and I together hefted Joseph up toward the top of the wall. Joseph grabbed the edges of the rocks. He pulled himself the rest of the way to the top.

"I see...I see the stream growing. We can climb over this wall and pick up the stream again. I see no danger here. We will be careful. Gokliya, let me pull you up with me."

Gokliya clambered up the wall. I handed our packs and weapons up. Joseph and Gokliya dropped them down to the ground beyond the wall. I heard the sound of them falling in a heap.

Then, they pulled me up.

I saw the stream in the next hall, as if it had woven underground water before popping out again at the wall like it had been a watery thread, sewn. It looked stronger there. I looked at all the walls around us from the top, and I picked our next pathway through the maze to follow the stream through the hills.

The maze continued on, forever and ever, beyond the horizon.

We let Gokliya down first, then me, and then Joseph.

The stream was near us. Before we picked up our packs, I bent to take a drink. The water tasted so cold, so sweet.

I gathered up my things.

My axe had snapped where it fell from the wall. The stone remained on the ground. The club end had bits of leather thread still clinging to the wood like damp fungus. The leathers had melted in the strain of damp snow and cold.

I showed it to my traveling companions silently. Gokliya picked up the stone and slipped it into a sack. Joseph pulled bits of string from his pocket, but we knew those small threads would not be enough to clutch the brick.

We had two spears left, and some spear tips, and the stone axe head, and a brick that had once been part of a brickbat. We had some skinning knives carved from either bone or minotaur horn. We had no other weapons.

Joseph lashed the rotting wooden handle to Gokliya's back with the thread from his pockets.

4: Happiness

I found tracks in the snow of four small hooves. Joseph and Gokliya and I moved silently through the snow after the creature.

A brown animal, with a long, alert face nibbled at the bark of a dead bush. The animal had a single giant flower bud sprouting from its white tail—closed in the winter—and giant wooden thorns sprouting from its head, with smaller sealed flower buds.

I threw the spear before the creature could bolt, where I knew it would run. It keened in death throes. Joseph threw the other spear. It gasped out its last breaths. Gokliya ran up to it with a bone dagger and sliced its throat. It died bleeding a sticky-sweet sap all over the ground.

Joseph stroked the dead thing's face.

It was like a deer. It was like a rose bush and a deer. What a strange creature.

We butchered the animal quickly. The sap blood tasted so sweet it was sickening, but the flesh was bitter and stiff. We set fire to the wooden antlers and did what cooking we could in that poor, short flame. We poured the sap over the bitter meat to make it edible. We ate it all right away. We were so hungry, we ate the entire thing between the three of us. We'd have eaten the bones if they'd had any marrow inside of them. They were bone, but they were more like a flower's stem inside than a meaty bone with marrow.

"This is a good sign," I said. "We have found something new to eat, and it is near the water. We can find more of them. We can hunt them all winter long."

Joseph shook his head. "We should find a way to raise them ourselves. Hunting is too dangerous, and too risky. If we grew the creatures ourselves, we could take control of our stomachs. We could grow them like corn and rice and the screaming oranges."

Gokliya fondled the damp bones. He sucked all the sap he could off of them. "Do you think these bones will burn like wood? We should keep them and see. Maybe they will start a great fire and warm us in the night."

I said nothing. I pulled my skins and leathers all around myself. I rubbed my tired bones. Weeks of walking, and winter hadn't broken, yet.

We had to get to the far edge of winter before we'd find my love, and we were almost there. We had to get out a little farther into the maze, to find her and her daughter.

We were almost there.

Gokliya asked his father for a story. Joseph yawned. Joseph asked me if there was any story I knew.

"I know nothing. I cannot help you. I will stay awake. I am not tired. I worry that we have not seen any monsters. Where are the wild men? Where are the minotaurs and manticores and hungry beasts? What larger things walk among these halls, beyond the halls we know? I will remain awake. I will wake you if I am tired, Joseph."

Gokliya said he wasn't tired, either, and that he would stay awake, too. He sang songs to himself in the evening twilight. The songs of the tribe were always songs about the tribe that the women and children sang to each other when they walked to the water, or scraped at the skins to make leather, or walked in groups to gather plants and roots and fruits and rice. They were sometimes about how to live in the maze and sometimes about us.

Gokliya sang both kinds of songs and sang songs deep into the night.

Djinni come for the children who wander too far from the tribe, and curse them or bless them. People wander in from the maze, telling stories of worlds we'll never know. Enyo Gyoja knows everything, and has lived in the maze all his life and all our lives and he will live on after our deaths, I know, older and with fewer teeth. Aia was a witch who could make a man fall in love with a woman. Sai would never share anything, unless you gave her something more valuable in return, and this is why she died that bad winter. All these songs, and more Gokliya sang.

I fell asleep to Gokliya's singing. I dreamed of the woman I have loved since I saw her in the water's eye.

She's lying in a pool of blood where I will find her. Then, I will see a caveman over her, erect and beating his chest and howling at me. I will kill the caveman with my bare hands. I will pick my beautiful one up from the floor and place her gently on a hammock. I will wrap her bleeding skull and I will raise her child, though I long to kill it.

This was a terrible dream, and I woke up weeping for what fate had in store for my beloved.

It was still dark when I woke up. I couldn't see a thing with the clouds in the night sky blocking out the moon and stars. I listened carefully. I heard Joseph snoring. I heard Gokliya breathing hard. I heard the sound of wind and creaking branches farther away and farther away and farther away and gone. I fell asleep again and dreamed of tomorrow, and how we would find the woman and her daughter climbing over walls. This dream was much better.

When daybreak came, Gokliya climbed up a wall to scout out the water again. The snow had melted in the sunlight. The water flowed without ice. Gokliya squinted his eyes.

"Hey, I see something on the wall!"

I held my breath.

"What?" said Joseph. "Get down!"

"No, it's…it looks like a girl. Hello! Hello over there!"

"Gokliya…!" said Joseph.

A girl's voice called back. It was a young girl's voice. She said words we didn't know. Then, there was a woman's voice.

My heart rose up in my throat.

I had loved this woman and this girl all the days of my life, though I did not know their names. The sound of their voices was the most beautiful thing I had ever heard.

The woman with her daughter and I with Joseph and Gokliya chased each other's voices most of the day. We ran down halls and shouted for each other, and we ran around halls and shouted. Where was the turn to take? Where was the right bend to follow in the path? How could we tell them where to walk when they did not speak our words and we did not speak theirs? I wanted them to just hold still! We who knew the maze could find a path to them if they held still!

We wound up in adjacent halls. The girl and Gokliya both climbed to the top of a high wall. He hugged the girl, happily. The girl was happy at first. Then, she was frightened. She saw us up close for the first time, and smelled our travels all over our filthy bodies.

The girl wore a clean, brown linen dress. A gold cross was sewn onto her chest and onto her back, below her long brown hair.

She looked down on Joseph and me with fear in her eyes. She pulled nervously away from Gokliya. The girl burst into tears. She tried to climb back down to the side away from us, toward her mother.

Gokliya chided her, gently. He clapped his hands. He picked her up below her arms and easily hefted the little child over the edge, down to Joseph and me.

Gokliya called down for a spear. He held the spear down over the wall and helped the woman there climb to the top, using the spear shaft like a rope. She emerged at the top, there.

She was more beautiful than I could ever remember.

I held my breath and looked up at her. Her blonde hair, her sharp, dark eyes and her clean, soft beauty was so pale in the winter cold. I couldn't move. I didn't want to move. I wanted to look at her, at the top of the wall, basking in the sunlight.

I will hold these two memories all the days of my life, in unison. First, the vision in the water's eye, when the woman first appeared to me on the wall, and I was a boy, and I was in love with her then. Second, the moment the woman appeared on the wall, and I was a man, and I was in love with her all over again; for the first and second time I was in love with her. Both memories merged in my love of her.

This was the happiest moment of my life.

The woman followed the girl down. Joseph helped her. She looked at the men she had found with fear all over her face, just like the girl had. She clenched her jaw and forced a friendly smile. She had gold crosses sewn to her brown dress, just like her daughter. Her hair was a long, tangled mess down to her waist. Her feet were bare and pale in the snow. We would need to wrap them in rags before she lost toes to frostbite. She said a word I didn't understand.

Joseph smiled. He bowed to the woman, slowly. "I know we must seem to be terrifying to you, covered in animal skins, and such hard and scarred men. But, we are the only ones who can keep you safe here. We will not hurt you."

I remembered. I had to make them laugh. I reached into my pack for a large bug I had found, as big as a thumb. I bit the beetle in half. I chewed and made happy eating noises. I knelt down. I held out the insect's other half to the girl. At first, she held very still. Then, she screamed and hid behind the woman's legs. The woman smacked the beetle away.

They were supposed to laugh at me.

I frowned. What could I do now, to make them laugh? Why didn't they laugh?

Joseph pulled me back from them.

"She thinks we are monsters, Xin. Perhaps, to her, we are monsters. She is beautiful and clean, and she has probably never seen anything so terrifying as us in all her life. Gokliya, sing a song for them, that they may know we are civilized."

They were supposed to laugh at me, eating the bug and offering it to the girl.

Gokliya clapped his hands. He sang.

When cavemen come, you know what's done?
Run, run, run and run
When manticores come, you know what's done?
Run, run, run, and run
When Aia comes, you know what's done?
Run, run, run, and run

Aia is big, and Aia is mean
Aia casts spells that make you green
Aia is nice, and I'm only playing
Because I'm afraid of her gods and her praying

When minotaurs come, you know what's done?
Run, run, run, and run
When panthers arrive, you know where to hide?
Run, run, run, and climb
When Aia comes, you know where to hide?
Nowhere to run, and nowhere to hide

Aia is big, and Aia is mean
Aia casts spells that make you green
Aia is nice, and I'm only playing
Because I'm afraid of her gods and her praying

I never liked that song.

They were supposed to laugh at me. They weren't laughing. I clapped and sang along halfway through Gokliya's song. I laughed in places I was supposed to laugh. I tried to be happy and help the women be happy. Joseph joined in.

The two women neither laughed nor clapped.

Joseph pulled out his water flask. He took a long drink. He poured some water on his hands. He rubbed his hands in the water, to clean them. He rubbed his wet hands on his face. He handed the flask to the woman.

She held it, awkwardly, because she was not used to handling water skins with her delicate palms. She sniffed at the melted snow mixed with stream water. She poured some carefully into her palm. She lifted it to her nose and sniffed at it. She stuck out a tongue and tasted it. She poured more into her hand and took a long drink. She did it again. She turned to the girl and told her something in their mysterious, lilting language. The girl leaned her head back like a baby bird. The woman poured water carefully down into the girl's mouth, straight from the source. The girl held her hands up when she was done. Then, the women drank more. She drank it all until nothing was left.

Gokliya offered his flask to the woman, too. She took it, but she did not drink it. She slung it over her shoulder, to keep it. Then, she leaned against the wall with one hand. She bent over at the waist. The girl was worried about the woman. The girl clung at the woman's side and spoke nervously in their language.

The woman vomited up clear, sick-looking water. I reached out a hand to her. Joseph reached out a hand to her. The woman took my hand in hers. She wiped her face with my hand. It was the first time I ever touched her, and she was using me to wipe away sickness. That wasn't correct. She was supposed to hold my hand for support. I pulled my hand away.

She laughed at me. She laughed at her prank. Then, she was crying. She fell deeper downward and she was crying and crying, and the girl was crying. They sat down against the wall and clutched their legs close and clutched each other and wept and wept.

Joseph sat down beside them. He told Gokliya to climb the wall with me and look for the water. They would need to find it again, soon, to replace the water that had been swallowed by these two new people.

Joseph stayed with the woman and the girl.

I held still, watching him hold the woman I loved, and he comforted her. I was supposed to hold her and comfort her.

The woman was so beautiful. She had a body unscarred by the maze and a face that had not been sunburnt between the sky and the snow. I saw the shadow of who she would be in her bone structure. I saw the scars to come, and I knew I would kiss them all in time.

I made no movement toward any stream.

I watched Joseph. I wanted to kill him.

Gokliya ignored his father's command, like I did. He tried to get the girl to play with him and clap hands and sing. She was too scared at first. She was so scared. Gokliya resorted to making faces at her, crossing his eyes and moving his lips and nose around with his hands.

The girl started crying again.

"Gokliya, leave her alone. Have some consideration for them. They were minding their own business when they arrived here. They do not know where they are. They are too soft to be natives of this terrible place. They are like me, when I first came here, before you were born. They are like Wang Xin."

I clenched my jaw. "I will go find the water, maybe find some food."

"Good man," said Joseph. "Take Gokliya. I'll stay with the women until they're themselves again. We'll have to wrap their feet against the snow."

I could have killed Joseph, then, but then how could she love me if I murdered a man who had comforted her? His death was coming soon enough, and all I had to do was walk him to the frozen lake and the creature that would destroy him, there.

I saw it all in my mind's eye—in the water's eye—when I walked away from them: Joseph screaming out death agonies I longed to hear right then, falling into the water with the giant monster, below the waves.

Then, she would have no one else to love but me.

Gokliya followed me away into the maze, searching after the stream we had lost chasing the women.

We found the icy stream, shimmery without any snow to conceal it. I smashed it open with the butt of my spear. I saw my face in the stagnant water.

The memory of Aia haunted me.

Gokliya gathered up the water. He did not seem to notice my emotions.

I gathered water with Gokliya. I dug through my pack for bits of meat. I searched hard for any trace or scrap fallen into the crevices of the lashes.

The love of my life, weeping where I could not hold her.

When Gokliya and I returned, we went directly to the women. I held out some dried meat for them. They took it. They sniffed it and split it between themselves and ate. They had terrified looks in their eyes.

"Why do they look at me like that? Why do they look like I am going to hurt them?" I said. "I have done nothing but help them, and they are afraid of me."

Joseph smiled. He told us to watch carefully, and be ready to jump after them if the women chose to run.

Gokliya laughed. "They think you are ugly and scary, Xin. I will make a song about how you frighten minotaurs and women and little girls and birds and everything. You are a mighty hunter, and you frighten everyone—everything."

Joseph stood up. "We need to keep searching. Our tribe is waiting for us to return. We need to find a camp along the water, where we can survive next winter in our growing numbers. These two women..." he said. "They will be hungry and they will make it harder for us to move quickly."

Gokliya looked up to the sky. "We've walked to the edge of winter, and we've found nothing." He scratched his head. "Father, we must turn back soon. We must go home and tell others of what we have found. Nothing. Nothing at all."

I curled my lip at Gokliya, as if I would strike him. "These women with us will make it harder for us when we return, because they are going to be hungry but they will not know how to help us find more food. They will slow us on our path home, because their feet are like babies' feet, and we will be unable to hunt with them stumbling noisily beside us. We must keep searching for a better place along the water. We will need more food just to make it back to Enyo Gyoja alive with these two noisy women."

Gokliya spoke again. "Let us climb to the top of the highest hill we can see. We will climb a wall there. We will look all around us at every-thing we can see. If we see nothing new, then we should turn home again, before we lose our way."

"Not yet," said Joseph. He clenched his hands on his spear. He looked all around. "I want to go home to your brother and sister, but I do not want to go home to them until I have found a way to help them sur-vive next winter. When Yi died..."

Silence followed. We all looked to our feet, then, remembering that winter. The woman broke the silence. She touched her own chest. She said, very slowly, very deliberately, "Ur...soux...lah..." She said it again. "Ursula."

Joseph bowed to her. "I've heard that name before, somewhere." He touched his own chest, as she had done. "Joseph." He did it again. "Joseph."

"Joseph?" She perked up and smiled. "Kristoos?"

Joseph thought carefully. He cocked his head and considered her word. Then, he placed a hand on his forehead, moved it to his heart, and then to each shoulder, in a cross.

She clapped and smiled. Her daughter knelt down in the muddy snow and clasped her hands, raising her eyes to the sky and laughing happily.

I scowled at him. "What do you think you are doing?"

"Her name is Ursula. I think she said she's a Christian. I was, too, once. Not Christian like her, exactly—not from the same place. She must think we are something wild. Look at us, Xin," he said. He pointed at himself, and then at me. "My name is Joseph. Introduce yourself, Xin."

I touched my own chest, as she and Joseph had done. "Wang Xin," I said. "Xin."

"Zin?" She frowned. "Zin?" She shook her head and babbled something harsh.

"Why does she act like that to me and clap and cheer for you? What did I do to deserve disgust when you are her hero?"

Joseph smirked. "Her religion has a name for the worst things you can do to other people, that their god hates more than anything in the world. Your name sounds very nearly the same. She must think you are some kind of monster."

Gokliya laughed. "You are a monster, Wang Xin. You frighten everything in the maze except for me."

He introduced himself to the girl. She introduced herself to him.

Catherine.

Ursula and Catherine.

Turn a corner in the maze and find death with open jaws. Turn another, and find a woman and a girl. Turn a thousand corners and find nothing.

I had never believed in a god. I saw no shape or pattern or will in all those stone bricks and passages beyond the water's eye. I saw nothing but the chaos of turning the corner in the hall and finding nothing or finding monsters, and a bicycle, and blood, and water, and trees, and now—like a madness—a woman and a girl, both in brown dresses with golden crosses and beautiful faces and long, clean blonde hair.

They walked around corners with us, back to the stream, on the path I had found to the water. They rested at the stream. They refilled water skins. The ice flowers in the shadows were wilted, but they were still edible. The days were too warm for the winter flowers. I plucked an ice flower and handed it to Ursula.

She smiled and placed it in her daughter's hair, behind her ear.

I shook my head. "No," I said. I snatched the flower and ate it. I showed her my chewing with my open lips. I plucked another flower, and I gave it to Ursula. She held it, confused, looking up at me with a cocked head and a frown. She put the flower behind her own ear. She plucked a new one for her daughter.

Catherine and Gokliya sang songs to each other. They could not speak the words each other spoke, but they could learn melodies. They could laugh.

Ursula walked close to Joseph. She mumbled to herself.

"What is she talking about? Is she insane?"

"I do not think so." Joseph smiled at her. "I think she is praying to her god. The Christian god—" (Ursula lit up at the words a moment, then returned to praying.) "—is far kinder in many ways than all the gods we know in the village, Aia's and everyone else's private gods. In other ways, this god is far crueler."

"God? There is no god. She wastes her voice on something foolish when she could be learning to speak to me. I want her to learn to speak, so I can tell her what she needs to know."

Ursula stopped to pick a second ice flower. She lifted the crystalline petals to her nose. She sniffed it. It was wilted and oozing water from the stem. She placed it in her hair, anyway, on the other ear to mirror the first. She plucked another one and placed it behind Catherine's empty ear.

She plucked an ice flower for Gokliya, and for Joseph. Finally, she plucked one for me. She smiled. She placed the flower behind my ear.

I frowned. I snatched it from my ear and tossed it into my mouth. "You're supposed to eat them," I said to her, deliberately slow, as if it would help her understand if I spoke slowly. "They'll keep the scurvy from you all winter long."

Ursula jumped away from me and hid on the other side of Joseph's body.

"What now? She is wasting perfectly good flowers."

"Wang Xin, you were never married to anyone. Be gentle. Be patient. Be kind."

"I am the greatest hunter in this maze. I kill the wild men of the caves alone. I kill minotaurs and drive back harpies and defeat the strangest monsters alone. She should be grateful to have me here, protecting her."

"She does not know that. She only knows that you are mean to her and you are named for something evil."

"Does your name mean anything to her?"

"My name is the same name as the kindly father of her God."

"Is Gokliya the name of her God?"

"No," he said. "Gokliya's name probably means nothing to her. I can tell you what his name means, if you'd like to know."

"I don't care."

"In the place where I was before I came here, there was a tribe that lived before my people on that land. The name 'Gokliya' was the name of a great leader, when he was a boy. It meant 'He Yawns a Lot' in their language. When the boy grew up, they changed his name to Geronimo, which meant that his arms were covered in the blood of his enemies."

"Gokliya is a better name for your boy than Geronimo."

Gokliya did not know he had become the topic of conversation. He was teaching a song to Catherine. They walked and sang songs and clapped their hands.

"He is young. He wants to be like you. He wants to be brave and strong. I'm glad to take him away from the village and keep him with me, where I can watch him become a man and try to teach him to be kind. I do not want to raise a Geronimo."

"I'm going to go on ahead and see if we are getting close to the stream again. Take my spear. It's better than yours. You can protect her with it. I don't need a spear to kill a minotaur or stop the gargoyles. I am Wang Xin, the mightiest hunter in these halls, and better than any Geronimo."

I ran ahead. My tired feet slapped on the dry places of the trail. I wasn't trying to keep quiet, just to be fast. I turned a corner, and turned another corner, and followed the echoes of flowing water in all that silence to find the stream where the water's eye had placed it in my mind. I dashed back through the curves and led them around to the path that would turn to water farther down the stream.

Sandstones, granite stones, pumice stones, black stones, red stones, and all of them bending against each other in bricks. Small vines wound through the desiccated mortaring. They were still brown from winter. They were brittle and hard.

I plucked a vine and touched it to my tongue. It tasted bitter and dead and brown. I held it between my teeth and chewed on it. Chewing on something eased thirst. Water swelled around the stem.

I looked down at the vine hanging from my mouth and saw it become green. I quickly pulled the stem from my mouth. A long, oozing tendril hung on from the cut stem, to my tongue. It siphoned water out of me. When my saliva had touched the stem, the vine greened down to the tip. The plant had been drinking from me. It continued to drink from me.

I tore the tendrils loose. I spit it all out. I threw the vine down. The plant sprouted legs like an insect and walked back to the wall. It adjusted itself against the nearest brown vine, and the green of my mouth fanned out into the vines, fading all color evenly along the long stems.

I thought, for just a moment, about sending him here, by himself. Joseph would die soon, on the lake of ice.

I turned back to them.

5: In Water's Eye, Your Death

When I got close to the sound of Gokliya singing, I jumped up as high as I could reach and snagged the top of a wall. I pulled hard and climbed up the bricks to peek over the top. I saw Gokliya and Catherine laughing and singing where they walked. They were waiting at the curve for me to return.

Ursula leaned against the wall below me. I heard her gentle voice. She and Joseph were trying words against each other, and learning to speak.

"Labrinto. Monsyoor. Catolesha."

"Labyrinth. Sir. Catholic."

I dropped back down. I leaned against the wall. I listened to the sound of the children singing and the parents learning to speak to each other.

I looked down on them, and I didn't know what to do but wait.

I climbed down off the wall. Eventually, I walked around the corner. I went without speaking to Joseph. I took my spear back from him.

Joseph patted my shoulder. "Any luck?"

"Yes. I found the water, but I think we can catch it later on if we take a different path. There's a dangerous, strange thing down this hall. I do not wish to learn more of it. Gokliya, what will we do with these women if we turn a corner and face something dangerous?"

"We will fight it."

"No," I said. "Catherine and Ursula will not fight. They will scream and get in the way and get themselves killed, and maybe get in our way and get us killed. We have to try to get them to understand that if we face danger, they must run away, and Gokliya, you should stay with them, to protect them. If we die, Joseph and I, then you should take them back to Enyo Gyoja and keep them safe."

The gravity of what I said slowly sunk into Gokliya's bones. He had been raised here in the maze. He understood what could happen in these halls. He nodded.

Joseph smiled up at the sky. He observed a passing cloud with gentle eyes. "I have been thinking about my past, Xin. I wonder if our village will be as we left it. You and I speak of bicycles. This woman here, her clothes are rough, and her teeth are as bad as ours. Her faith is too strong and too open for a woman of my time. He ran a hand down her hair. She did not understand what he was saying. She let him touch her wild hair like that. She did not stop him.

I stomped my foot. I smashed my spear onto the ground hard enough to crack the wood at the bottom.

I glared at Joseph, and my anger poured over everyone. The women cowered back from me. Gokliya straightened where he stood. Joseph did not flinch.

"Joseph, I have to tell you this, Joseph, and I want you to not forget this. You have your children and had your great love. I have none, and have had none. I am in love with this woman." It is not in the water's eye that I do these things. Everything is wrong, now. I don't want things to be different. "I am in love with Ursula, and I do not want you leading her on. Your sons and daughter will care for you in your old age, but I have none of these things. This woman is beautiful, and I can see her gentle nature."

"Wang Xin, listen to me, this is important."

"No, listen to me. If you take her from me, I will hurt you. I will hurt you in ways you cannot imagine. I desire this woman. She will be mine."

"That's fine, Wang Xin. I will not fight you for her heart. I will not challenge you for her. Just listen; she is not from the same time as we are. She is from far in the past. I wonder how time works here, in this maze—how the sunrises and sunsets sometimes bend. Is east still east? Is west still west? Are north and south bent each morning with the bending of the halls?"

"I don't care about that." I grabbed his arm, hard. I yanked him away from my beautiful Ursula. "I don't know what you are talking about, and I don't care."

Ursula slapped me in the face. Then, Catherine stormed up to me and kicked my shin as hard as she could. She shouted at me in her strange language.

I frowned at both of them, the woman and the girl.

Joseph pulled the women away from me. "Xin, you scared them. You were threatening to them. Aia lives among the maze, and has lived here her whole life. Even she hates to be bullied like that. She'd kill you if she could. What do you expect of gentle creatures like these two, here with us?"

I frowned at the little child, who was still angrily gazing up at me. I wanted her to smile, and to laugh, and to be happy to see me. I wanted her to know how hard I strived to keep her safe, and how much I loved her and her mother. Instead, she had her little fists on her hips, and she was ready to kick me again if I showed the slightest inclination toward anger.

I looked to the clouds above. I looked to the stones. I looked to my own hands, hard as stones and grinding into my broken spear.

I let go. I leaned the rotting wooden shaft against the wall.

"Joseph, ahead there is a vine, but it is not a vine. It is an insect that seeks to steal water. It looks brown and like a vine, but if you pluck it and try to eat it, it will steal water from your mouth and turn green. Then, it will run back to the vine and spread your water out among the vine. I do not think we should test the limits of that strange vine."

"We shall avoid it, then. Who knows what else it does? You are good to warn us of this."

"I do not want to scare them. Tell them that I am kind and I do not want to scare them."

"I don't speak their language."

"Tell them that I am their friend."

"Tell them yourself. I will scout ahead next time. You can stay back with the women. Try talking to her. Try teaching her to speak our language."

Down the hall, down the next, to the water. Only small bits of food left. Dead maggots. Rotted strips of meat.

I smacked the girl's hand, lightly. Her mother didn't stop me, because she saw what her daughter was trying to do.

"Never eat the stones. They will not ease your pain. Only suck on them. They will pull water into your mouth and you will not feel so thirsty, and you will not feel so hungry. Drink the water when you are hungry."

"Water?"

"Yes, this is water. We're following the water out. Do you understand that?"

"Non."

"You will learn."

The sun warmed the walls. Was winter over? Was this the break in the cold that eased all our disasters until the final storm and the ice lake? The water's eye had showed me a great storm, as horrible as any in the wintertime.

I have lost all faith in the water's eye, though.

The women I love cower and tremble before me.

At night, after dark, I slip away from them all. I find a place where I can push the black place in my chest with my hand, and try to quell that blackness. In this place, I weep.

I do not want anyone to see me weeping, especially Joseph and Gokliya.

We found some trees growing where the hall fattened enough to let their acorns take root in the sunlight. We plucked their budding leaves from their stems. The new ones were shaped like hands. Each one we peeled matched each of our hands, exactly whomever peeled open the leaf bud.

The wound in the tree oozed a white milk. We rolled the leaves up and ate them. We licked the milk from the trees. It tasted horrible, but we were in no place to choose, and we had all eaten far worse.

These six trees, each no taller than Gokliya, pressed against the stones, with long, long, long roots that reached to the stream and the water down the hall.

We tried out a long branch as a possible spear shaft, but the oozing milk was too thick, and the wood was too rubbery in our hands. It wouldn't even burn.

We meandered around the maze, searching for the water again. When we found it, we heard it long before we saw it. The water seemed to be growing stronger along this vein. We couldn't hop over it in one step. We had to get at least one foot wet to the knee to get across the stream.

We danced with the growing stream, away and back, away and back. We chased the water down the halls that filled these hills, this world.

I killed a small animal that hid from me in a dark rock. I had the tiny thing cornered. It swiped at me with claws. I ignored the claws. They could not pierce my leathery skin. I snatched it by the scruff and yanked it out, shaking it and smashing it against the wall, dead in moments.

Joseph pulled it out of my hands as soon as he saw it. He stroked it along its dead back.

He called it a "Cat."

Ursula took it from him, next, and stroked the dead thing's neck just as Joseph had. Catherine began to cry for it.

I frowned at her. I yanked it out of her arms. I handed the dead animal to Gokliya. I told Gokliya to skin it. I told Gokliya to dry the meat on a rock. We had no fuel to burn it, so we were going to dry the meat as best we could, and eat it raw.

The creature was gaunt. Its meat was grey and putrid.

Ursula and Catherine wouldn't eat it. Gokliya tried to chew on it with his mouth open, making noises as if it was good—and it wasn't good. Catherine ran behind Ursula's ragged skirt, crying.

Gokliya swallowed what was left. He spit out the flavor and drank water.

The sun was up. The sun was high. Winter was a memory.

I watched Ursula. She should have been proud of me. She should have been grateful I had found something for her to eat. Even Joseph ate it.

"Aren't they hungry?" I said.

Joseph took little Catherine's hand. He told her to walk with him a while, and they'd find something else for her to eat. She didn't understand anything, but she did it anyway.

Ursula touched Joseph's back. She rested a hand on his shoulder blade. She muttered her prayers under her breath.

Joseph walked a while and stopped, digging behind rocks for food. He emerged with cat meat in his palm, and pretended like he had found it for her.

Catherine ate it. Ursula looked on with empty eyes.

"Did we walk back in time?" said Joseph. "Look to the clouds, and see the storms coming. Gokliya, tell me what you see."

"It looks bad, father."

"How do clouds sneak up on us like that? Where did all the clouds come from? Do you see Catherine? Do you see the clouds?"

The women looked at the clouds, but they didn't see anything. They seemed confused.

It had been warm yesterday, but today the wind rolled over the passageways and hung over us like vultures.

Cold snaps come. Snow returns.

"Did we walk through time itself, Wang Xin?"

"I do not know, Joseph. I do not worry of these things. When we go back, we shall go back and see what season it is for our people. Do you wish to go back now and share all your observations with Enyo Gyoja?"

"Of course not."

I looked around for Gokliya. He was ahead of us, skipping with Catherine and learning her songs. Ursula stood ahead of us, and it didn't matter if she heard me because she could barely speak a word of our language after only a few short weeks. "Joseph, I should tell you something. Listen, Joseph, this is important."

His lips pressed together. He took a deep breath. "Yes?"

"Listen," I said. "When I was very young, I once put my head in a bucket of water. A Djinni was there, in the water. It tumbled deep into my eye. I see many things. I see so many things."

He smirked. He didn't believe me. He had birthed one, he had said, from his lung. "A Djinni?" he said. "When was this?"

"A very long time ago. Listen, I know that you will not turn back, yet. I know the snow comes soon. I know our path is true. I know many things, Joseph, because I saw my whole life flash in my eye when the Djinni entered it."

"Where was this Djinni?"

"In a bucket of water, when I was young, and Selah put my head inside the bucket to teach me of his god. But, he did not know what was in the water. A Djinni spoke to me in the water. It entered my eye, and my whole life was revealed to me, and I cannot forget it. Listen, we need to be ready for the snow. The storm will come. It will be a terrible storm. We will need shelter for two days before we can walk out again. Then, we will reach the place where the ice lake reaches our feet. I have seen every beast that I have killed, and every beast I shall kill. I have seen every hall I have traveled, and every hall I will travel. I have seen my first night with Ursula, how she looks up at me. Joseph, I have seen your death."

"Xin, you should never speak of these lies."

"Listen, we must prepare for the snow. It will come fast and hard from these clouds that sneak up on us. Already, the wind drops colder than we have known for days. We should gather all the water we can and find a place where the sun will warm us when it returns."

"Wang Xin, you do not need to see the future to know it will snow hard. We will speak again of these strange things you claim when we have some time alone, away from the others—especially Gokliya."

"Of course we will," I said. "Your death is soon, Joseph."

What did my eye see?

I saw Ursula leaning into Joseph's shoulder. She held him close. She wept softly, so she would not wake the children. (Is Gokliya still a child after this journey? He sleeps like one now.) Joseph stroked Ursula's hair with his filthy hands. He did not try to calm her, or contain her, or end her tears.

What did the Djinni in the water show me?

Ursula leaning into my arms, weeping. Beautiful Ursula with her thin, white hands grabbing at my back and holding me, Wang Xin, the mightiest hunter in these halls, and she would touch my lips with hers in the darkness when even Joseph was asleep. Ursula, beautiful Ursula, was supposed to fall in love with me here. That is what the Djinni showed me, when my head was pushed into the water and the Djinni tumbled into my eye.

When Ursula finished weeping, Joseph did not steal any kisses from her. I know because I was awake long after Joseph was supposed to have been asleep. He lowered Ursula gently to the cool mud beside the sleeping children. Gokliya and Catherine huddled together like baby rabbits, young and innocent where their skins pressed into each other for warmth.

I could not see Joseph's eyes in the dark cave of snow we had made. I knew he was searching for mine. I knew we were both trying to look each other in the eye.

"What's wrong, Wang Xin?" he whispered.

"The Djinni lied to me, all those years ago. The Djinni lied to me. I have done all I saw until now. How could she fall into your arms when I am here and younger and stronger and in love with her?"

Joseph shook his head. "The maze makes no promises, Wang Xin. I have buried more loves than you have ever known. I've buried children. Tell me, Wang Xin, did the Djinni show you your own face when you looked into its waters?"

"Of course not. I saw only what I would see. This path has become all wrong. I do not know when it happened, but I have fallen off the path of my own life, and it hurts me more than I have ever been hurt in my life to watch my wife fall asleep in your arms when I have waited so long to meet her. I wish I could kill you, but I know when your death will come. She will love me when you are gone. She is supposed to love me."

"You have a cruel face, Wang Xin. When you look at people, you do not smile. You do not have kind eyes. Why should anyone love a man with a cruel face?"

"Aia let me love her," I whispered.

"You're a fool to think that, Xin," he said. "She begged for your death. I...think she might be right."

"Gokliya loves me," I said, not whispering at all. "Your son has always loved me."

Joseph was still whispering. "Gokliya wants strength, because he is a boy," said Joseph. "Years from now, he will no longer love you. He will see you for what you are."

Catherine stirred. I heard her dress rustling. I whispered, again. "I am Wang Xin, the mightiest hunter in the maze. I know my whole life until my death. Joseph, your death is near."

"Death is always close to us here," he said. "It will be enough for me to know that most of my children live. Tell me, Wang Xin, who has seen all our fates inside his own, how much longer until we find what we seek? Do we find anything at all?"

"When the snowfall breaks at last, the ice will remain. We will walk out where the streams merge and freeze into an ice lake as large as the sky. We will travel over the thick ice where the flowers grow to the dam beyond it. There will be an empty riverbed beyond the dam. We will follow the riverbed until we find what we seek. You won't be with us, anymore."

"We can't go on like this forever," he said. "We'll die if we do. Our people will die without us."

"You will not survive the ice lake, Joseph. There will be a terrible monster there, waiting for you, and you will die that your son may live on. You die well, and bravely. Gokliya will never forget your bravery that day. Nor will any of us."

"You're lying."

"When you see what is on the ice lake—and the ice lake is the only way to find what we seek—you will know that death is the only way to save your son."

We sat in darkness. We slept. We only left our shelter to keep our doorway clear of falling snow, into the open air, that we would not suffocate.

The way we had made our shelter was this: we piled up a high mound of snow. We poured water over it, to freeze the shape together. We dug out the middle of the pile carefully, so we had room for us all inside.

For two long days, we ate what was left of the food we had gathered: bits of bark and leaf buds, and rotten meat from a cat.

Ursula was not in love with me. I had to watch her, but I could not touch her face.

These were the worst two days of my life.

At last, when the sun came out, the roof of our snow shelter began to leak. The sides were still iced hard where the sun wasn't direct. We clambered as best we could out from the little shelter. We breathed deep the fresh air. We felt the sun, still cold enough to keep the streams in ice, but warm enough to drive the snow back into the shadowed places.

I pointed ahead. I spoke, for the first time in two days.

"This way," I said. "We are almost at the place where the lake rises up the sides of the hills around the dam. We are almost at our final destination, in the riverbed."

"What are you talking about?" said Gokliya.

Joseph took Catherine's hand. "You say that I will die down this trail?" he said.

"I have seen it in the water's eye."

"I still don't believe you, Wang Xin," he said. "Gokliya, listen to me, because this is very important. If I die today, you will be the one to take care of Ursula and Catherine. You know Wang Xin is too cruel for such a task. You will have to care for them. He believes that Ursula will love him. He is wrong. She will never love him."

Gokliya cocked his head. "Father, I don't understand."

"We don't have time for this," I said. "Let us walk to your death, and then you will see what the water's eye has shown me. This monster will be like nothing we've ever seen. It will be like a tree, but not a tree at all. It will walk naked over the ice and stand between us and our true destination, where we will live in peace all the days of our lives. Past your death, Joseph, is a better life for our people, and exactly what we seek."

Ursula took Catherine's free hand. Catherine's other hand was in Joseph's. I looked at them, walking as if they were a family, and Gokliya behind them, glancing always over his shoulder.

Perhaps he had become a man, for no one needed to tell him to take up the rear, to watch behind us for danger.

I led us down the halls, where the ice flowed below the snow. I kicked snowdrifts aside sometimes, to show them that I knew where we walked. I knew exactly where we walked.

I led them to where the water expanded slowly in the hall. It was not deep, but it was wide. In places, the sun had melted the ice, and a sluice of slushy, muddy water looked like a scrape in the flesh of the winter.

The snow started again, but it wasn't bad.

"Joseph, I have loved this beautiful one my whole life. I have dreamed of her for nearly twenty years. You must understand this to know how much I hate that she walks with you, where I should be walking, and that her daughter holds your hand instead of mine. I long to reach the lake where you will die."

"Wang Xin, I believe your emotions, but I do not believe in what you claim to have seen. If you know where we will find a better home for our people, lead us there and ignore the rest. What you describe is not a Djinni like what I knew, but something else. Who knows what it really was? Speak to Enyo Gyoja if you see him again, for he is the oldest and wisest one in all the maze."

"I will speak to him, then, and until then, we will take the right path to the lake and the dam and the empty river. You will die on the lake, Joseph. When we get there, say goodbye to your son and the women you stole from me."

Gokliya spoke to me, then. I turned and looked him in his face. He looked like a man. When had this boy become a man? "If you try to hurt my father," he said, "I will stop you from hurting him. You are not mightier than both of us, together."

I saw it all over his face. He rejected me, to defend his father.

I turned away from the young man's cold gaze. I had only enemies, now. In the water's eye, I should have had a lover, a daughter, the respect of my fellow men.

I led them down the hall, where the streams fattened and remained frozen. I listened to the sound of the winter wind in the halls. I listened to our footfalls crunching through snow and ice.

I wondered what sounds the monster would make when we found it, at last. I wondered what its heavy feet would sound like, smashing through the ice flowers along the frozen lake, and what screams it would make while it drowned with Joseph.

We turned a corner and zig-zagged around some narrow places, all the while worried a minotaur might surprise us where we could not sidestep its animal charge. We followed the water. I led them through the maze, toward the thickening ice.

Ice flowers grew in bunches where the snow and ice were thick enough to hold their roots. We walked through them quickly. Their petals jangled like small bells where our legs knocked them around.

I felt Gokliya's eyes burning into the back of my head. I felt Joseph's eyes, too. I wondered what Ursula and Catherine were thinking about, right then. They were silent, so they must have noticed the tension among men.

I walked faster and faster, longing for her love.

The snow picked up as the day cooled into late afternoon.

Before nightfall, the streams had widened to fill the halls with water. The bending walls of the maze descended down below the ice sheet of the frozen lake.

The lake, a field of ice flowers blooming late into winter where the ice was thick, was a long, unbroken horizon.

We all looked at it. We all held our breath. We had not seen such a thing since coming to the maze: a long, even plain before us with no walls as far as the eye could see. We gazed out at the ice and the field of ice flowers growing there. The flowers tumbled into each other in a strong wind. The cloudy sky and the falling snow filled our eyes with whiteness. We gazed around us in wonder at the sight of the maze halls clutched by the ice and dropping away into the lake. At the end of the lake, where I knew there would be a tall dam like the edge of a plateau where the ice ended, we saw nothing at all but sky.

We had never seen such a thing, a world open before us like that.

Gokliya fell to one knee. He held his breath. When he breathed again, he was pale in awe. Joseph touched his head, in wonder like his son.

Ursula already tested the strength of the ice, gingerly stepping out and testing one step ahead with her foot.

I had dreamed of this day all my life, and this glorious white vision of openness, and a field of ice flowers.

The clouds reached the lake, too. They poured snow down onto us. The wind dropped into a deep chill, nearly enough to drive us into another shelter. I would not allow such a thing, though, and I announced as much.

"I agree with you, Wang Xin," said Joseph. "If there is a monster here, we should face it now, and seek shelter later."

Ursula returned to us from her ventures on the ice, smiling and unafraid. She did not understand why we men were grim. She handed us ice flowers to eat. She placed them in Gokliya and Catherine's hair. Joseph took her hand and tried to communicate that she should stay close to Gokliya.

"I would rather face this monster. I would rather face your prophecy right now, Wang Xin. Tell me, is there anything that you see that might save my life?"

"No. We cannot fight this monster, but you lead it away from your son and the women. You lead the monster to the thin ice where the flowers cannot take root. There, you plunge through the ice with it, and together you both die."

"I will try to jump, then. I will try to jump. Maybe you are wrong. Your prophecies have been wrong before."

"No," I said. "Not this one."

I looked at Ursula. I held her eyes until she looked away, to her feet. She looked up again and saw my gaze. Then she muttered a prayer and looked away. She moved her hands in the sign of the cross.

"Can't you feel it, even now, Joseph? Do you feel that prickle in your spine and the tension in your palms?"

"I do," he said. "We are old hunters, you and I. We know these things, these feelings."

Gokliya stood tall at his father's side. "Father, I will take your place. I will lead the monster away to the shallows."

"Don't be foolish, Gokliya," said Joseph. "This is what it means to be a man, Gokliya: to face death for your sons and daughters and all the women. Do not forget this. When you return to our people, you will be a man, and it is important to remember what men do for their families. It is a father's place to face death instead of his children, whenever he can. It is my place to face this monster. Do not fear Wang Xin's prophecies. He admits he has been wrong many times."

Ursula did not know what we said. How could she? She knew that Joseph said something serious. She touched his face and murmured her prayers. She took his hand, and moved it in the sign of the cross, and murmured her prayers. She did not let go of his hand when she was done.

"Let's go," I said.

The snow listened to me. The clouds opened up sheets of snow, blowing in the wind like a fog.

Our trepidation was contagious among the women. Catherine sobbed and slowed down. Gokliya let her ride on his back.

"Stay together," I said. "We have to stay together."

(I remembered footprints I could not recognize—a bicycle broken and blood pooling in the strange footprints in the snow. I held the image of those footprints and considered what the Djinni had shown me of the monster's legs.)

"What hunts us, Wang Xin? Tell me." Joseph walked backward next to me, scanning the empty world upon the ice, behind us and around us.

Gokliya was quiet. He was supposed to speak and gesture wildly about how large the world looked when there were no walls to hem us in. He was supposed to talk about the size of the sky with his hands pointing everywhere. He said nothing. He carried Catherine on his back. Did the Djinni lie to me, all those years past? He was not supposed to be carrying her. They were supposed to be laughing and happy about this large field of ice flowers that rang like bells when they ran through the flowers, and they banged around each other in the wake of the children.

(I considered the footprints we had seen when we had found the half-eaten minotaur, and did not know what had claimed it.)

I felt its eyes upon me, and felt the fear.

We were being hunted. I could feel it deep inside my cold bones. We'd been hunted a long time. It had been stalking us along the trails and searching for our village.

What caveman or minotaur was so cunning? What gargoyle or manticore would bother with such a thing in deep winter, when food was scarce and must be taken when it is there to be taken?

Joseph held beautiful Ursula's hand. I was supposed to be holding her hand. I snarled at him. He didn't notice. He scanned the horizon for this monster that would come.

Soon, it wouldn't matter whose hand she held.

I saw it before they did. Of course I did. I had seen it in the water's eye. It had stalked my nightmares all the days of my life. I knew what shape to seek in the snow. I knew the hulking brute's outline, lumbering like a dead tree with legs—a mangled, giant thing.

There.

I pointed toward a shape in the snow. Along the ice sheet, there were no halls and passageways to give it shadow, no corners and angled passages to hide the sound of its heavy footfall.

There.

It lumbered from side to side, smashing the field of ice flowers into a crystalline glass cackle of ruined flowers. It was a tree with legs, but it was not a tree at all. It was white with guano and snow and icicles, and shaped like a man melded with a tree with long limbs and spiky hair and huge black eyes. Its hair shot up at sharp angles down its hunched back like a mane. Its horrible long face was expressionless. It dragged its long hands along the ground where it walked. Its feet lifted and stomped and lifted and stomped, and though it did not look fast, it was very tall, and it walked urgently, and this was faster than a man could run.

There.

Joseph let go of Ursula—I knew he would—and moved beside me, pointing toward the monster. It looked like a thin, wooden…thing.

I turned toward Gokliya. "We will find a riverbed and walk down it, together. We do not have to watch to see your father's fate."

Joseph touched my arm. "It's getting closer. I can see its face. It doesn't look like a thing at all. It looks almost like a man."

Beautiful Ursula exhaled a frightened moan. Then she screamed. I reached for her because we were supposed to flee from this together. She pulled away from me. She started to run alone.

"Wait!"

Gokliya ran, too, with Catherine still on his back, after Ursula. He shouted for her to wait.

I shouted, then, as loud as I could. "Gokliya, that's the wrong way! You have to go east from here! East, do you hear me? You're running south!"

Joseph had the remains of a spear-point in one hand. He hefted a heavy brick in his other. "I don't care what your prophecy showed you. We can kill this thing between us, whatever it is. Do you want what's left of the spear or what's left of the brickbat?"

I took the stone. "This is all wrong! We can't kill this with sticks and stones. We're both going to die here, and the village won't find the grove!"

"I have decided that I don't believe in your prophecies, Wang Xin. I will take the spear point. You're stronger than I am. You can use the brick."

"Listen, the water's eye has led us this far and shown me your death here. Listen to me!"

"We should name this beast before we kill it. It looks like a troll, to me. I think we should call it a troll."

The monster took long, heavy steps through the snow. It swung huge, clawed hands. It was nearly upon us in the wide-open field of ice flowers.

Joseph sidestepped away from me to flank.

Fifty strides away.

I spread my legs out to steady my stance.

I hefted the brick up to my shoulder. Where could I strike it that it was weak?

Thirty strides away.

The monster kept on a straight line toward me. It wasn't supposed to do that. It was supposed to follow Joseph. Why did it come now for me?

(Misery of miseries, and death of deaths, I had stood at the front of our group when we stepped onto the ice, not Joseph. I had seen the monster first, and it had seen me first. Even now, when Joseph stepped away from me, the monster kept toward me. Beautiful Ursula had slowed Joseph down, pulling on his arm instead of mine.

Fates of the maze, laugh at me now. Gods of this horrible place, laugh at me now.

I had charged blindly down a path that I had had burned into my memory. I had walked blindly to death all the days of my life.)

I saw the glimmer of the putrid blue icicle saliva from the mouth of the huge nightmare.

Ten strides.

"Are you listening to me, Joseph?"

"I'm listening."

"Go get your son, and lead him and the women east to the grove. Take care of Ursula. I loved her my whole life. I don't expect you to understand that, and I don't expect her to understand that, but I loved her my whole life."

I ducked under the first heavy backhand of the monster. I jumped up into its face and smashed the brick into one of its eyes. The eye was hard as bark. My blow didn't even knock the creature back. Its other hand swung up toward my face. I jumped back in time to catch only the tips of the claws along my leather shirt. Nothing tore, yet.

Joseph circled, searching for his opening.

"Listen, Joseph, I will kill it alone! I have seen its death, and I know how to kill it on the ice! Go get your son! Walk along the empty riverbed to the east! Lead our people there in spring! Take care of Ursula and her children! You do not have to die today! Hurry!"

I hopped backward, careful not to lose my footing. The monster swung at the air. I was too fast for it. I prayed I wouldn't slip on a slick spot of the ice, where the snow wasn't packed deep enough to keep the ice from my feet and ice flower stems didn't give me traction. I was careful not to let my feet get tangled in the singing ice flowers, as well, that banged away from my legs.

(A sweet battle song of ice flowers, the most beautiful thing I had ever heard. The beast's percussive stomps, and my sweeping windchime leaps.)

The monster was not so lucky. Its huge feet stepped down upon the flowers instead of moving lowly through them. The flowers cracked and leaked their liquids. The thing's root-like feet shot out from under it. It flipped onto its back, huge arms and legs splayed open, snatching at air.

Joseph lunged. He smashed the spear-tip into an eye just once. The monster flailed a heavy arm and knocked Joseph backward through the air. Joseph fell hard on the ice.

I stood still, waiting for the monster's next move, and waiting for Joseph to stand up. I longed for the monster to choose Joseph. I longed for Joseph to stand up and escape. How could I long for his life and his death at the same time?

"Joseph..."

The troll rolled over and placed its huge stump-feet upon the packed snow and ice. It turned its black eyes to me.

I back-stepped carefully. The weak ice would be where the sun was strongest, and the water had reason to flow. I had to go north, where the lowest hills bounded the lake with moving waters, and the ice flowers could not grow.

Joseph was slow to find his feet. The monster ignored him, steadying its feet upon the slick places it had found on the ice. It leaned forward, toward me, as if it would fall onto me like a felled tree.

I threw my brick at the monster's face. The brick hit the thing on its shoulder and bounced off of it like a pebble.

It fell forward, arms and legs flailing.

I jumped away, untouched.

"Joseph, listen, go get your son before he gets himself killed! You will only die here if you fight with me."

The thing crawled on all fours, awkwardly.

"I will kill this. I am Wang Xin, mightiest hunter in the maze."

I jumped away from it again, pulling my stomach back from the claws that reached for me. It fell onto its chest on the ice on the futile back-swing, and struggled to get its feet below it again. I stepped slowly and steadily, then jumped and dodged the wild swings, moving backward, toward the north and the weaker ice.

"The monster's death is known to me, Joseph. I will kill it. Go to the grove at the end of the empty riverbed. Then, return to the village. I will meet you in the village, and I will tell you the story of how I killed this terrible thing."

I jumped away from another swing. The troll was moving faster, now, more confident in its balance, and I had to move faster, too. I couldn't outrun it. I knew I couldn't outrun it. I could dodge the wild swings and lead it back to the weak ice.

"I am Wang Xin! I am the mightiest hunter in these halls!"

I saw Joseph, behind the troll's flailing body, standing still where he had been struck, and smiling.

I felt like I had seen him for the first time, standing beyond his death and smiling at me. We were friends, after all. We had always been friends. "Wang Xin," he shouted, "I have never seen you so happy!"

I ducked a swing. I jumped away from a hard kick. I kept moving backward, to the weak place in the ice, where the troll would fall into the water and drown. The ice flowers dwindled at my legs. I was getting closer and closer.

Joseph watched me, and he would wait for me, until the end. His son was a man now, and could care for the women. Joseph waited for me, his friend, unconcerned about Gokliya and Catherine and Ursula while I fought for my life.

I jumped and dodged and ducked and tumbled. I took a strike to the stomach instead of the face. I took a kick to my legs that cracked the bone. I kept jumping and dodging on the broken leg. It was easier to ignore the pain in all that freezing cold and snow.

I saw the monster closer than it had ever appeared in the water's eye. It had a face, but it did not have any expressions. Its skin was hard as tree bark. It could not smile or growl. It could only chew and turn its head to gaze around it like an insect.

I stepped backward, always backward.

I felt the ice flowers disappear below my feet. The music of their petals, tinkling like wind chimes where I stepped, was gone.

There was only the monster, throwing its limbs at me. I heard ice crackling instead of the ice flowers. I bled where I had been cut. My leg hurt badly. I knew I couldn't put much weight on it. I had to struggle to dodge the monster. It caught my ear with its claws. I felt blood pouring down my neck. It sliced through my leathers and found my stomach. Blood spilled there, too.

I kept jumping backward on my good leg, as much as I could.

The troll threw a foot at my chest. I jumped backward and caught the kick with my arms, using my own backward jump to mute the strike. It still rattled me all through my chest. I tumbled onto my back. When I landed, I heard the ice cracking beneath me. I rolled to the side as fast as I could, away, without thinking. An arm swung down from the sky. It slammed where I had been before I could have seen it coming.

The ice cracked more. It sounded like the ice flower petals at first, but it was the ice sheet, and it wasn't musical now. It was only the sound of imminent collapse.

I rolled away again and again. I found my good leg beneath me. I limped on the bad one. I ran farther down the weak ice, toward the sound of the cracking.

MAZE

I ran toward my own death, in the breaking ice. I could not jump to escape the fall with a broken leg. I knew I couldn't. I didn't care. Ursula didn't love me. Aia would hate me all the days of her life. My people would never be what I saw of their fates anymore. I ran as fast as I could toward the sound of the breaking ice.

I couldn't run fast at all.

The monster took three long strides that rattled the ice below my feet. The creature caught me around my neck.

Death wrapped around my throat. I was lifted into the air by my neck. I was turned to face the monster.

(What intelligence and cunning it must have had to look me in the face when it wished to kill me. No brute beast would have bothered to look me in the face. I hope Joseph watched this and carried this knowledge back to the village to warn them of this cunning monster.)

Death crackled in the ice below my feet, louder and louder, before even one bite could be taken from my flesh.

Of course we fell through the ice, into the deep water. Of course we did, both the monster and me. I was lost to it, in the freezing water. We both sank in.

I saw the water, then, like a late twilight sky, all darkest blue, stained through with my spraying blood where my throat had been sliced by a claw. It was warm where I had been cut, and cold everywhere else.

A broken bicycle—what is it doing here, you awful maze gods, in your horrible jest?—floated up toward the crack in the ice. A broken bicycle swimming like a fish in the dirty water, like my own personal curse.

Was that water burning in my lungs, or was my throat cut?

I saw all paths in the water's eye of my youth all at once, in the freezing water on the brink of my death.

But I was wrong about the old water's eye. I was wrong about the maze. I was wrong about everything.

This maze is not a maze.

There is only one path here, and all the twists and tesseracts and bending halls are built upon the lie of all mazes—that there are many paths to choose.

There is only one hallway, maze or no, for all feet that walk and people that move in life. That hall is the slow walk to death, in a line as straight as the path of the sun across the sky.

Still, the water's eye filled my sight with a past, a future.

I saw all things I had ever known, then, from both pathways before me as if they were one, united.

I loved Ursula my whole life, from when I was just a small boy and saw her face in the water. I loved her my whole life. I wanted to meet her.

I wanted to live through all the things I saw in the water's eye. I wanted to be happy with her. I wanted to fall asleep with beautiful Ursula beside me, and her arms around me, and her lullaby, and close my eyes wrapped in her love in the winter of my death.

When I was a boy, I dreamed of her smile and imagined the sound of her song. It hung over me like a moon in the night through all my youthful memories. The love tainted my loss when I fell from my bicycle into the maze. I saw Aia as she truly was, and as how she was meant to be. Both faces merged into a stillness neither happiness nor sorrow. In between, her face showed me only neutrality and stillness. In Ursula's face, her fear melted away the love we should have shared, but could not diminish the love that burned in my heart, stronger than any frozen lake. When I was a boy, I dreamed of her smile, and it hung over me like a moon in the night. When I was a young man, I dreamed of her smile, and it hung over me like a moon in the night.

Even now, a giant fish bends toward me in the water in a ripple of beautiful, flashing silver like a moon, and I think of Ursula. I can't feel my legs, my arms. My lungs have burned away to stillness with the aqualungs. The sunlight seeps through the breech in the ice ceiling. My words scream from the infinite moments near death.

The fish's mouth opens, larger than my whole body. Its scales flash like stars in the filtered sunlight, and this is Ursula's light.

She sings a lullaby to me.

I know the sound of her voice, now, and how her lips move to make sounds. I can hear every word she speaks to me. We are in the hut I built with my own two hands. Our grandsons are with us. My son by Aia, named Ascalon when Ursula calls him and I read her lips and imagine her voice from those lips, had many children. Ursula's only surviving son's children are there, too.

Even the raping monster's grandchild that we kept and raised because we are Christians—proud, ugly Lucius—sleeps among our grandchildren for he is our grandchild, too. We sleep in our hut so we can all huddle together for warmth on a cold winter's night, early in winter, before the plagues. Our beautiful sons walk the moonlight, to keep our people safe in our good grove in these awful halls. Our sons are brave and strong. Even the caveman's boy, who is a child of violence, does us proud, for we raise him as our son, and his strength is our strength, and his goodness is our goodness.

And Ursula watches me drift toward sleep in our hut. She runs her hands along my face, then down my old body's old bones. She's smiling at me. We are still in love, even after decades have passed. We are lying together, with our grandchildren all around us, and she is still beautiful to me and we are still in love.

The last thing I remember doing is this: I tell my beautiful wife that I love her.

I tell her that I love her loud enough that she can hear, but soft enough that it won't wake our grandchildren. Then, I close my eyes to sleep.

That's the last thing I remember, and I feel her love all around me.

I feel Ursula's love.

I feel the Djinni's love, too.

Then, the light leaves me, and I know it will go deep into the shadows of the water. The light will carry my heart down into the deep water, flow with the streams to new places and new eyes.

Many years will pass.

Many years.

Ursula will have children, who will have children.

They will live. They will all live in the grove, in peace and joy and I'm so happy.

Julie
Station's
Maze

1: Life in the Grove

My name is Julie Station. My mother's name was Maia Station. I don't know who my father is. I don't know anything about my grandparents.

Lucius Caveman and I were cast out of the village and abandoned to the maze all around us. We stood past the barricades of the humans' marshy lakebed. The stone maze halls in front of Lucius and me echoed the birdsongs from the trees behind us like half-heard memories.

Lucius and I held hands. We stepped into the hallways, alone.

What else could we do?

At first, it felt like a patrol. We were out on patrol, running one of the loops, together. I usually had patrolled with my husband, Gokliya, but this time I was with Lucius, like I had been the first time I had gone out on patrol. The air was full of the mortar dust that I had known my whole life, but only noticed strongly outside the grove—outside, where the maze scattered pathways of old, old stones.

The wind was still, here. The world was still, and cold. Winter had broken, but it wasn't over, yet. The cold would grip us for weeks and weeks.

Lucius Caveman led the way to the edge of the known trails. I didn't know where we were going, and I don't think he did, either.

I wasn't scared. I should have been. Ours was like a death sentence, to be cast out of the humans' village and grove and marshlands in our dried-up lakebed inside the maze.

My name is Julie Station.

If a creature survived in the maze beyond our barricades, the creature must be dangerous. Even birds had sharp talons and sharp beaks. Even the tiniest insects bit with tiny poisons.

Trolls, with sap for veins and bodies like wooden bones, walked among my nightmares more than most monsters.

I once hid in a very lonely oak tree and held my breath while two trolls ate the girl who wasn't as fast as me. I took small sips of air, and I clutched at the highest branches that I dared climb. The trolls didn't look up at me. They had someone to eat in their hands. They probably thought I had turned a corner out of the grove, and then another and then another until my trail was lost where the trees ended in the broken barricades and the stone halls continued beyond the far horizon.

Then, the men came with fire and brickbats and drove the trolls away. Four people died, that time, and two of them were from where the barricade had been broken.

The trolls were fibrous like dead trees. They covered their wooden bodies in bird guano. You could smell the guano if they got close enough, that acrid stink that hid their natural scents. When they walked, they sounded like branches creaking in winds too strong for these twisted halls.

Minotaurs, too, hunted for meat among the stones. They usually traveled in packs, but hunted alone. I never saw one alive—thank Lucius' God—but I saw plenty dead. They tasted terrible, but they didn't make you sick, and when winter came every ounce of meat jerky helped us survive the snowfall. Minotaurs had big, brutish heads with long snouts and black hairs, but their bodies looked almost human. Their horns were wild and curved up toward the sky. When they fought their prey, they gored their victims on their horns and then ate the bodies raw, from the stomach out.

The last time we caught a minotaur was many seasons ago. Saitan was out on patrol with an older man named Brim. Together they smashed the minotaur into a pulp with their brickbats. I could barely make out its skull, but I recognized the horns Saitan carried and the nearly human body of the dead monster.

Brim, eldest son of Robert, had been gored by it. He held his own intestines in with one hand and leaned on his brickbat with the other, using it like a cane. Saitan dragged the dead minotaur behind him. Two trails of blood led off into the maze until the rain washed the blood away. Brim went straight to his hut, and his wife. She bathed him three times a day. She fed him by hand for a week. Everything he ate fell out of his stomach, half-digested.

Brim never cried out. He just stayed there, in his hut with his wife, for thirteen days, lingering. When he died, his wife, Justine, sliced off all her hair. She poured it over his body where we had left the body for the crows and vultures and bugs.

Justine cried a long time. I worked with her sewing nets, and she couldn't stop crying. Geraldine yelled at her for crying on the birds we had caught. Geraldine said it was bad luck to weep while we pulled our supper from the nets. Justine called Geraldine all sorts of names. Geraldine returned with worse names. In the end, Justine ran off with her sister and didn't come back to the nets for a long time.

When the minotaur meat was done smoking, we wanted to give Justine more of it, but she wouldn't touch any of it, even if it meant starving. When winter came, all we had for a week was dried minotaur. She still wouldn't eat it. She got sick. Enyo put her out in a hut by herself so she wouldn't get the rest of us sick. She missed the children dancing in the vulture feathers because she was sick.

When the solstice flies finally came, Enyo brought all he could to her in her hut and nursed her back himself.

Justine didn't talk very much, after that.

Stone cows aren't vicious, and don't eat men, but they're still dangerous. They're huge beasts and covered in a thick brick hide. They walk the halls, nibbling on pebbles and rocks and fallen stones. When they find plants, they eat among the roots, until the roots dwindle like naked, muddy ropes struggling to hold their plants in place, failing, falling down, and then there is no more tree. Stone cows move in huge herds. They must be pressed back with strong spears and barricades of wood, lest they come into our grove and eat our trees to death with the dumb, plodding thoroughness of herding beasts. We have not found a way to kill them, but they are not immune to the push and pester of our sticks. We shout and whack at them and shove at them. They fall back against their herd. Their herd falls back into the halls. They wander away from us.

I've heard they can trample someone to death if they get really scared and all start running, but I've never seen it.

There are men who aren't like us. We call them cavemen. Lucius' father was one of those men. They have flattened foreheads, and grotesque noses, and thick ridges over their eyebrows, and beastly, toothy maws where they should have mouths. Their ears are huge and floppy. They can't really talk like we can, in any language. They don't seem to think like we do.

They'd be funny if they weren't so terrible. They used to send out raiders, naked and painted in feces and lime, and they tried to break past our barricades or hunt our patrols down in our known halls to rape and eat the dead.

We haven't seen those men in a long time.

Lucius' father was one of those men, who had come to us seeking to steal our food, our belongings, our women. He snuck in alone in the dark. Lucius' mother was taken, and left for dead by the beast, all her belongings smashed and blood all over her floor. Enyo killed the beast man with a spear, they say.

Anyone else would have killed the child. Lucius' mother refused to kill an unborn because she was a Cathar. She raised the creature like a son. She taught it stories from her life before the maze, about a man who so loved his people that he died once and took all death upon his shoulders. This child she bore grew up tall and strong and ugly. She named him Lucius, and we called him Lucius Caveman.

Nobody really trusted Lucius until he had fought back and killed some of the men who weren't like us. Lucius' mother died trying to squeeze out one more child. Lucius' father and sister filled his little head with the stories of his mother's Languedoc, a place as mystical as a dream, where there were fields and fields as far as the eye could see, full of wheat and trees and a Savior that took all death upon His shoulders.

I don't know about saviors. I don't really bother with Lucius' god, or any other of our gods.

There are other gods, here. We have as many gods as we have families, and we try not to argue about them, because we need everyone to fight and work and stay together. Some of us, like me, have no gods.

My mother told me that gods are illusions that people cling to because they aren't strong enough to hope without one. My mother told me science was her god before she found herself here. I don't know what science is, or how to worship it, but I won't worship anything, even science, because it sent my grandmother here.

There are even other gods, here, than just the gods of the humans.

The tiny beasts with four legs and two arms and heads like large bugs set up shrines everywhere they go, pulled together from the bones of their meat—mostly rats. They bow and worship their altars. They bring them rotten meat. When people on patrol find the tiny ones, they know that all they have to do is kick down the shrine and the tiny ones will stop fighting and leave our places, for we have killed their god. They mourn loudly when we kick the shrines down. They scatter, defeated, into the maze as fast as their legs can run. They taste as bad as harpy.

Harpy meat makes you sick, and they scare off the birds we can eat. If any get caught in our nets, we kill them and feed them to vultures. It makes the vultures sick, too, which makes them easier to catch.

Vulture tastes awful, but sometimes they're all we have. In winter, you eat what you have and you're grateful for it.

Before winter came, the breeze quickened and dropped colder. The leaves on the trees died and fell to the ground to get blown around in the wind. Through the halls, the leaves collected in corners and rotted. The smell got worse in the rain. Tiny ants ate the mold. They were drawn to the stink of rotting leaves and feasted on the mold, carrying off tiny pieces of the leaves with the rot to—I assume—grow mold in their ant mound in the winter.

There were spiders, too, but not very big ones. They had reddish-burgundy bodies like bloody teardrops. They made webs in any place where the flies and gnats came. The spiders were very poisonous. A single bite could kill a child. A grown-up would be sick for days. We left them alone if they were out of reach of children. They ate the flies that liked to plant maggots in our flour, after all, but we chased them back from the hands of our children with ferocity. Women with brooms battled them constantly. I imagine a spider's nightmare involved an old woman with a stooped back and a broom in her hand. The kindly smile that warmed a grandchild's heart was nothing but teeth bared to a spider. They kept to the rafters. They kept to the corners and the far places in the trees. We warned all the children climbing trees to tell someone about a spider web and come down quickly so an older child could kill the thing.

There were mosquitoes. Like miniature, insect-faced gargoyles, they sipped our blood with impunity. We killed them if we could. Mostly, we couldn't. In the summertime, when the mosquitoes came, we covered our skin with mud. We burned fires near the edge of the marsh because mosquitoes tended to move toward the smell of smoke, and lots of the mosquitoes died in the flame.

Gargoyles never moved if you were looking at them. They crept slowly around the tops of the walls like stray panthers, with hideous faces and sharp claws. They were the same color as the stone. They were easy to kill, as long as you could see them in time, because they wouldn't move away from the brickbat that crushed their bony skulls if you were looking at them. They always seemed to come from the east when they came, and even if they surprised someone, the worst they'd do is get a few scrapes in before they were seen and turned to stone where they stood.

Gokliya, a few seasons back, had taken the heads of smashed gargoyles with their stony eyes still intact and lined the walls of the barricades and the walls around us, so the eyes looked out over the halls and saw everything. We haven't seen any gargoyles in our village since, but I hesitate to assume the cause and effect are ours. (My mother taught me that.) Maybe something happened in the east.

Spirits walk the halls, too, and I think they probably have their gods and as many as we do. Ghosts of no origin, no tribe, walk past our barricades as if passing through walls. They wander, stopping to gaze at things that aren't there, ignoring everyone, gesturing and speaking with mute mouths. Then, they wander off.

My mother said not to think that they're ghosts and dead, because we don't have any proof of what they are. They could just be people in the universe, finding a thin place where the tesseracts bend toward the maze. They could be a hallucination of my overactive mind.

I'd believe her if so many of the ghosts weren't so horribly cut up, wounded, pale, and grotesque. One night, I woke up, and a ghost was at the foot of my cot, looking at me. I thought I would scream, but I couldn't breathe enough while I was so afraid.

The ghost looked drowned, bloated and green and rotten. I stumbled from my bed, away from the ghost, but it kept staring at the place where I had been. Then, it reached down, and its hand went through my cot, into the place beneath it. The ghost stood back up, and it had a baby in its arms, crying and crying though I couldn't hear the phantom child.

I shook my mother awake. Together we watched the ghost rock the crying babe to sleep. Both of the ghosts looked drowned. Then, when the babe was calm, the ghost walked through the wall with the ghost child. I peered out the door to watch them walk away. They walked through the next hut as if it wasn't there, into the orchard, and then gone.

My mother said only one thing to me before going back to sleep. "Don't assume that child belongs to that woman. You have no proof. The evidence is circumstantial, no matter what the other women of the village might say. Remember the scientific method, Julie. Go back to sleep. Ghosts don't bother anyone if you just ignore them."

My mother's dead. I miss her terribly, but I don't know what she would say about Lucius and me, and part of me is glad she will never know my shameful acts.

Our rabbits attracted trouble, of course: harpies and vultures and the little manticores that snuck around the halls like cats—oh, and of course, cats were nothing but trouble with the rabbits.

We kept our rabbits in pens, below the trees. We knew when winter was coming because the rabbits grew thick fur. They burrowed deep into their pens—we had layers of fencing to keep them from escaping underground, and it mostly worked—but instead of coming back up somewhere else, they stayed down there, unless we dug them out for our dinner. We hated to eat rabbits in winter because we needed them alive in spring.

We caught all kinds of things in our nets, but none of them were particularly dangerous.

Some of the women peeled the cats from our nets and kept them in their huts. Their black and white and mottled and striped and orange and grey shapes dart away from me, because they knew I didn't have anything for them but contempt. They kept the rats and roaches away, but they would take a rabbit if given a chance. Still, the geckos and spiders and other things were no match for a bored feline, and I didn't try to kill the cats with rocks like when I was young. As long as we watched the rabbits closely, the cats were permitted.

Sara has five cats. She lets them sleep on her body. They were kittens in the web when she found them. Now they're like her children.

She names them like her children, anyway. All her human children are long dead. Two got sick and didn't get better. One disappeared when no one was watching him closely enough. One drowned in the marsh. The last one lived for five years, until trolls smashed through a barricade and one of them got into where we kept the kids and the chickens and rabbits. The boy—I've forgotten his face, but I remember his name was Jon because of the cat—got kicked in the head and never got up again. Now Sara has five cats, and her husband is too old and too tired to wrestle her for more children. He still patrols with the young men, but soon he will be too old, and he will stay with the women winding tree bark and vines into ropes, and ropes into nets.

Either that, or Geraldine'll run him off and he'll fish for insects and frogs in the marsh water and look after the rabbits and chickens. Then, if he lives as long as Enyo Gyoja, he might sit on the stump and wear leaves sewn into a hat and cloak and let the young men fight about who should go where and what should be done to prepare for this season's dangers.

(I don't think he'll live that long. Hardly anyone does. I don't think he'll survive the winter. Winter eats the old and the young. Winter is the worst of the monsters here.)

The one nice thing about having all the cats around is that you can snap their necks and roast them in a pinch, like greasy, bitter rabbit meat. I don't think Sara has the heart for that, but she's surprised me before. When she learned about Gokliya and me, she smirked and patted my cheek and congratulated me, before she knew Lucius and I would be cast out for it. I expected her to hate me, and to yell at me, and to never speak to me again, because that's what people were doing when they found out about my love affair.

Maybe Sarah would eat one of her cats if she had to. I've heard that the reason we give our dead to vultures is so we never feel tempted to eat them ourselves. I wonder if Sara could eat one of her cats. I wonder if she's ever felt the temptation in the long, cold winter night to eat those creatures that she loves.

Cats don't taste very good, but sometimes it's all you have, and you have to be grateful that you have anything at all, sometimes.

Saitan showed me a mouse, once, that was very small even for a mouse. When I peered close to the tiny thing in his palm, I saw its face was not a mouse's face at all, nor was its tail anything resembling a mouse's tail. The head was a beautiful purple carapace, like an insect's, with little insect eyes. The tail was segmented like pink chains, and chitinous. It seemed to be where the tiny creature was breathing. The furry mouse body in between the head and tail was soft and downy, and clearly mouse. I leaned in close. I cupped my own hands. Saitan handed me the little insect mouse. He told me that he had found it when he was patrolling.

"What is it like, beyond the barricades?" I asked.

He smiled down at me. He had a beautiful smile. "It is better in here. There's trees, and flowers, and food. Outside, it is dangerous, and there's nothing in those hallways but things that want to eat you."

I looked up at Saitan from the insect mouse in my palm. I did not know where his family had been before the maze. Most families didn't. I only knew where my mother had been.

Saitan was tall—but not as tall as Lucius—and very handsome. He was gentle with us, too. I heard the men say he was ferocious with a brick-bat, but I had trouble imagining the Saitan I knew facing down trolls with fear and anger swimming together in his courageous face, and his muscles trembling.

He had brought me the insect mouse for my pleasure. It rested in my palm. A tiny insect proboscis uncurled from the pincer mouth and tasted my skin as if I were a flower. Then, disappointed in my flavor, it opened the shell of its face and hovered up, while the little mouse body dangled like something captured. The bug flew away and away, falling in a breeze and away.

I laughed at the strange thing.

Saitan asked me what we should call it if we ever found it again.

I suggested we call it "Saitan's Treasure," which he did not find amusing in the slightest.

There are deer, here, and they're very tasty. They all have horns along their heads and backs. White roses sprout from their tails. It's hard to tell where the plant-like thorns end and the bone-like horns begin. They taste a little sour, but if you pour their own uncooked thorn sap upon them, they taste sweet and sticky.

There are oranges that are very tasty, too. They scream when you bite them.

We have bushes that grow all sorts of berries in every color I can imagine, and they each have different seasons. The dainty little purple berries are first, coming at the end of winter, while snow is still on the ground. Then, the red berries shaped like thumbs. Then, the red berries shaped like bells. Then, the blue berries that have more seeds than flesh and we have to boil them and filter them to get to the edible pieces.

We catch lobsters in the marsh. They aren't as big as chickens. Enyo Gyoja—every time he sees one—talks about a time when he was young and the lobsters were nearly as big as a small child. Now, after generations of us throwing our traps into the water, the lobsters aren't so big anymore. Before I was born, they were eaten all the time. Now, with them always so small, we wish to let them grow large again. We only eat them once a year, right before harvest, when people marry.

We make drums and rattles and sing songs and celebrate all the new couples. We eat lobsters then. Each new couple divides one down the center with a sharp stone axe. The meat gets smashed more than cut. The couples scrape the meat off the chopping block. They take their scrapings into their huts. They close the curtains to the cheers of all who stay in the yard, dancing and pounding drums and eating the smaller, softer lobsters, shell and all, with boiled fish.

When Gokliya and I married, he missed the lobster on his first swing, and I had to take the second swing and finish the cut. I didn't quite hit it right, either. The axe was too heavy for me.

We laughed.

Everyone laughed.

We took our smashed meal into our basket, and I carried it into our hut. I put it down. I was too scared to be hungry. Gokliya was too scared not to eat. We sat in silence while he ate all the bits of lobster meat, afraid to look up at me. Then, he rinsed his mouth out with water. He tried to touch my hand, and it was sticky from the lobster. I pulled away. I made him rinse his hands in water before I let him touch me like a husband.

He apologized when he learned that I had stopped him because of his hands. I told him not to worry about it. He was so embarrassed. I told him not to worry. I washed his hands better. Then, I washed his feet. Then, he washed my feet. We nervously attempted the thing everyone had been talking about for weeks and everyone had assured us was great fun, or great annoyance, or both.

Afterward, I don't know what Gokliya was thinking, but I could only wonder what the point was, and why everyone thought that was something worth all the bother.

It hurt a bit, at first—of course it did—and then it was over. Gokliya cried. I held him. He had had another wife before, Lucius' sister, who was much older than Lucius. I don't know what was going through his mind when he was with me. I know I didn't like it that he was crying. I was hungry and wanted to eat something, but there was nothing to eat in his hut. I wanted to go out and get something to eat, but I didn't think there'd be anything out there until morning, when the older women got the oven burning again for their flatbread. Besides, I didn't want people looking at me, teasing me, knowing what I had done and talking about it with me.

I wanted to be by myself. I didn't even want Gokliya there.

I watched a spider in the corner of the hut making a web. I watched something small and black—some sort of gnat or fly?—fall into the spider's web. The spider went toward its new prize. The prize immediately swallowed the spider with a tiny slurp, sucked up the web, and then the insect flittered off through a hole in the hut's thatching. I had never seen anything like that before, and I wondered what it was. There were so many things here, with us in this maze. How could anyone know them all?

We knew the ones that scared us best. We knew the ones that helped us through the winter best, like rose deer, like rabbits, like solstice flies.

The solstice flies only lived for one brief day in winter. Their razor-sharp pincers cut through the ice, and they burst into the grey sky like giant snowflakes falling in the wrong direction. We caught as many as we could in nets. We could never catch all of them, which I guess is a good thing because then we wouldn't have them the next year. The birds of the labyrinth clustered around the pools and lakes, waiting for the one day when the solstice flies would emerge from the frozen water.

They weren't very big, when you smashed them up. Alive, they were about as large as a palm. But they were thin and mostly made of chitin razors and paper wings. You could catch dozens of them—hundreds of them—and smash them up into a paste and cook them with ground-up acorns into a crunchy flatbread. It barely counted as a meal.

In the winter, in the maze, every little bit helped.

Lucius Caveman pointed at the birds flying above the solstice flies. "We should be after the birds," he said. "They're bigger. They're meatier."

"They're quicker and smarter," I said.

I was wrapped in his brown leather jacket, which was far, far too big for me. Lucius made me wear it because he said that women were the weaker sex. In the summertime, I'd hit him if he said that, and we'd probably be joking with each other. In the winter, I let him say anything he wanted if he gave me his jacket because I was freezing and his huge jacket was still warm from his body heat and it was like swimming in huge warmth for a little while.

We burned dead trolls. We burned vines. We burned leaves. We burned feathers. We burned worn-out clothes too gone to be used as rags. We burned everything we could.

Lucius didn't seem to mind the cold. Why would he? One of his grandfathers was a monster of lime and feces and violence who ran naked even in the coldest winters.

His mother had come to the maze from a place called Languedoc, fleeing monsters who flung every heretic into the cold with golden crosses sewn into their clothes. On the back of his jacket, he had sewn a golden cross, pulled together from woven golden feathers and spare string.

He believed the world was flat. He thought I was insane to talk about my mother's space station, above a round world. He told me that the flesh was the work of the devil, and the spirit was the true realm of the divine.

He told me I was a weak little woman. He brought me little gifts, some-times. He let me wear his jacket in the worst of the maze winters if Gok-liya wasn't around. He let me sleep pressed into him for warmth when I snuck away from Gokliya a while. He told me I was beautiful, and liked me as I was—a woman among the men, and strange.

I didn't really care that he had that squat, malformed caveman hiding in the fringes of his huge face. I was in love with Lucius Caveman.

Julie Station is my name, like I said.

My mother came from the sky. Most people told me that my mother was lying about where we were from, and I didn't worry either way what was real or not in her history. She came here pregnant with me.

I was born in the maze. The maze is all I know.

"This maze touches all places," Enyo Gyoja had said, "all times." Everything can turn a corner and fall headlong into one of the endless tesseracts that end in the maze, where stone halls and dangerous traps and hungry beasts wait for all strays.

Who made the maze?

My mother had said aliens. Lucius' sister had preached about Nephilim and Lucifer. Sarah said Loki, the trickster god. Ascalon's wife sang of a spider king, weaving stone webs and sleeping unseen in our grove, eating souls that had fallen into his web.

We hadn't had anyone new find our village since I was a little girl, and that one died before I got to know him and ask him about things.

Enyo Gyoja was in charge, if anyone was. He was an old, yellow man, draped in a cloak of green leaves, and a hat of green leaves, and a staff of wood and metal. He wore sandals that kept his feet high off the ground in all seasons. Enyo wasn't as tall as anyone else—not even me, and I was shorter than most of the women.

Enyo Gyoja refused to bother with the source of our world. I agreed with him. I didn't worry about the why of things, either. This was the only place I knew. I woke up in a hut built between stone walls made up of the stone walls we had torn down, inside halls our tribe had barricaded with stones and wooden spikes. I worked in our defended grove, growing berries and wheat and catching birds in nets and raising what animals we could where we could raise them.

I even went out on patrols, with Gokliya, and sat in the watchtowers, staring into the stone pathways that spread out beyond the horizon.

Maybe Enyo Gyoja was the one who was here first, and people collected here over time because Enyo showed them how to live with the leaf nets, the patches of fruits and nuts, acorn-bread, and the chickens, and the barricades, and the harvesting of stones from the walls that penned us all in so we could pen the maze out. We took apart walls one brick at a time, and turned them into houses and barricades. We ground them loose from their ancient mortar with sharp rocks and persistence, and we pulled the walls down. (Maybe that's how the maze started, a long time ago, when all these bricks were lying around, and people and creatures rebuilt them and rebuilt them and rebuilt them until nothing was left of the original shape of the world but the maze.)

Maybe Enyo Gyoja was also the one to make the order of things when the village began and nobody knew how to survive in the maze until they found the old man on a felled log, raising rose deer and sewing bird nets. He was old enough for it.

He told me stories of when my mother was beautiful and young, like me, and big with child, and she came to this place alone.

My mother never left the tribal barricades. Why would she? We had a good place. She had come from outside of it—where no one was safe, and no one had a friend to watch for trouble in the halls—carrying me in her belly.

We have a safe place. We have trees, a marsh with a small lake that gives us fresh water, and sometimes fish.

A river used to flow into our small lake. The stone walls of the maze reach above a dry riverbed. At the bottom, the bones of very deadly-looking fish wait for the rain to grind them to dust with empty eyes. Their teeth are larger than their heads, and their heads are the size of small melons. We use their teeth for knives and spear-tips along the barricades. We send patrols along the riverbed to watch for things that might slither through the gap, directly to our grove in the dry lakebed.

When I was old enough, I patrolled the riverbed with Lucius. I had never really spoken to Lucius before, except now and then, and even then only a little. I was intimidated by him. Who wouldn't be? He was huge and quiet and the people gave him room, gave him respect. But, when I was old enough to consider my place in the maze, I decided I wanted to see more of it than just the grove. I wanted to travel out into the stone hallways. Lucius took me the first time.

I remember I went in the early morning to the place where men went who were going to patrol. I stood, uncomfortably, among them.

"What are you doing here?" said Lucius.

Enyo Gyoja, who told everyone what path to take, looked at me. All the other young men looked at me. I felt very small.

"You seek for me, Julie Station?" said Enyo Gyoja. "Wait until after patrols go."

I braced myself. "I want to go out on patrol," I said. "I'm big enough. I'm old enough."

"You're a girl," said Lucius.

"So? I want to go out on patrols."

What I didn't say was the truth. It wasn't that I wanted to go on patrol. It was, in truth, that I was curious to see the world beyond our huts and gardens and the well-known paths and barricaded places.

If I went alone, I likely wouldn't return. If I went with a patrol, I'd be on a known path—just not known to me—with a fighting man. My impulse had been a spontaneous one, thoroughly unplanned, that had come upon me one morning while considering another day with Geraldine at the nets. In my line of vision, while I had walked to another day at the nets, Gokliya had walked toward Enyo Gyoja with a brickbat slung over his powerful shoulder like a fishing rod.

I wasn't thinking. I went to Enyo Gyoja, with the men. I announced my decision.

Lucius grunted. "I'll take you with me, if you want," he said. "Most days and nights, nothing happens. No harm in walking around a bit on one of those days."

Enyo Gyoja sighed at me. He shook his head. I knew he disapproved of me, but he rarely spoke against the will of another if it did not endanger the whole of us. Lucius volunteered to take me, so I could go, and only Lucius was endangered by my foolishness, by his own choice.

We went down to the dry riverbed. He told me to pick out a good tooth for a spearhead. When I did, he slipped the tooth into a pocket of his giant coat. Then, we walked along the river, picking our way carefully through the sharp bones of the fish.

"Be sure you don't just look down," said Lucius. "If something hunts us here, it's coming from above." He pointed to the slopes where the stone walls of the maze ended at the river, and footbridges curved over our heads. Some of the bridges and walls had broken, and their bricks littered the dust at our feet among the fish bones.

We walked the riverbed all morning. We stopped only once. Lucius saw something in the dirt he didn't like. It looked like a smooth grey stone, but it wasn't a stone, because when Lucius jabbed at it with his spear, it swallowed the bone tip like wet mud. He grunted. "It's been gone a while," he said. "Good."

"What is it?"

"If you find one of those, and you stab it and it's as hard as a stone, run back to the village as fast as you can and scream for help at the top of your lungs. That, or hide."

"What is it, Lucius?"

He ignored my question. He scraped his spear off on the nearest bones. He continued down the path. We carefully chose our path through the bones until the sun was high above us.

"Lucius," I said, "Will we be heading back soon? I'm hungry."

"You didn't bring anything to eat?"

"I didn't know I was supposed to."

He reached into his big brown coat and pulled out some dried meat. "Next time, bring your own." He threw it to me. I tried to catch it. I missed. I picked it up from the ground and dusted it off.

"Is it always so quiet out here?"

"Most days," he said. The air was dead of all sound. The wind was too gentle to howl. There weren't any trees to push around. No insects taunted birds. No birds sang war songs about hunting insects. Not even the vultures cackled at us for walking among bones. "Best not to talk so much. You want to hear them before they hear you. We're almost at the end of the path."

We walked along farther and farther among the fish bones, in the shadows of old bridges. The sun was hot, and I was sweaty and tired. Lucius never took off his huge jacket. I fell a little behind him. He told me to place a hand on the feathered cross upon his back, and never take my hand off, if I was going to be behind him.

I asked him why.

He said that he needed to know I was still there, or if something had come along to snatch me up.

I took that as a signal to get beside him again.

Then, a wall of stones taller than the river, and taller than the walls of the maze around the river, cut a path above everything else.

Lucius pointed at the top with his spear. "You want to rest a bit before we turn back?"

I looked at the wall and the fat, squat bricks that stood end over end, all the way to the top, ten times as tall as me. I walked up to the wall. I grabbed at the stones, testing my weight on them.

"Have you ever seen the other side of this wall?" I asked.

Lucius grunted at me. I don't know what his grunt meant.

"You rest a bit," I said. "I'll be right back."

I started to climb.

"What do you think you're doing?" said Lucius.

I ignored him. I kept picking my path among the knobby stones. These weren't bricks, like the walls of the maze. These were rocks. They were packed together, water-tight, with quality mortaring. The rocks were different sizes and shapes and colors.

Lucius shouted after me. Then, he dragged himself slowly up the wall after me. I was faster than he was. I was smaller and lighter and driven by my fear of being caught. I wasn't weighed down by his huge coat, and all the things hidden in his pockets, and the spear tied to his back. He was heavy. His hands had trouble finding the corners and angles of stones. He had thick, meaty hands.

When I reached the top, I slung one leg over the edge and looked all around. This wall cut over the maze. The paths of the stones continued on either side as if nothing was different from one side to the other. Something was different. On the side of the wall were I had come from, there was no water. On the other side, the river rolled through some higher hills and swelled in the valley below the wall. I gazed in wonder at the paths of the maze descending into the murky depths.

Lucius finally pulled himself next to me. He was breathing hard. He was scowling. He straddled the wall, facing me. He looked down on me like he was about to push me off.

"I've never been up here," he said.

I smiled at him. "What do you think of the world, Lucius Caveman?" I gestured with one hand to the maze below us, the water, and the sky.

He looked around, with a concentrated face.

He said the last thing I ever expected him to say. "Thank you," he said, and he sounded like he meant it. He reached out a hand and pressed it over mine on the wall. "It's beautiful. Thank you," he said, again.

Then, he tried to kiss me.

I pulled away from him.

He stopped. He looked down at our hands. He lifted his giant hand off my tiny mouse palm. He pulled away from me. "You're beautiful," he said. Then, he mumbled something. I understood it after he said it. "I'm sorry."

I swung myself around. I began to climb down, carefully. "We'd best head back," I said. "We don't want to take too long, or people will worry about us."

The climb down the wall took longer than the climb up. I couldn't see where I was putting my feet, exactly, no matter how hard I tried. I had to climb just by feel. Lucius lingered at the top, looking all around. Then, he climbed down, gracefully.

When he got to the ground, he wouldn't look at me. He just looked back toward the village. "We should head back now," he said. "Watch for trouble. Who knows what's changed since we came out this way? You see anything different from before, you tell me."

We went back up the riverbed until we saw the trees and the riverbed's sides that lost their sharp edges. The sides sloped up gently to the grove. I think this place, our little grove, was once a small pond full of the awful fish until someone put the dam in place and closed off the river. After the dam, the trees grew. We didn't stay in the trees—too dangerous in the open—but we did make our huts from the branches and keep our birds and rabbits in the open space. We had armed guards with clappers circling the edges.

Lucius called out to the men circling the grove—Jim and Gokliya— and they called back. Lucius called them over.

"Watch the riverbed for trouble," said Lucius. "I found a troll dropping. It was old, and almost melted out, but I found it out there a ways. They might try to sneak up this way. One troll for sure, maybe more."

My eyes opened. "Trolls?" I said.

"I wouldn't have left you," he said. "I bet you run faster than I do. Trolls stop chasing to eat what they've caught."

Gokliya frowned. He scratched his scraggly chin and squinted at the defenses. He was nearsighted. "Running is good," he said. "Fire is better. Maybe they're going to feint this way, and come after us from one of the walls. Best tell Enyo, and see what he says."

Gokliya went to gather torches and stoke fires at the barricades.

Lucius and I went to Enyo and told him about the trolls.

Enyo Gyoja closed his eyes when we told him. "The seasons change, and winter comes soon," he said. "Trolls look to store up their sap before winter sleep." Enyo picked at his remaining tooth with a bone dagger. He looked up at Lucius. "I am an old man," said Enyo. "I cannot always know the answer, or else when I die the answers die with me. What do we do, Lucius?"

"It was mostly melted away when I found it. One troll dropping doesn't mean much. Could be anything. We prepare the fire at the barricades. We keep patrolling."

"Who went down the riverbed yesterday? Was it Gokliya and Jim? Gokliya is blind. Jim is useless. Tomorrow, Lucius, take Saitan with you along the riverbed. Two men like you will find anything worth finding. Little girl, go back to the nets and the fields. Perhaps you can have another adventure when this bad season passes."

"She could go with my brother on the short loop," said Lucius. "Jim is useless, but Gokliya isn't. He's just nearsighted. Julie's got good eyes. Good enough for the short loop."

Enyo yawned and fanned his face with a leaf. "Sending women out on patrols is unwise. They carry our future inside their bellies. They are small and weak, like old men, and they can make many strong, young men to keep us safe."

Lucius nodded at me. "Come back tomorrow," he said.

The next day I went out with Gokliya. Lucius gave me a brickbat to carry, to get used to the weight. The stone fell free of the vine lashes about halfway down the trail. They didn't spare me a very good brickbat with trolls along the riverbed.

I didn't bother to pick up the lost brick. I carried just the stick. Gokliya didn't notice. He squinted into the halls and walked me around the groves of our empty lakebed. I never stopped hearing the sound of the birds. In the sky above, birds flew to the trees and freshwater marshland in the middle of our grove.

Gokliya didn't talk much, and he didn't try to kiss me. Mostly, he looked like he was thinking very hard about the path in front of him, which suited me fine. He squinted all the time. It made him look pensive.

We saw nothing but the winding stone hallways, and birds, and blue sky. The ground was littered with dirt and small clumps of brown grass.

The path was marked with the gaps where we had been scavenging for fresh stones for generations. We had created a maze within the maze where we had torn gaps in the walls. We kept this spiderweb of trails clear because the mortaring here was the easiest to break.

Lucius and Saitan found more troll droppings in the riverbed. Saitan was shivering with rage. Lucius was dead calm. Enyo Gyoja nodded.

"I am too old to know what to do all the time. What do you think we should do, both of you?"

Saitan shook his head. "They're coming," he said.

"Maybe they are going," said Enyo. "Not everything is about us. Perhaps the trolls do the same that we do and believe we are coming for them."

Lucius nodded. "We wait," he said. "We keep the fires ready. We pull our patrols in close a while. We don't fight them unless they come after us."

"Saitan, do you agree with Lucius?"

Saitan shook his head. "They aren't many by their droppings. I think we should hunt them down. We can find them and kill them before they find us. Then, we could store their bodies for the winter to burn like wood."

Enyo smirked. "When I was very young and we were wandering the halls with no home to call our own, do you know what we did with the green birds?"

We waited. No one spoke.

"We gave them the lame, and the sick. When they had eaten their fill for the winter season, they flew away until the next winter season."

Ascalon, the one with a carefully trimmed beard that formed a single red line to his knees, frowned at Enyo. Ascalon shook his head and tsk-ed. "We should do what Lucius says. We're stronger where we've built defenses."

The men divided into two camps. Some thought Saitan's plan was best, to fight the trolls on their ground before the trolls fought here, near the women and children. Some thought Lucius was the wisest. Lucius said nothing while the arguments rolled from mouth to mouth. Ascalon did all the yelling for Lucius. Lucius glared at me. I glared back.

Finally, Lucius curled his lip into a moment's pause among the shouts. "What do you think, Julie Station? You want to be one of the men; you should speak up, too."

"I don't..." I looked around at all the men. There were at least a dozen who said nothing, and all looked at me. "I don't know."

"You would go out on patrols with us. Would you fight trolls with us? Would you swing a brickbat, while they're eating me, or my brother, Gokliya, next to me?"

I looked down at my feet.

Lucius snorted at me. He turned to the men. "We do not know where the trolls are. They know where we are. We've been here for generations. We should prepare for them, right here, where they will attack us if they go hunting for men."

Saitan placed a hand on my shoulder. He squeezed it like a friend. He argued vociferously that trolls could be found. The angry words continued all around me.

The other men talked and talked and talked above my head.

I didn't pay any more attention to them. I slipped away from Saitan's hand, and from the group. I went to the women sewing nets from reeds and tree bark. I told them about the trolls, and Lucius and Saitan.

"Enyo's way would be better," said Geraldine. "Like with the bird. They wouldn't survive the winter, anyway. If Saitan has his way, we'll lose the strongest men. If the cavemen come, or the other beasts, we'll need Saitan's strength."

The others were silent for a time, and I was, too. I wove the net. I wove the net. I wove the net. I thought about how good it was to be a woman right then, and surrounded by strong men who would protect me, and I could sit here and weave a net.

Then, I was very angry, and I didn't know why. I wove the net. I wove the net. I wove the net. Then, I knew why I was angry.

When I was done with the net, I went to Lucius. He squatted on the shore of the pond in the grove, scraping bark off thick saplings for new brickbats, spears, and fishing poles. He looked up at me and said nothing to me.

I kicked him in the face.

He fell back onto his back. "What was that for?" he said.

I kicked him again, in the leg. I was kicking him as hard as I could, and he didn't even flinch. If I hadn't caught him by surprise, I would not have knocked him over at all. "Don't taunt me like that," I said.

"Taunt you?" he said. "When did I taunt you?"

"Think about it, Lucius Caveman." I said. I picked up one of the saplings. I hefted it in my hands like a club. It was going to need to be cut back, and it would need a brick at the end to make any impact against trolls and minotaurs and worse, but I still held it up and tested it as if it were a bat that I would be swinging soon. "I want to fight, too."

"We're not going to fight trolls," he said. "Enyo wouldn't let us. Saitan and Gokliya are going to find out where they are and what they're doing so close to us. I don't think you should go with them."

"Why not?"

"You're fooling yourself, little girl." he said. "Bring me some bricks. I'm making brickbats. If the trolls come, we'll need plenty of new ones for the boys to fight beside the men. I'll make you a brickbat."

I threw his sapling back to him. I walked away, saying nothing. I didn't bring him any bricks.

He made me a brickbat. He left it outside my hut for me to find in the morning.

Saitan and Gokliya couldn't find the trolls, the next day.

Enyo politely refused to let them go out again looking for the trolls. Enyo looked up to the sun. He squinted. "We'll see the stone cow herds, soon. We should double the men at the barricades and build long spears. We'll stop patrolling far afield. We should only patrol the short loop, along the cliff, and the long loop. Keep fires ready in case trolls do show up, but we have to prepare for the stone cow herds. If even one gets into the fields..."

Saitan pounded his chest with the hilt of a brickbat. "I can go out alone and keep looking for the trolls myself."

Gokliya placed a hand on Saitan's shoulder. "No one will stop you, Saitan. I won't go with you. I don't think anyone should. We have to hold what we have. We should not assume the trolls are after us. Maybe they are after stone cows, or the minotaurs have driven them back, or something else far worse creeps up to our barricades, unknown to us."

"I'll go with you, Saitan," I said.

Saitan looked at Lucius, and at me. "I'll go by myself, Julie Station. Why don't you stay behind with Lucius and help him."

He picked up a brickbat and slung it over his shoulder. He walked out beyond the barricade at the dry riverbed. He kept going.

I went on patrol with Gokliya on the short loop. I thought about death and jumped at small noises. Gokliya didn't tease me for it. He seemed kind about my fear and told me to worry about what I saw and let him worry about what we heard. For three days, I patrolled with Gokliya and the men.

We never saw Saitan again.

I went back to the women for a little while, after that, sewing nets. I gathered white roses from the tails of tame deer and smashed the petals in water for their perfume. I collected bird eggs from the trees with the young boys and girls.

Then, because I felt like a coward, I went back to the men who patrolled. Ascalon grabbed my arm before I could arrive at Enyo Gyoja's tree stump. Ascalon threw me into an empty hut. I realized it was Saitan's hut, empty now.

Ascalon told me why Saitan had been so eager to fight. When Lucius and Saitan had gone out together, they had argued over who would win beautiful Julie Station's heart. Gruff, mean Lucius had told brave, beautiful Saitan about kissing me on the river's dam.

I decided not to argue the kiss with Ascalon. His friend had died because of that lie.

I listened to Ascalon spit words at me a while, telling me to stay away from the patrols. I decided, then, that I'd never speak to Lucius again, if I could avoid it, and certainly never alone.

Then, I went to a tree. I climbed it. I hid among the branches. The green leaves hid me. After much deep thought about my place in the village, and how everyone would feel about Saitan dying because of me, and more deep thought about Geraldine and the women at the nets, who would be saying all sorts of snide things about the girl who would go patrol with the strong, young men, and cause their deaths with her flirtations, after all that thinking, I wondered what life would be like if my mother was still alive. I missed her, terribly. I imagined being a girl again, forever, playing in the fields and laughing carefree all spring, and all summer, and never feeling winter creep icy tentacles of wind and snow over the grove again.

After even more deep thought, the rest of the day had passed. Enyo's flute sang the moons into the sky by sundown.

In evening twilight, with Enyo's flute singing, I went to Gokliya's hut and asked Gokliya about his first wife. Her name had been Catherine, and she'd had blonde hair, like mine.

I told Gokliya that Lucius was lying, and I had never let him kiss me.

Gokliya looked up at me without squinting. He leaned in close, where he could see me better. I smelled his nut-brown skin. I looked him in his glossy, kind eyes, and let him look in mine.

Like every girl who thinks she can outsmart her heart, I placed a man's hand on my cheek, and I tried to convince myself that this was for the best.

I was wrong.

4: The Wedding

I was wrong about Lucius Caveman, the Cathar, and so was Ascalon.

When winter came, and Lucius and I were hiding out from Gokliya in an abandoned hut in the cold, in the night, I told all of this to Lucius, about how mad I was at him for killing Saitan.

"I never told him that we had kissed."

"Liar."

"What I told him was that you took me to the top of the wall, and I held your hand. I didn't tell Saitan that we had kissed."

"Lucius, you told him that we had kissed because you thought it would make him think you had already won my heart."

"I didn't kill him, Julie."

"You caused his death."

"He didn't have to go chasing trolls by himself."

"He was angry, Lucius, and he wanted to strike out. He wanted to prove he was a man. He wanted to prove to me that he was a better man than you."

Lucius had sad eyes. He looked up at the holes in the thatching. "Do you think he was a better man than me?"

"I would have never picked him over you," I said.

Silence hung in the air, like mosquitoes, sucking out all the blood from the naked places in our skin.

"I have to go back, before anyone sees us," I said.

Then, we kissed one last time. We pulled our clothes back together. I left first, alone. Lucius would wait until I was long gone. Maybe he'd sleep there, wake up draped in snow, and lose fingertips to frostbite, like my mother had lost toes.

I went back to my husband's hut. He slept with his face to the wall. He snored. I pressed next to Gokliya for warmth. His hand found my hand in his sleep. I bit his shoulder, gently. He did nothing.

I had chosen Gokliya because he had always seemed so kind.

After Saitan disappeared, and I had chosen my husband, I only went on patrols when I was going with Gokliya. Of course, that's because we were to be married, and if I had gone with anyone else, there would have been gossip.

I spent my time on the watchtowers, like one of the boys or the old men, staring out over the walls, watching for motion and danger in halls as silent as the rocks that formed the walls. I liked the watchtowers because I could sit with anyone, then, and I could even just sit by myself.

Before I was like the men, I wove nets with the women.

The blossoms brought the bugs. The bugs moved in and out of our nets easily. The birds chased the bugs. The nets caught the birds' feet and wings.

The nets tightly twisted up when birds pulled at them. Birds either escaped or became tangled. Then, the women took the edges of the nets and rolled them back to ground. We killed most of the birds. We clipped the wings of some and kept them in pens like rabbits.

If they did not produce eggs and more birds, we ate them and dried the extra meat for winter. Usually, we ate the birds. Their feathers were used for fletching and clothing and pillows and mattresses and blankets.

I didn't like sewing nets.

Geraldine told everyone what to do. She was a fat little woman with five children running around the grove and a husband always fishing.

Geraldine went to the nets every morning to see what had been caught. She shouted at others to help her unwrap the trees. For many children—like me—this was the sound that woke us in the morning: Geraldine shouting at women to help her with nets.

I went to watch the rose deer. The men there asked me why I wasn't at the nets. They asked me because everyone knew I had nimble hands and could twist the knots smooth and strong. I didn't know what to tell them that Geraldine wasn't saying behind my back. They'd hear soon enough, from their wives.

I didn't like caring for rose deer, either. They were quick to scratch someone with a thorn or a horn. They seemed to know, deep down in their roots, that someday the men would take them off and it wouldn't be the rosebuds in their tails that would be plucked.

I did like planting their seeds. I liked them when they were young, and still growing into deer from furry, brambled bushes. I walked among the young rose deer as they wiggled their braying bodies into the sun and breeze. I clipped the first growths of their flower buds, so the flowers would grow back larger. I clipped them back to their roots if they emerged from the ground before winter.

Young girls did this, and I did it with them. Geraldine's daughters seemed nice. We talked about their husbands among the boys and used bone daggers to clip the roses. We talked about the shapes of clouds, and the things we would name our children if they were boys, or if they were girls. I had heard a pretty name once, and I repeated it for the girls. Catherine, I had said.

Sometimes, I went back to the nets, but it always a whim, and I always regretted it. But, I was getting too old for the rose deer and the little girls.

Other girls my age already sent their daughters out among the rose deer.

Then, one day, at the nets, I heard a woman talk about how it sounded like I was going to marry Gokliya, Geraldine's brother, because I wanted to name my daughter the same as his dead wife.

Geraldine's daughters had told Geraldine. Geraldine had told the women of the nets, with the snide way she had of speaking about women, as if she knew everything, and none of the young people would ever be as wise as she.

I stopped talking very much with Geraldine's daughters among the deer.

I was sneaking through the night to the water after Lucius. I heard noise. I hid. I looked. I saw Geraldine's husband.

He was washing the salty loam off his skin in the marsh, looking around for anyone who might see his nakedness. I hid from him behind a tree. I watched one of Geraldine's friends, just another stooped old woman, slip out of the water with the moonlight all over her wrinkled back.

I tried to choke down my laughter. I wondered if the village, at night, was full of adulterers hiding from each other, and all of us spying on each other, and all of us keeping quiet about each other. When those two left the water, I went to the same place in the marsh and poured water over my naked skin, and rosewater. I hurried because I knew I wouldn't be the only one on a warm autumn night, in between the rains.

To be a child again.

Why would children worry if they didn't have to? They climbed trees. They chased after insects. Many of the older boys went fishing for bugs and frogs with their fathers. The girls usually tended the rose deer and the rabbits.

Unless we had a harvest, we did not need them. They would just be in the way. Better that the children play—especially boys, who played rough and hurt each other sometimes and it got them ready to patrol with the men, so no one minded rough boys.

When harvest came, no one played. We needed everyone. Older siblings looked after younger siblings. Some went to the orchard and pulled the apples down, one by one. Some went to the wheat and cut at the stalks. Older siblings guided younger siblings. Only children—like I had been—worked with their closest relations. I had no cousins to work with. I worked with Lucius. He and his father, Geraldine and Gokliya's father walked the wheat.

Lucius showed me how to cut with my bone dagger to catch sheaves of wheat in handfuls. Lucius taught me to put the wheat in the big baskets. Lucius threatened to hit me if I didn't pick up the small stalks I had dropped.

Lucius' father told his son never to hit a woman. Lucius sneered at me. I asked Lucius' father if I could hit Lucius. Lucius' father assured me that if I hit Lucius, the boy probably deserved it. I stuck my tongue out at Lucius. Lucius looked at his feet. Hit me, then.

"I'll hit you when you least expect it!" I said.

Even then, he towered over me. He was not yet old enough, brave enough, to patrol the halls with the men. He was just a big kid, who didn't know how to get along with other kids.

Then, my hands blistered with the blade. My back ached. I sat down. Lucius Caveman stopped working long enough to scowl at me. "What are you doing?" he said. "We have to keep harvesting. Everyone has to keep harvesting."

I showed him my hands, covered in pinkish-yellow blisters. "I can't," I said.

He showed me his hands, a mirror of my own blisters made giant on his huge palms. "You can," he said. "But if you want to give up, I won't stop you." He turned back to work. He cut into the wheat where I had stopped. "You're just a little kid," he said.

I watched him working, and rested my hands.

I can't remember what happened next. Shouldn't I remember what happened next? There's his back turned at an angle to me, so I can almost see his face, and he isn't wearing his father's brown jacket, yet, so I can see the muscles on his back, below the baby fat, glistening in sweat and browned from the sun, and the pantaloons stitched up from old clothes and rabbit leather, whipping with the windy wheat stalks, and his brow wracked with pained concentration.

Now that I'm older, I know what that look on his face means. That's what he looks like when he's trying to say he loves me, but he can't quite spit it out. That's what he looks like when he's smashing something with his brickbat, or slicing something with his spear, or digging himself into me like a spear, or anything at all that gets his pulse racing and the blood up in his ears.

But, back then, he was just a kid, and I was just a kid, and I can't remember what happened next that harvest. I can remember him, though, in that gesture, in that pose, yanking his blade over the sheaves of wheat, trying to cut the stalks with the tooth of a predatory fish, long dead, and the sun on his sweaty, muscular back.

The next year, I was working with girls my own age. We sneaked off when we got tired, and Ascalon caught us. His wife whipped us all for shirking, and then we had to work until our hands were bleeding enough to run down the blades, and risk ruining the wheat. We were crying, and no one seemed to care.

The year after that, we got our hands ready. We climbed trees with tough bark to harden our palms

Everyone worked during the harvest. It wasn't just wheat. It was fruit, and rose deer, and rabbits, and fish, and lobster, and birds, and everything we could find that we could store up for the long, dark, cold times.

I can see him, Lucius Caveman, bent down with the sickle in his hands, and his huge back and his face like he's choking on something that hurts him.

I remember Lucius, wrapped in his huge coat, whittling at the edges of our fires. He hummed psalms under his breath. He only remembered some of the words, but he could remember all the melodies. His voice was as rough as bark. He wasn't paying attention to the songs we sang closer to the fire, or the stories we told, stories we had learned from before we were all here in this grove, in this marsh, in this maze.

Was it because I wanted to pull him into the fire? To peel the coat from his back and reveal his beautiful naked shoulders to everyone, so strong and working so hard for us?

No. He was always one of us. He wrestled with Saitan, and with older boys, and played a game with them with a stick in the tail. Each boy put a stick in the back of his pants. He held it in place with one hand. They faced each other, usually smiling opportunistically, and feinted…feinted…feinted…to grab the other's stick from behind and pull it away before the other boy could grab his own stick and pull it away. Two boys circled each other. Lucius, left-handed, had an unfair advantage. He held the stick behind him with his right hand. His left arm pushed away the mirrored hand. He clamped down on the right wrist of his opponent and yanked until—overpowering even his father's son, Gokliya, decades older than he—Lucius could whip his right hand around to the stick in his opponent's belt and break it in half, whack his opponent with it, shouting victory. Finally, when the boy released the stick to defend his aching head, Lucius grabbed the stump in back.

Lucius was victorious forever until the boys decided a new rule was that you couldn't break the stick anymore, otherwise Lucius would always win.

Lucius still had an advantage because he was left-handed, because he was bigger than everyone, and because he was a little mean. But, he wasn't ostracized. He was respected. Boys respect strength. Lucius was strong, and he was rough, but he wasn't mean enough to be called cruel. He was a Cathar. He believed everyone had a soul, glowing in the rot and decay of their mortal flesh, and deserved respect for that, if nothing else.

The morning after I married Gokliya, I couldn't sleep very long. Gokliya slept hard. The lobster had given him gas, and he was farting. My body was damp with sweat where our skin had been pressed together in the night. I peeled away from him and let him fall into the space where I had been. I washed my skin with a wet rag dipped in rosewater. I turned to look at Gokliya. I had not had a chance to really look at him the night before. He was lean and strong, and his skin had felt like sandstone against me, with all that salt and dust and sweat and brown skin that smelled like stone heat. He breathed. His ribs moved. His eyes were closed. His mouth was open, his body rolled back and more naked than I had ever seen. He was just flesh, naked and breathing.

I put my pants on, and my shirt. I put my leather tunic on. I pulled my moccasins over my feet. I shook my hair and wondered if I would smell like Gokliya now, forever, in the hair that had been pushed against his skin all night, where his sweat and tears had washed over me.

I went to the nets. Where else would I go? I was a woman now, and I wanted to be with the women. I had accepted my path. I imagined that someday I would be the one guiding young hands at the nets, showing them how to twist the vines, and untwist the vines, and snap a bird's neck, and peel away all the feathers and down, and gut it, and save the guts for the fish, and never gossip the way Geraldine gossiped, and the way the older women gossiped because life shouldn't be full of so much meanness when it was already so hard.

The new wives worked there already, and I was the last to arrive. There were six of us, and every one but me was trying hard to hide the stupid grin on her face. I wasn't smiling. I was just working.

Geraldine asked me if I was all right.

"What?" I said.

"Are you all right, little sister? You look angry. Is everything all right?"

As if I'd tell her. "Everything's fine. Why are you looking at me so much? Is something wrong with my knots?"

Of course people talked. Of course Gokliya heard it.

And Lucius, the man I loved though I didn't know it at the time, was gone on patrols. He was gone on long patrols. He was fishing. He was whittling wood on the far sides of the grove, where he had to swim over marshes and climb over logs to find a place away from the people.

Geraldine said it was because he had asked someone to marry him, and she had said no. She had heard it was one of the girls who had only just bled woman, and the girl was still playing with the children, and how dare he ask someone so much younger when women his age were unwed. For instance, Sarah's husband had died last winter. Sarah wasn't pretty, but neither was Lucius.

I stayed as long as I could stand, listening to all that talk. When I thought they wouldn't suspect why I was so mad, I got up and left.

I was mad because Lucius hadn't married like I had, and he was older than I was. I was mad because he was off hiding, and it was his fault I had married Gokliya, because Lucius had gotten Saitan killed with stupid gossip. It was all Lucius' fault.

I went looking for Lucius.

I started at the gates, where I knew he spent long hours whittling wooden sticks into tools and staring into the maze halls. Men asked me if I had seen Gokliya, because he hadn't woken up, yet. They joked about the night.

I didn't blush. I didn't say anything. I just kept walking, looking for Lucius.

I still didn't understand what they were japing about. What I had experienced the night before had been strange, awkward, and a little painful, and I didn't know how I felt about the whole nonsense, but I knew it wasn't anything like what they were talking about. Gokliya had cried, and all that sweat.

I went to the deer fields, watched little girls petting the deer. The last of the season's baby deer wriggled incessantly in the breeze, but they were rooted down hard. We wouldn't cut the last crop loose.. They'd remain in the ground as long into winter as we could stand it.

Qiang and Geraldine's husband, Renaldo, were repairing the fence around the deer. I asked these men where I could find Lucius.

They didn't ask me why I was looking for Lucius. They told me Lucius was out praying, and I'd best leave him alone when he was doing that.

"Where?" I asked. "I wanted to ask him something important. He is my husband's youngest brother."

They pointed into the deep marsh, where the trees pressed against the far wall of the maze, and we had placed spikes and traps and gargoyle heads.

A large watchtower was on the top of a tall tree. I climbed to the top.

He wasn't there. Nobody was. I sat down, alone. I looked at the maze, long and far away, and the rolling hills of stone walls.

I started to cry, then. I wished people wouldn't talk about me.

I wiped my eyes on my sleeve. I plucked leaves from the tree to blow my nose. I kept crying.

A brown coat, and his arm, wrapped around me. I leaned into his shoulder. I kept crying. I hit Lucius a little bit, but he didn't stop me. He rocked me a little. He stroked my face and wiped away the tears with the sleeve of his coat.

At last, I said, "They're talking about you."

"Let them talk," he said.

"They say terrible things. They want you to marry Sara."

"I will never marry," he said. "The flesh is an impurity, and an abomination. I will live in the spirit world, for God. Then, someday, my devotion to the realm of the spirit will liberate me from this place. I'll return to the hills of Languedoc, where my mother's family had their farm."

"I was looking for you," I said.

"You have found me."

We sat still like that a long time. He had his arm around me, his big duster jacket.

"Are you going to try to kiss me again?"

"No."

"Do you want to?"

"Yes, but I can't. Gokliya's my brother."

"He's my husband. I don't want you to kiss me. I just want a friend who doesn't want to judge me or tell me what I should do. People are so mean to each other. Isn't it hard enough here without all those people being mean to each other? What I always liked about you is how you were never talking about people. You never talked to anyone unless they wanted you to."

"We'd be banished if we were caught."

"I can't believe he's my husband. It's all your fault. And Saitan's."

"Saitan and I used to love this spot. We could sit out here and be away from everyone. He was my friend, too. Everyone is my friend. You and I are friends, Julie Station."

The words faded into the songbird breeze. I looked out and saw the maze before me. I saw something moving from the corner of my eye. I pointed at it.

"What's that?" I said.

His arm stiffened around me. He peeled away from me. He stood up.

"Strike the rock," he said. "I'm going to get the men."

I squinted toward the distance. I couldn't quite make it out among the rocks. Then, I saw the spikes and creaking branches. I saw the way the spikes moved to indicate the rest of the body below the wall.

Troll.

At the farther outposts, we used sticks against hollow stones so people would know from where the alarm called. I grabbed the stick and smashed the rock. I heard the sound of men gathering and shouting. I watched the men of the village armed with brickbats. You had to smash a troll with a brickbat or a club; a spear would do nothing but push it back a little. I saw them passing around torches. Trolls burned like wood.

The men clumped at the gate, where Lucius led them. I watched from the far outpost as the bristling hairs lumbered through the hall. I waited, holding the stick to my body like I was holding all the men of our village against my heart.

The troll was alone. It lumbered along on its wood-like legs. The monster reached the spot on the path where it could see the men waiting for it with brickbats.

I saw the monster stop in its path. I waited for it to move forward or backward. I heard the sound of men shouting and smashing their brickbats menacingly against the stone walls.

The troll turned away from us. It walked back the way it came.

I stayed where I was, because it could come back any second with allies.

Lucius returned to me, in the tower.

"We don't have enough men to keep an eye on everything. You should join us patrolling, and watching from the towers. We need all the help we can get until the troll threat passes."

I didn't give Lucius an answer. I gave him his stick back. Then, I said, "Where's Gokliya?"

"He's already out on patrol. He went with Renaldo to check our other side. We've been flanked before by trolls."

I stepped down from the watchtower.

I went back to the nets, where the women worked on like nothing had happened. I stayed there until we finished with the birds and the sewing. I took my share of the food back to Gokliya's hut.

When Gokliya returned, he asked me if I had baked any bread for him. I didn't know how to bake anything.

He urged me to learn.

I should have stayed at the nets, and learned to bake bread, and let the men take care of me—of all of us.

Instead, I joined Gokliya on short patrols, where I was his eyes and he was my ears and strength. I took to the guard towers and gazed out into the maze, watching for anything that moved.

Enyo Gyoja posted double sentries at all the gates, all day and night. We had to be ready in case the trolls came back.

What did we eat instead of bread, Gokliya and me? We ate everything we could. We were both patrolling. We were both guarding. Qiang, who butchered the deer, brought us a liver or a heart, still sweet with red sap. Simran offered us an extra fish from time to time. Before nightfall, we took turns scouring the marsh for cattails and ripe rice patches. We boiled all these things together.

I know the men teased Gokliya because his wife was not cooking bread, was out among the men, carrying a spear and watching the halls.

With Saitan gone, and all the strong that had been laid to rest the past winter, Enyo Gyoja agreed with Lucius that I was useful to the men for now. Ascalon agreed with Enyo Gyoja. Gokliya took no side—which, I suspect, indicated that he did not support me at all, but refused to take away this indulgence from me.

I learned the short loop like the back of my own hand. I rarely went out farther. I kept watch from the distant patrol towers at the fringe of the marsh because I was small and nimble and could climb the creaky old wooden branches of trees, and my weight never risked the green, rotten wood, like the men's weight did, in the far places of our grove.

Two of Geraldine's daughters—both unmarried, but old enough to be asked next autumn—decided to follow my example.

I can only imagine the horrible things said at the nets about me, pulling girls away from their places, endangering them like men.

After nightfall, Gokliya reached for me, and I let him. I held still. I waited for him to finish. I ran my hands through his hair and wondered what all this was for, all this intrusion and sweat and a feeling of emptiness, after. I didn't want him to touch me, after. I didn't want to feel his skin on mine or smell him or hear him breathing, but I did not know how to peel away from him while he slept.

Lucius and I didn't speak alone again for a long time. Always busy, always guarding, he took the longer trails, usually with Ascalon or men I barely knew enough to recall their names.

The troll threat faded slowly. We found no new droppings. We saw no sign of them on patrol. The wind changed. Winter stalked us now, and it was far worse than trolls. What else was there to say of the time, then, when all hands gathered up our food?

I kept to the watchtowers.

Gokliya said nothing. He squinted into the stew we had made. He took to trading meat for bread from Geraldine. In the night, he touched my stomach and asked me questions I did not know how to answer.

"Do you feel well? Do you feel anything inside of you? Do you want to try again?"

"I'm fine. No. I just want to sleep, Gokliya. Can't we just lie here, stay warm, and try to sleep?"

"Do you love me?"

"I don't know. I just want to get some sleep."

"Someday you will. I'm sure you will. It just takes time."

Lucius gave me a cloak he had made from rose deer leather. He found me in a watchtower, gazing out over the maze, with the cold chill in the air blowing over me.

"The wind gets rough up there, sometimes," he said. "Especially in winter."

When I took it from him, I touched the back of his hand. He had gigantic hands. He had warm hands. I pulled one up to my face, to warm me. "I'm freezing," I said.

He jerked away from me. "I'll be back later. Enyo wants to keep people watching the gates at night, with spears. He wonders where the stone cows are. He's worried they'll come in the night this time. We don't know if they sleep like us or not. You can come, if you want."

I smelled Lucius in the jacket. I remembered being with Gokliya, how it was like his smell filled my whole consciousness, and I still wasn't sure if I liked that smell of him. I smelled Lucius' jacket, and I liked Lucius' smell.

And, the world was so cold. And, I hadn't been to the nets in so long. And, if Lucius had returned, I would have done things with him, and I wouldn't have cared.

When he did not return to me, I folded his big jacket up and carried it over my arm. I didn't want to walk into town wearing his jacket. I wanted to say he had left his jacket at the post before I got there, and I was bringing it back to him. I went to his hut. I knocked on his door. He pulled aside the reeds and looked at me. I looked into his eyes. I held up the jacket.

He reached a hand beneath the jacket, to take it from me, folded.

I smiled. I touched his naked arm with my hand, underneath the cloth. I clutched at his hand. He took mine in his. We stood still, too long. He blinked. He pulled his arm and his jacket away from me.

He took a deep breath.

We held still, looking at each other.

"Thanks," he said.

"Gokliya is probably hungry."

"He is hungry. So am I."

The reeds closed. I didn't turn away right then. I waited for the sound of him leaving his own doorway. I did not hear the sound of him returning to his stool or hammock. I thought I could sense him—smell him—just past the reed curtain.

I whispered into the room. "Meet me at the watchtower tonight."

I didn't know if he heard me or not. My heart raced just whispering it.

I went home to Gokliya. He had started a fire. Another rose deer had been slaughtered. Gokliya cooked the liver in its own sticky sap. He had grape leaves and sea fruits to wrap with the meat. He handed a wrapped piece to me.

"Are you hungry?" he said.

"No," I said.

"What will you do if the trolls come, or a caveman, or a minotaur? Will you fight with the men?"

"I'll fight."

"I don't want you to fight with us."

"I'm sorry."

"I don't want to fight with you," he said. He held up the meat and fruit wrapped in leaves. "Just promise me you will go back to the women if the dangerous things come. There will be more men, soon. There will be boys growing up into men. Do you know why Enyo Gyoja does not like to let women join the men?"

"We are small, weak—"

"No. Don't be silly. One woman carries a dozen men inside of her belly. Once upon a time, Enyo says that there were many women for each man, because so many men had died. But, Enyo says that if the opposite had happened, and most of the women had died, then there would be no village and no people and all of us would dwindle off to death. That is why women stay behind and do not fight."

Gokliya touched my stomach.

"You're being silly," I said. I ate the food he had cooked.

He said, "I don't want to fight with you. Before, with...We fought all the time. I hated it that we were always fighting. When she died, we were fighting. We weren't speaking to each other because we were fighting."

I chewed. I swallowed. I said nothing.

Gokliya and I weren't speaking to each other, and it was because we weren't fighting.

"Are you mad at me?" he said.

I touched his arm. "Of course not, Gokliya." It was the truth.

It was his turn not to speak. He ate his food. He reclined in the bedding. He gazed up at the thatching.

I sat up in the night. I did not join him in bed. I watched him watching me—I sat on a stool across from him—and I waited for his eyes to close. I waited for him to snore.

I left in the dark, for the far outpost.

We kept our watchmen closer to the village in the dark. We didn't have many keeping watch unless we expected trouble. We had the men at the barricades, mostly, ready for stone cows in the night, and burning fires to scare off trolls. Most of the beasts of the maze were not nocturnal. It was hard enough to see in the moonlight without the shadows everywhere from all the walls, blocking out moonlight, starlight, all light.

Lucius was there, before me.

Sitting in the tree, and looking out to the maze in the dark, where all the paths had fallen into black below the thin moon.

Lucius was waiting for me.

Gokliya never said anything. I slipped out in the night. How could he not know I was slipping out in the night, when my body kept him warm in the late autumn chill? How could he not wonder about me at the far guard posts each morning and evening, looking into the slanting twilight, alone?

Before the trolls came, he told me something, when I thought he was lounging half-asleep in the morning. "Everyone says I'm blind. I'm not blind," he said. "I'm just nearsighted. I can see what's right in front of my face." He rolled over. He reached a hand and touched the cold stone wall. He stroked the cold stones. He said it again. "I can see what's right in front of my face."

I thought of replying to him. I did not. I thought about going to bake bread. I thought about filling the bread with small stones and letting him chew rocks and bricks and swallow rocks and bricks and bleed.

Of course the stone cows came. I saw them from the guard post on a bright, cold morning. I cried out. I rang the bells.

Everyone gathered sticks and spears—man, woman, child—and ran to the gates. We had to push them back or they would eat all the rocks from the roots and kill all the trees.

We were all there, helping or watching, even Enyo Gyoja. We weren't watching behind us. Why would we? We had to fight the stone cows. We had a threat right in front of us.

We pushed them from our barricade with long, sturdy spears. We shouted and pushed. The stone herd milled about, pushing against us with the weight of their numbers. The strongest men took to the front to dig their heels in and really push.

Nine trolls crept up behind us while none of us carried a brickbat, and none of us were watching the back gate, and our fires weren't ready.

I was close to the back, holding a long stick. I heard a scream behind me. I turned.

I screamed, too.

The trolls already had Geraldine's youngest daughter, two old women, and Ascalon's wife. I saw their limp bodies torn to parts and blood spray.

I remember thinking, before the men came from fighting back the stone cow herds, about how all the dead were women, and how that wasn't the right way. Men were supposed to die protecting women. Women weren't supposed to die this way.

Gokliya and Enyo Gyoja charged with spears first, shouting back to the men and boys and everyone to fight while the women and children held back the stone cows.

I blinked. I took a deep breath. I was too afraid to charge like my husband. I grabbed at the ground for rocks and sticks. I threw them. I shouted for everyone to throw rocks, to attack.

Gokliya smashed his spear on the chest of a troll, but it didn't hurt the monster. The troll swung a long clawed arm; a child dangled from its mouth. My rock knocked loose the part of the dead body dangling from the teeth. The troll wheezed. Human blood splattered from the gaps in its wooden teeth.

Enyo Gyoja whacked at the trolls, futilely. He ducked the swung claw but couldn't easily get back up again to counter-attack.

The monster swung at another man, and Enyo still struggled to find his footing on his old legs and his old sandals. I gathered enough courage for him. I jumped into the battle. I grabbed Enyo Gyoja's arm. I pulled him up to standing. I dragged him back from the fight.

More men came. I pulled Enyo back to the women. His spear clattered around in the air, uselessly. I took his spear from him. I turned my back to him.

Gokliya, Lucius, Ascalon, Jim, Simran, Qiang, and all the others had a couple of trolls down. Lucius smashed one's head in with a bat while men with spears pinned the troll's arms. Lucius had his jacket off. He had a large cut down his back, but he didn't stop swinging his bat.

I heard women weeping. I heard Enyo Gyoja shout at me to stay back with the women. He screamed at me to stay there. He clutched at his spear and tried to pull it from me.

I yanked it away from him. I told him to stay there. I jumped into the fight, at last.

Ascalon swung his brickbat wildly at the troll that had killed his wife. The other men fought smarter, using spears to hold trolls back and pester them until a good brickbat could get a swing in. Ascalon was out beyond the spears. Trolls were being beaten back, but they were still snatching at bodies, at legs. They snatched spears and pulled them away. They swung claws. People were struck, and fell.

(And the cows, at the barricade: women pushed and struggled to push and push back the hungry herd without the strength of men. Everybody screamed except for me.)

Ascalon swung his bat without spearmen to aid him. He ducked the troll's claws. He swung again, wild.

I jammed my spear against the troll's shoulder. I tried to stab it in the heart.

I had to be careful Ascalon didn't hit me on a backswing.

Gokliya appeared beside me. He guided my spear lower. He shouted at me. I didn't hear him. Ascalon's brickbat was snatched away by a different troll. This troll threw it at Lucius' head—Lucius snatched it in mid-air, one-handed—and the troll swung an arm at Ascalon. Ascalon took the blow across his face. He fell down. He didn't get up. More men were there, from the troll they had just killed.

Gokliya shouted something again. He tried to move my spear—I kept pushing it and pushing it at the troll but it wasn't doing anything, and I thought I was weak—and he tried to move my spear again, lower. I noticed others doing the same with spears, aiming low at legs and hips. I heard what Gokliya was saying, then. "Trip the troll for Lucius!"

I aimed low. A man went down, blood pouring from his nose. Another troll went down.

The trolls that were left snagged one man between them. A man, I call him, but he was no man. He was a boy younger than I was. The trolls ran for the gate.

Lucius shouted that we had to keep the stone cows out.

Enyo Gyoja shouted for all the spears to return to the stone cows, but I don't think anyone heard him over the wailing of the women. They heard Lucius, though, with a voice booming like a minotaur's roar over all of us.

Gokliya and a few other men chased after the trolls, carrying torches and brickbats and spears. Enyo Gyoja hobbled up to me to take back his spear. I did not let him take it.

I ran to the barriers, and to the stone cows. I jabbed them in their eyes and necks, and I pushed with all my might to turn the herd away.

None had gotten through when we had turned to fight off the trolls. Women and children had been the ones holding them back, and not a single cow had gotten through.

Men were hurt, but none of the good, strong men were badly hurt. Women and children had died.

I never wanted to go back to being a woman again, the way Enyo Gyoja wanted us to be.

I wanted to fight.

I think, in the end, it wasn't the cheating that caused us to be banished. I think it was because I left Enyo Gyoja among the women. I had wounded an old man's pride.

I had not even bothered to look him in the face when he was shouting and grabbing at me. I don't know what his eyes had looked like. I imagine they looked like what a man's eyes looked like when, for the first time in his life, his orders went disobeyed to his face, in front of all those people.

6: Winter

We mourned the dead. Of course we did. The boy who had been taken wasn't brought back to us alive. Part of his leg came back to us. Gokliya carried the leg wrapped in rags for the vultures to take their share, where we could catch them.

Lucius limped back to us, leaning on his brickbat. He had lost blood along his back. He had been cut along one of his legs and in his face. I wanted to weep for him, and scream and hold him and hug him and take his blood all over my skin in mourning. I touched Gokliya's hand. I forced myself to look in Gokliya's eyes, and to kiss him, lightly.

Ascalon was cut, but he wasn't dead. His nose was broken, and he had been knocked unconscious, but he was alive. Geraldine set the bone. Geraldine held in the tears for her lost child long enough to heal the living. She wrapped Lucius' wounds in flattened sweet cane. She took care of the ones who had no wives or mothers.

Then, she held her lost daughter. She wept into the girl's hair. Her husband had been killed, too, though no one could find Renaldo's body. He was an old man, hobbling and hoary, and he had probably been at the back. He had probably been the first one the trolls took.

We gave our dead to the vultures. They laughed at us while devouring our lost.

Winter came too soon. It always did. We were never truly ready. We had stored up dried meat. We protected our rice and our wheat from bugs and mice and wetness with cats and vigilance. We pulled our deer and rabbits into huts. We let some out with nets all around them to catch the predators that came after them. We smoked the predators' meat and added to our stores.

The air turned first, from cold to a deep cold that climbed inside the skin. That's when we knew the snow was coming. The snow clouds came soon after, like a veil of fog above us that dropped bits of chilled cloud down to the ground.

We huddled in close for the winter.

We watched for trouble at the watchtowers. When I knew I wanted to be with Lucius, I went to one at night, where I had to sit in the dark and watch for movement in the moonlight. I had to wrap myself in the rags that others no longer wore, and the cloaks made like netting from bits of tree bark and reeds.

Lucius came for me in the dark. He wrapped me in his jacket. He held me close. I pressed my head against his chest and heard his heartbeat. I let my eyes close.

Lucius told me about his God.

The world of the flesh was broken and warped. The world of the spirit was the truth. We were more than our skin, more than our blood, and more than our misdeeds. God wanted us to be good. He brought us to this horrible place to test us. If we stayed true to his teachings, we would never die. Even in death, we would only be abandoning our disgusting bags of flesh to this world.

He believed that I was destroying his soul. It did not bother him enough to stop.

I happened to like the world of flesh. I didn't want to be a spirit without flesh.

Ghosts walked through the barricades and snowdrifts. They passed through trees and through boundaries. Lucius said that ghosts were the dead who were not pure enough to become one with the Lord. The devil corrupted the world of God and brought us all into His damnation, the maze.

I let him sing the hymns his mother sang, like lullabies—words nearly forgotten, or garbled in his memory such that they made little sense. I listened to his prayers. I never tried to remember them. To me, they were a rumble in his chest when my eyes were closed at the edge of my dreams.

He didn't always want to make love because the flesh was sinful, and adultery was sinful. He made love anyway because he couldn't help himself. Love was greater than a song in the dark, and a prayer no one else cared to hear.

We made love when we should have been watching the frigid night. We told each other our dreams.

Gokliya, my husband, was pitied by the married women. They brought him extra bread and helped him with the winter weavings. I had tried my best at the weavings, but my hands had known spears and practiced with slings. What could these calloused hands know of delicately threaded needles and repairing cloth with reed threads?

I wondered if we were cheating on each other, he and I. All those women, many he had known longer than I had been alive, who pitied him when his first wife had died and now saw a young wife that refused to be a woman. I was caught before he was. I'll never know the truth.

Winter was awful. We were always hungry and never ate to fill because we knew we had to make the food last.

People died because they got sick. They coughed and coughed, and then something flowered in their chests, and weeds sprouted from their open mouths and they were dead. People got fevers and died in sweltering heat while the world around them was ice. Cuts became gangrenous. Little babies and old people died more than the rest.

We used their dead bodies to trap vultures and crows.

We ate one of Sara's cats. I don't know if she ate any of them herself or not. She wasn't around when we killed it, skinned it and cooked it.

The solstice flies came and went, deep into the winter.

Enyo Gyoja came down with a cough that rattled his chest, but it didn't kill him like it did the others.

We peeled bark from old trees and boiled it with snow until we could chew it like a hairy, long nut.

Gokliya noticed I was missing because he was cold. He woke up from the cold. He came looking for me. I was walking in the dark, sneaking my way back to him from one of the abandoned huts where an old woman had died. Her roof had been taken away for kindling.

"Is that you, Julie Station?" he said. "Is my wife sneaking around in the dark like a ghost?"

I touched Gokliya's cheek. "I couldn't sleep," I said. "That's all. I couldn't sleep, and I went for a walk."

"It's freezing out here. How can you possibly go for a walk in this?"

His hands trembled in the cold. He clenched them into balls. I thought it was to keep them warmer.

"Love," he said. "My father loved my mother. My sister loved her husband. Catherine loved me, for a time." Then, knuckles found my left eye. "I will know him by the bruise on your face. The man who hates me in the morning will be him who pulls you from your husband on a cold night, when you should be warming him to whom you swore your life."

My tears melted snow. I couldn't believe they didn't freeze on my face. I looked up at Gokliya in the darkness, a tall, lean shadow with no face. He was more terrifying than a troll.

"I can smell him all over you, whoever he is," said Gokliya. "I always could."

He bent down to take me by the arm. He picked me up from the snow. He pulled me close to him. He led me home, to our hut. He placed me on the stone bed. The hot coals we had placed beneath our bed still held some warmth in the dark.

I said nothing to him, ever again. I looked at the wall. I waited for him to press against me.

He didn't for a long time. He sat on the edge of the warmed stones. He looked down at me, wrapped in blankets and leaves and rags, pressing as much of my body into the warmed stone as I could, and staring away from him.

I glanced up at him, when I wondered why he was taking so long, and there he was, looking at me. I looked away from him quickly. I didn't want to look him in the face.

He said, before finally joining me in the bed. "You came to me, Julie Station. I never knew why. I still don't. Why would you cleave to me and then leave me in the night? What did I do to you to deserve this?"

I pretended to be asleep.

In the morning, I hid from the village. I didn't want anyone to see my bruised eye. I could feel my face swollen up like a fruit. I had trouble seeing out of the eye where I had been struck.

Gokliya returned from his patrol. He took my hair in one hand, my arm in another. He pulled me out into the village. He led me around the whole village, with my bruised eye. Lucius had gone from a patrol to a watchtower.

Lucius didn't see. Lucius didn't know.

Though I never did find out exactly who told Lucius, I have always imagined that it was Geraldine. Geraldine rose from her nets upon seeing me. She stopped her day's labor and sought out Lucius Caveman, and told him that Gokliya had struck me in the face and paraded me around the village to show everyone my bruised eye.

I hid from the world inside Gokliya's hut—my hut. Gokliya brought me food that night. He talked to fill the silence. He told me he was sorry. He told me he thought it would end soon enough and I would return to him, my sworn husband. He told me he wouldn't have cared if he had to raise another man's child, as long as things ended and he could have me—all of me.

He told me he loved me.

I chewed what he brought me to eat. A handful of dried meat as foul as I could stomach. Boiled bark soup as cold as ice by the time it came to my hut.

In the morning, Geraldine came to me. She touched my hair. She tried to hug me. I pushed her away. She told me that she knew about Lucius, and all he had done to her brothers.

She said that Lucius and I would have our fates decided by Gokliya, for he had been wronged by us.

I told Geraldine that I had made a mistake.

"You have made so many mistakes, Julie," she said. "But that's all right. People make mistakes. Perhaps now you will settle down with your husband. Gokliya's a good man."

"No!" I said. "I married the wrong man. That's the only mistake I have ever made. I married the wrong man. I am in love with Lucius. I was mad at him once and did something stupid, and I shouldn't have married Gokliya. I never should have married Gokliya. I hate him."

Geraldine pursed her lips. She looked down on me with very sad eyes. She left me there.

Gokliya did not decide my fate.

Enyo Gyoja did.

I stayed in the hut a long time, alone. Gokliya came and went but did not speak to me. People brought me food, if there was food to spare and if they didn't hate me.

Sara, she of five cats instead of five children, brought me food. She was one of the very few who did. Sometimes I left the hut in search of it, but no one spoke to me but Sara. Not even Geraldine spoke to me anymore, and usually she couldn't shut up.

Lucius came to me, and he said that he didn't care what people thought of us even though I knew he was lying. He cared. He was ashamed of what he'd done to his eldest brother.

He told me that he had nearly killed Gokliya on a patrol after hearing about what had happened to my eye. Lucius had surprised Gokliya and tied him up and left him in the maze, on a long patrol.

Gokliya had escaped and made his way back to the village before Lucius did.

We shared all our secrets, then, all our regrets. He came to me openly, in what used to be Gokliya's hut. No one spoke to us. When we came looking for food, we were looked at as if we were stealing.

I had betrayed my husband. Lucius had tried to kill him.

It wasn't long, then. A week, maybe two. Winter had broken and warmed a little, but not much. It was getting warmer, and the snow had mostly melted, but there was ice on the rocks and grasses every morning.

It felt like a long time because I knew Gokliya was making a decision, and the village had already made it for him and they were merely convincing Gokliya that it was his decision.

I knew what was going to happen to us.

The men came to the hut one morning before Lucius and I could wake up. They had spears. They had cold eyes. They didn't speak to Lucius and me. The men surrounded us with their spears.

We were to be abandoned in the maze, like Lucius had tried to do to Gokliya.

We were led to the nearest barricade by the circle of spears.

I was relieved that we were done waiting. I don't know why it took them so long to decide to cast us out.

Lucius and I walked out alone, with only what we could grab on our way toward the barricade. A brickbat. A few skins of frozen water. The flint in Lucius' jacket pocket. The spear I grabbed and strapped to my back as we walked past the extra spears of the barricade.

When we had walked beyond the village of the men, Lucius asked me if I wanted to pray with him for our salvation.

I didn't know the words, but I listened to him, praying for us both.

We kept moving the first day, beyond the known halls. We found three dead ends and backtracked almost to where we had started to find our next path. When night fell, we huddled close inside Lucius' jacket. We should have kept watch. We didn't.

I don't really think either one of us cared if a troll found us in the night.

On the second day, Lucius handed me jerky. I swallowed half and gave the rest back to him. He refused it. "It's all we have left. You eat it. I don't even like how minotaur tastes when I'm hungry."

I probably should have saved it, but it was in my hand and I was hungry and I was thirsty, and I didn't think. I placed it in my mouth. I chewed. I swallowed.

We were lucky when we wound up at the large lake the second day. Where we stood, Lucius could reach up and touch the top of the dam. With the melting snows, the water level was near the top. We climbed up easily. The top of the lake was still iced over from the winter chill in the air. We couldn't straddle the dam with the water level so high. We sat carefully, keeping our feet away from the ice. Ice flowers grew in a field. It reminded me of the grove. We ate all we could grab, until we were full of water and bitter petals and stems.

Lucius had a water skin in his jacket. He filled it up with the ice flower water.

He pointed to a side of the lake. "Remember the first time we saw this lake? We were over there."

I looked. I wrapped my arms around Lucius' neck. We kissed.

When we had all the water we could carry, we climbed back down. We kept moving. We sucked on ice until we ran out.

We walked around a bend, into a herd of gargoyles. Dozens of them looked up and suddenly turned to stone before us. We stopped in our tracks.

"Can we go another way?" I said. "Can we track back and try a different path?"

If we just kept looking at them, maybe we could catch one. Lucius hooked an arm in mine, and then got behind me. He hooked another arm.

"I'll watch our back. Don't stop looking at them."

I was scared into stillness. Lucius' huge body pressed me, stumbling, toward the gargoyles.

I let him push me. We walked into them, and over them, always looking at them. We darted our eyes all around. Sometimes we lost sight of a few from the corners of our eyes, but they couldn't orient themselves on us long enough to attack before they were stone again, and we had moved forward.

Lucius kicked over any we had to step across.

When we got past them, Lucius told me to wait a minute. He ran back to the gargoyles and plucked one, still stone, into the air. He held it up in front of his face with both hands, to keep it stone. It was bigger than a cat and heavy as bricks.

We ran off from the gargoyles, always looking over our shoulders, until we came to a forking path. We chose randomly. Then, eight steps in, we backtracked and took a different path, always keeping the gargoyle held up in front of our eyes, a stone.

Lucius took my spear by the base of the bone tip. He placed the gargoyle on its back on the ground. He carefully chose a place for the spear tip, right over the monster's heart. He told me to step back. I did. He started to push with his spear, and turned his head. "Close your eyes," he said.

When I opened them again, he had a gargoyle, limp and bloody, on the end of the spear. He tore out the heart. He swallowed it raw. He handed me an organ. "It tastes terrible," he said. "I think I'm going to be sick."

I took what he gave me and swallowed it without chewing. I didn't care what it tasted like. I hadn't eaten in two days.

We found a dead vulture. We weren't brave enough to attempt that dried, rotting flesh raw. Lucius set fire to it. We held strips of gargoyle flesh over the flame to cook that, too. Our fire didn't get hot enough or last long enough to cook anything, but we felt better for trying. It burned away the worst flavors of the vulture meat, at least. It just tasted burnt after that.

We had blood all over our mouths and our clothes.

We huddled into each other for warmth. We closed our eyes and tried to sleep. A strong wind could wake us. A cloud tumbling over the moon could wake us.

We kept on.

If we found a dead end, we backtracked until we found something that wasn't a dead end. We stepped over holes filled with bones; they had probably been traps, once. We peeled leaves from vines and ate them. If the root itself wasn't too thick, we ate that, too.

We kept moving.

We looked up toward a cliff on the third day after we ate the gargoyle. We saw caves carved into the sides of the cliff. We were too weak to climb up and look inside. The caves were large, so I said—my voice weak and cracking because we were almost out of water—to Lucius, "Better not. They're big, like us. They'll probably eat us."

We kept walking, below the cliff. We kept glancing above us for signs of things hunting after us.

Later that day we found a bush full of berries. We were too hungry to worry if it was poisonous or not. When we plucked the fruit from the branches, we saw that it wasn't fruit growing here, but red larva. We ate them anyway, wriggling in our mouths and damp with a sickly-sweet sap. It reminded me of the rose deer.

We didn't vomit. We didn't die. We plucked as many as we could fit into our pockets. We stripped the plant nearly bare. Lucius cut off a large branch covered in the little red larvae, and he carried it over his shoulder.

We kept moving. We hadn't seen anything else alive since the gargoyles.

Then, we found a small stream of water flowing uphill. We refilled our water skins. We refilled our bellies, too. We stayed there a day and a night, at the stream, eating the larva berries. We drank so much water.

At night, our hands wandered places we hadn't been since we were cast out. Then, he told me he wanted to baptize me, not make love to me. He wanted to save my soul.

He took water from the stream. He placed it on my head. "Do you hate this world, and everything evil in it?"

"Hold me tighter."

"Do you accept the light; the purest light?"

"Lucius, I love you."

"Do you accept your true self, your true nature, free of the pollutions of this flesh?"

He was choking down tears. I took water from the stream. I washed his eyes. I kissed them. I held him while Lucius Caveman cried. "Please, Julie...Do you accept Christ, who died on the Cross to release all of us into the light?"

"I'm here, Lucius. I'm here. We're together. I don't know what you want. I just know I love you."

"I tried to kill Gokliya. He was a good man, and it's not his fault what happened. I committed adultery, and I tried to kill him. Oh, Christ, forgive me. I deserve this hell."

"Lucius, it's not your fault. It's my fault, and I'm not sorry. I love you, and I'd rather be here than anywhere near those horrible people who hate us for trying to be happy."

"Christ, forgive me for the pollutions of this flesh."

All night like that, with some sleep. The morning came, and we rolled out of the shadows to warm ourselves in the sun and to try to bring our limbs back to life. The night was so cold. The shadows were still so cold. Our bodies were so stiff, so cold.

We heard the sound of giant wings in the distance, flapping. We couldn't see anything over our heads.

"We need to keep moving," said Lucius. "Other things will come here for the water."

We saw a hill—maybe a mountain; I had heard the largest hills were called mountains—and there was a huge building at the top, surrounded by lower buildings that were still very large, and around that were piles of trash and ruined buildings and bleached bones like naked trees from monstrous beasts both giant and unknown.

Of course we climbed to the top. Of course we did. What else was there for us to do?

We had lost Lucius' brickbat. We were too weak to carry it. We had lost my spear. We still had some of the larvae in Lucius' pockets. We still had a little bit of water. We stepped carefully over the rocks. Tiny, angry things snapped at us, but disappeared into the rocks without biting us. They looked like men and like snakes and like insects all at once, no larger than a finger. Spiders and worms huddled into the dark places between fallen rocks.

We moved carefully and slowly over all those broken walls. We had to use hands and feet.

The village at the top—I recognized that it was a village—was abandoned. There used to be a wall around it, but we had climbed over what was left of that wall to reach the top of the hill—the mountain.

Lucius touched a door taller than he was. He pushed it. It crumbled to dust at his touch. I peered into the first hut. It was very large, like two huts stacked on top of each other. A bone ladder led up to the second hut. I didn't try my weight on it.

The place smelled of dust. The huts had nothing else inside but dust and the smell of dust. Not even bones were inside the huts.

We went to the largest built place. It was like a dozen huts all piled on top of each other, with crumbling walls piled on top of the huts.

Of course we went inside.

There was a long room with white pillars taller than trees. There was a chair in the middle of the room.

In the chair was a man.

Enyo Gyoja sat in the chair. He looked at us with such tired eyes.

Enyo Gyoja, old since I was young, old as long as anyone remembered him, old with his leaf cape to keep him warm and his walking staff with the metal charms.

He looked at us.

We looked at him.

Lucius reeled, pressing his whole weight into me. He pushed me to my knees. "And you are the devil, himself, Enyo? You are the devil of this miserable world?"

Enyo laughed at that. "I am just an old man," he said.

"Can you help us go home?" said Lucius. "The devil has his magic. Send us home."

Enyo scowled down at us from his huge chair. He leaned forward. "You were born in this maze. This is your home. I am not the devil. I have made the best life I can in this place. That is all anyone can do."

I touched my cheek. I was crying. "How can we trust you?" I said. "Looking at you here, we believe you are some kind of monster, like the cavemen or the minotaur or the legendary Djinni. How can we trust you?"

Enyo leaned back in the throne. He looked out the holes in the walls at the maze all around him, filling the valleys and the hills in the morning light.

"'Djinni,' she says. Julie Station, I have forgotten more than you will ever know," he said. "I have met myself so many times that I do not know where I began, anymore. When I was young, I was alone, like you. I was hungry and scared. But I have forgotten so many things." He lifted up a sandal and struck at it with his spear. It didn't come off. He struck it again and pushed at it with the spear. He sighed. He put his feet down. "There are too many mysterious things. Julie Station, I think you are the monster. You did something monstrous, didn't you?"

I picked up a jagged stone. I held it in my hand, and it was heavy. I stood up.

"I am an old man. Before I die, I want to make sure you can survive without me. What do you think we should do, Lucius? Travel to some strange place we don't know? This maze is our home. It is all we have ever known."

I walked slowly, at first, toward the throne. Then, I wasn't walking. Then, I was running.

Enyo Gyoja raised his staff, but he was too old and too slow. I was young and fast. I hit him so many times with that rock. I hit him until his blood was everywhere, spilling out from his leaf hat and over his leaf cloak and all over his clothes.

I hit him so many times.

Lucius said nothing. He just watched.

Lucius took off his jacket. He took off his woven reeds of shirt. He used his shirt like a rag to wipe the blood from my face, my hands, my body. He threw the shirt over the blood on the ground, where Enyo's brains looked like anyone else's brains smashed open. Lucius put his jacket back on his naked shoulders.

Then, Lucius took the body from the big hut. He dragged it out to the hillside with all the fallen walls. He returned with the cape, the hat rinsed clean, and the staff. He gave them to me.

I was trembling and cold and that's why he gave me Enyo's hat and cape.

Lucius picked me up in his strong arms. He sat me down in the huge chair that grew out of the very ground. He sat at my feet.

I felt better. I felt better than I ever had in my whole life.

"Lucius," I said.

Lucius Caveman, the man I loved, placed his face in his hands. He didn't want me to see him weeping.

"Lucius…?"

He turned his body away from me.

I touched his shoulder.

"Lucius, I'm sorry."

I rubbed his shoulder.

"Please, Lucius…"

Finally, he spoke. "Please don't touch me right now, Julie."

We just sat there, like that.

We sat there a long time.

The days to come would be hardship and joy and more hardship.

I knew. I always knew.

Lucius, who longed to be a creature without flesh, would never understand how much I hungered for it.

Even now, I can see how much he hates the swelling of life inside of me. I can see how lost he is because of it.

I was not afraid of the towers. My mother was a scientist and taught me to test things. I did, and I found my way to the highest place in the maze, at the top of this strange tower where times and spaces bend and flow away from each other like the valves of a heart. I look out through the gap in the wall, and I can see the maze and the maze and the maze all over the horizon and beyond, and the sunlight bathes the stone in glistening moss, and there's so much life hidden here, and it's so beautiful.

There's Lucius, in a hallway, carrying water back to me and back to the light inside of my swollen belly.

At night, our infant glows with light. Lucius touches my pink skin, and he's terrified because babies aren't supposed to glow like that. But, I tell him that my mother was born in a space station, among the stars.

"Do not claim to be an angel," he said.

"I don't know what that is," I said. "I'm not one of those. I'm only me, nothing else."

"You're a monster," he said. "You're the devil himself."

"No, I'm not, Lucius. Don't call me names. I am only me, Julie Station."

He frowned, quiet and cold. He turned away from me. He covered his eyes to sleep near the glowing of me.

I studied my stomach's veins in the dark, and their own glowing light, branching pathways under my skin, where I knew the blood flowed—my blood.

Then, I knew: not a village, but a city, like my mother had told me about, far larger than villages, and full of life pushed into every corner, like how my blood was alive with tiny, living things that grew and swelled and lived and died.

Lucius Caveman, I can see the light in you, now. I can see that your skin is just a city of darkness, and I am just a city of light, and we are both lost in this city of mazes.

I can see how we lie down to sleep but never lose our dreams. We wake with empty minds. I want to tell everyone in the village, and everyone lost in the village, and Lucius and the swell of child's light inside of me. I want to tell them all. I can only tell the light, and the light is listening; I know it is always listening.

Listen, time and blood are as one, and never-ending. I want to bring time and blood to everyone. The paths I know through these stone halls, and the paths I will never know, and all the people who are and who are going to be and who never were, and everything will echo with what I know. Listen, you must all hear me.

Life never ends here.

Feel this life inside of you.

Live.

Breathe deep.

Biography

J M McDermott is the author of *Last Dragon*, *Disintegration Visions*, *The Dogsland Trilogy*, and *Women and Monsters*. He holds an MFA from the Stonecoast Program from the University of Southern Maine. He lives in San Antonio, Texas.

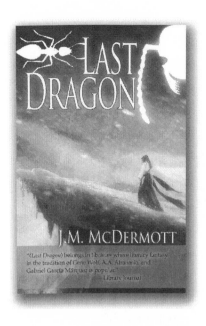